Bloodlines

SHIREEN MAGEDIN

AUSXIP PUBLISHING

www.ausxippublishing.com

Edited by Rosa Alonso
Cover Design by Mary Draganis
Interior design by AUSXIP Publishing

Published by AUSXIP Publishing
www.ausxippublishing.com

DEDICATION

*I dedicate **Bloodlines** to both of my parents.*

To my mother, because she always encouraged and believed in me. To my father, who loved to explore and travel, and the best part was that he always took us along with him.

ACKNOWLEDGMENTS

From the first day that I started to type **Bloodlines**, Taylor Rickard, an eminent bestselling author with many years' experience, was at my side. She encouraged, coached, and commented on my chapters as I fired them off to her when they were ready. Taylor showed me how to make my characters three dimensional, and I started to live and breathe them. To my mind, saying only thank you is not enough, but I want her to know how much her help and friendship is appreciated.

Mary Draganis, thank you for your confidence in me and your continuing encouragement. As I keep saying, I wouldn't have come on this track if it weren't for you.

Rosa, you have also been encouraging, and I was thrilled when you said that you liked Bloodlines. As you have mentioned many times, it was a roller coaster ride. Thanks a lot.

My beta readers, Allison Slowski and Mariam Balley, are the best. I did incorporate their very valid suggestions into the story.

Last but not least, I would like to thank my sister Janie and my brother Yusuf, who encouraged me with love and typical criticism that only a sibling can give to another. I love you both so much.

I would also like to thank my readers who enjoyed **Lifelines** and hope they will like the journey **Bloodlines** will take them on to.

SARAH & TANYA'S JOURNEY

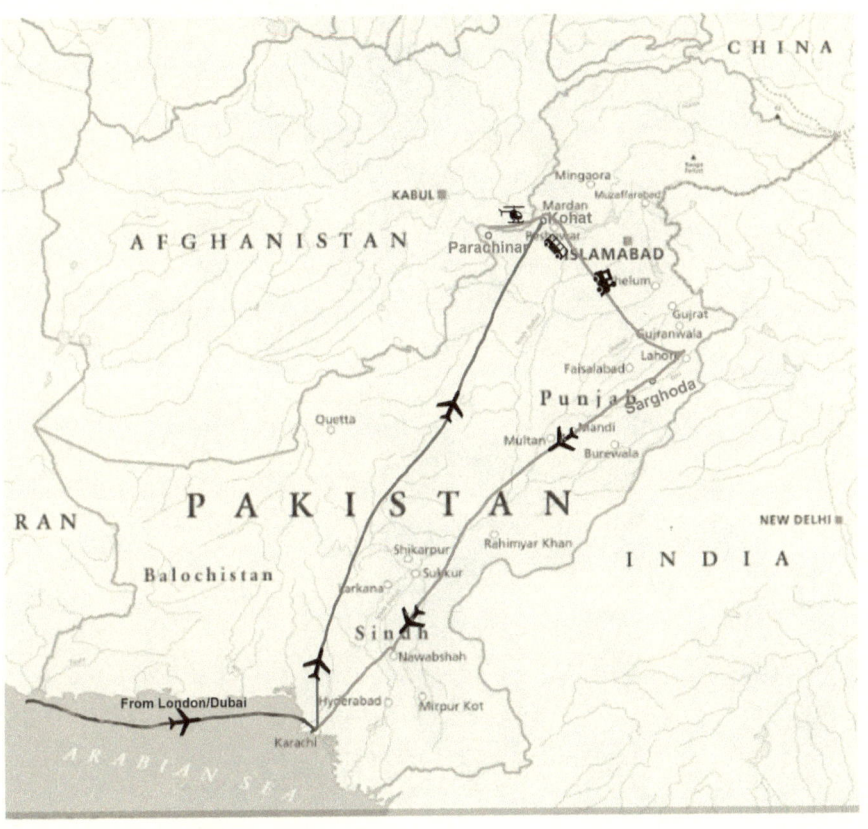

The Hippocratic Oath

The **Hippocratic Oath** is an oath of ethics historically taken by physicians all over the world. It is one of the most widely known Greek medical texts. In its original form, it requires a new physician to swear to uphold specific ethical standards. The earliest expression of this oath establishes several principles of medical ethics which remain of paramount significance even today. These include the principles of medical confidentiality and non-maleficence. Swearing a modified form of the oath remains a rite of passage for medical graduates in many countries all over the world, and is a requirement enshrined in legal statutes of many international jurisdictions. For example, in some countries, violations of the oath may carry criminal or other liability beyond the oath's symbolic nature.

The main premise of this oath is to do no harm!

CHAPTER 1

CONSANGUINITY

"True kindness is a pure divine affinity. Not founded upon human consanguinity. It is a spirit, not blood relation. Superior to family and station." ~ Henry David Thoreau!

Sarah

I LOVED THE ENGLISH COUNTRYSIDE IN SPRING, when it was very evident that Mother Nature was finally waking up after a long hard winter. There was nothing subtle about it. She woke up with an explosion; no, a kaleidoscope of colors. There were the crocuses and the bluebells that heralded spring, but I simply adored the way the daffodils popped up everywhere almost overnight and were in abundance in every little nook and cranny where their bulbs had covertly spread the spring before. Most of all, I loved having a bouquet of them on my kitchen table. Tanya knew this, and she brought me a bouquet nearly every day after her usual jog around the neighborhood in the morning. They brightened up the room while bringing a message of hope and cheer of spring indoors. Especially after a long and hard winter. She would always do small things like that to continuously show her affection. There was no doubt at all that I felt cared for and treasured.

Yes, I love the countryside, the greenery, and the fact that we lived in Surrey just twenty minutes away from London by train. While we worked in one of the busiest cities in the world, our home was the epitome of harmony and tranquility, which was something that we relished when we made our ways back in the evening. It was our safe place, our sanctuary. We were committed to one another, and we were at peace with the world. My Tanya, intrepid member of Interpol, was my friend, my lover, and my wife. Though it hurt me immensely that I had lost contact with my parents and my brothers, I knew that Tanya would always be there for me. No matter what. After all, we had gone through trials of fire just to be with each other. We were each other's family. Families hold together. At least that's what they are supposed to do...

We usually went to work together, getting Cornish pasties and coffee from a nearby bakery as we walked to the railway station, but that day I had to go alone because Tanya had to leave for the city much earlier for one of her usual high-powered meetings. In fact, there was also an important clinico-pathological conference that I had been told was mandatory for me to attend. While I sat in the "quiet" compartment of the train that was taking me to Waterloo Station, I thought about my patient, the one I knew we were going to discuss at the meeting.

Baby Amina was born with congenital hydrocephalus, which is a buildup of excess cerebrospinal fluid (CSF) in the brain at birth. The extra fluid can increase pressure in the baby's brain, causing brain damage and mental and physical problems. Her parents were British Pakistanis, and the trend of consanguinity was deeply inherent in their families. Not only were her parents cousins, but also her grandparents as well as her great grandparents. That is, as far as they could be traced. I was sure that if her genetic lineage were further investigated, the consanguinity trait could be traced even farther back than that.

Amina was the third child in her family who had been born with this defect. Her older siblings had already gone through the whole rigamarole of multiple surgeries and insertions of shunts to prevent pressure damage. These procedures were absolutely necessary to protect the brain from the rapid buildup of cerebrospinal fluid. Her eldest brother had died quite recently due to the consequences of this disorder, and her parents were understandably devastated. However, in spite of being counselled and told that the possibility of having another child with this birth defect was extremely high, they still had Amina, and had left everything "in God's hands." The problem was that even though the NHS supported them and paid for their medical expenses, the psychological stress and implications were taking its toll on them. While the couple had been extensively counselled again and again, the elders of their family would continue to pressure them to have another child and "not to listen to the white man's advice, since they don't know our culture."

Now faced with Amina, they had dealt with the problem in a most immature and harrowing way. They had abandoned the baby at the hospital and had left the country without any known forwarding address or destination. For now, they were untraceable. In their convoluted minds, they thought that either the NHS and/or child services would look after the baby, or perhaps they had the morbid hope that she would mercifully die soon.

That got me thinking about the personalities of families in ethnic settings and as a whole... were they all like that? Were people so caught up in their set ways and egos that they would rather let their daughter die than live with "defects"? Were they all just like my family? They also thought that I was defective and had tried to "fix" my proclivities by forcing me to marry that lech Dr. Farooq. And yet they shared DNA with me, which is why I still loved them. I used to have a good relationship with my Baba, but that seemed to change once they found out about my sexuality. Yet, I was the same person. Did I not deserve to be loved by my parents? Realizing that I was sinking into a familiar melancholy that sporadically surfaced when I thought of my family, I shook myself and turned towards happy thoughts.

That day was Tanya's and my anniversary—not our marriage anniversary, but the anniversary of the first day we laid our eyes on each other ten years before—that day in the summer of 1974 when Tanya looked at me over the crowd and she almost drove her jeep into our college gate. Our eyes met then, and somehow, we had an almost spiritual connection and knew that we were destined for each other.

Tanya assured me that she would try to get home earlier, and I had already arranged with a colleague to take over my evening duty hours. We planned to have a relaxed albeit romantic evening together. We tried to do that as much as we could since our work schedules were sometimes quite hectic and erratic. More often than not, she would be called away to travel around the globe chasing culprits and bringing them to justice. I was so proud of her... Both of us had come a long way.

As I got off at Waterloo station, I was grateful that I didn't have to rush like the other commuters to catch any more trains with the London Underground. There was just a ten-minute walk to the hospital and I enjoyed the fresh air. It was only when the weather didn't behave itself that I tried to catch a taxi so that I didn't look a soggy mess when I arrived at work.

"Good morning, Dr. Shah," our porter called out. "It's a lovely day today. Just the weather you like, isn't it?"

"That it is, Mr. Jones. How is your wife today?"

"She is getting better, thank you. I am glad to say that she is up and about now."

I smiled and waved at him while I pushed my way through the heavy doors and into my familiar domain. The ambience, the smells, and the sounds energized and calmed me at the same time. This was where I was in my element.

"Dr. Shah to the pediatrics conference room, please. Dr. Shah to the pediatrics conference room, please!" the paging speaker blared loudly. I ran to the nearest inhouse phone and dialed the conference room number. My boss, the head of the pediatrics department answered almost immediately.

"Where are you, Sarah? We are waiting for you. Please, come as soon as you can." He sounded quite irritable, but I knew I was not the cause of his exasperation because, according to my watch, I was actually thirty minutes early.

"I have just walked in and I will be there as soon as I have deposited my bag in the locker," I said.

He harumphed and just told me to hurry up, after which he firmly put down the phone.

After flinging my bag haphazardly into my locker and taking a clean white coat with my name embroidered on the left breast pocket from the hanger, I hurried to the conference room to see what had upset my usually calm boss this morning.

When I walked in, I sensed the mood in the room was somber. As an empath, I feel the atmosphere of situations around me, and this was not a happy feeling. There were a few people sitting around the conference table, two of whom were of obvious Pakistani descent. The MRI and CT scan reports of Amina were set up in chronological order on the panel of light boxes that took up most of the wall on the left side of the room.

"Come in, Sarah," said Professor Bingham, waving his hands towards the couple. "These people are Mr. and Mrs. Kamal Siddiqui. They are Amina's uncle and aunt."

"Salam, how do you do?" I asked politely.

"Do you speak Urdu?" asked Mr. Siddiqui looking at me hopefully.

"Yes, I do," I answered warily. I didn't want to talk to them in a language my professor didn't understand. It was clear that Mr. Siddiqui spoke English, albeit with a cockney accent that indicated he had lived in London for a long time.

"Please, go ahead and talk to them in their language," Professor Bingham said with a deep sigh. "Mrs. Siddiqui is not that fluent in English and would like to know what we are going to do about our little patient."

"Where are Amina's parents?" I asked the uncle in Urdu. I knew the parents were untraceable, but we needed to know what had happened from the relatives, so I pressed on. "They also need to be here. We called this meeting to discuss the treatment and prognosis of their daughter and what measures need to be taken to prevent more babies to be born with similar conditions."

I looked pointedly at the couple, but they couldn't meet my eyes. They didn't seem to know what to say or where to look...

"We can't find Amina's parents; they disappeared overnight and left their son with their neighbor, Mrs. McCarthy, who sometimes babysits for them. She is a retired nurse and looks after Murad quite efficiently," Mrs. Siddiqui blurted out in Urdu. "But now we are worried about the baby and don't know what to do about her. We are poor people and we can't afford another mouth to feed. Moreover, she will be needing special care. I can't do it, and neither can Kamal. She needs her parents." She twisted her chiffon scarf into knots in agitation and didn't look up when she spoke. "After Taimur, their older son, died a week ago, they just quietly packed their bags and left in the night without telling anyone. Murad will now be shifted to his grandparents' home in Leeds. He can't stay permanently with Mrs. McCarthy. The point is that everyone is now worried about Amina, but no one wants to take responsibility for her."

I quickly translated for my professor, and he was justified to be worried. We needed parental permission to insert a shunt and for any subsequent surgeries if they were required. Amina was already showing the typical "sunset sign" of her eyes, which indicated that her intra cranial pressure was increasing. She needed help immediately.

"May we give our consent for the operation?" asked Mr.

Siddiqui. "After all, she has been left behind by her parents and we are, for now, the nearest relatives she has."

After translating once more, I looked towards my boss to see what he would say. He tersely nodded his consent and the requisite papers were promptly signed and witnessed by me.

Professor Bingham left the room immediately afterwards. However, before he did, he drew me aside and asked me to talk to the couple to see if I could find out more about the absconding parents.

"I have informed the police, and since they think Amina's parents might have left the country, they are sending over someone from Interpol this morning to talk to them," he said indicating with his head towards the couple, who were frantically whispering and gesticulating to each other. "Interpol said their representative will be here by ten o'clock, so that's approximately in the next ten minutes. Go and see what you can get out of them." With that, he turned around briskly and walked off towards the Neonatal Intensive Care Unit (NICU).

I sat down with the couple and offered them a cup of tea, which they gratefully accepted. I had a feeling they knew exactly where the baby's parents were. They were probably scared of the authorities and, like many ethnic families, they were very close-knit and kept their secrets to themselves. Even though I didn't know them, I had this feeling that they were from a very obscure village in Punjab. When I handed Mrs. Siddiqui a cup of tea, my hand accidently brushed against the back of her hand. All of a sudden, I saw the name of the village in my mind's eye—Gojra. That name kept echoing and bouncing about in my mind. I wasn't even sure that such a place existed, but I did see a hamlet with fertile fields, cattle, and sunshine.

Talking solely in Urdu, I tried to get as much information as possible from the couple, but they were quite tight lipped. I was about to lose my patience when there was a sharp rap on the door of the conference room and Tanya walked in.

"Now, why am I not surprised that you are involved in this strange situation, Dr. Sarah Shah?" she said as she sat down at the conference table with a broad smile. "Can you also get me a cup of tea, please? The wind has started to bluster and it's getting a bit chilly outside."

Tanya

MY LIFE WAS COMPLETE. Those past few years, in spite of the usual peaks and valleys, had been idyllic, especially our life together in the home we bought. It was always comforting to come home to a lovely home and a stunning wife. We were no doubt busy with our respective careers, but the most important thing was that we were together. The nightmare from five years before seemed to be fading from our memories. Sarah kept telling me that she knew her family and she didn't think they would give up so easily. Therefore we shouldn't get too complacent. She believed her parents might strike unexpectedly, probably when she finally finished her pediatric specialization in London.

My training at Interpol was grueling but interesting and I was posted to the Interpol headquarters in London. I had been put in charge of the Human Trafficking Cell. It was a multi-billion-dollar form of organized crime, constituting of modern day slavery, with a total disregard for human dignity and rights towards the hapless victims. Because of my origins and language skills, I had been given the responsibility for South Asia and the Middle East. I needed to travel a lot for my job, but I was comforted that Sarah was well liked at work and our neighbors were helpful and kind. Therefore, my periodic travelling didn't bother us too much and I could leave for my official trips with a peaceful mind.

Because of Sarah's feelings of disquiet that popped up sporadically, we had memorized our private and work telephone numbers so that we could try to get to a phone and call if anything happened to either of us. It was the least we could do and it calmed Sarah to some extent, but she was still anxious and kept looking over her shoulder. I tried to reassure her that we were now British subjects and we would be taken care of by the Crown if anything were to happen to us.

Besides the Human Trafficking Cell, I was at times handed cases of child abuse, abandonment, and kidnapping, especially of British Pakistani girls. Such cases were increasing day by day, so much so that the local police had started to depend heavily on Interpol to help them. Apparently, the girls were taken on false pretenses to Pakistan, India, and Bangladesh, where they were forced to marry cousins or unknown men chosen for them by none other than their parents. A few of them were sometimes lucky enough to live a comfortable life, but then there were those young women who were raped and mistreated by their spouses. Many were never found again because they were taken deep into the mountains or the tribal areas where legal jurisdictions were dicey if at all present. The few that were found were either too scared of their family to go back or they developed the typical signs of Stockholm syndrome and opted to stay with their spouse and children. I personally thought it was the children that held them back.

I was called in to a meeting that morning by my superiors. They were worried about parents who abandoned their children with birth defects at NHS facilities and then disappeared. With the increase of congenital malformations as a result of consanguinity, such cases of abandonment were tragically on the rise. The emotional and financial implications were at times too distressing for some parents, and so they just gave up and left things to fate or any other entity that they considered holy or divine. The only plus point in the UK was that Child Protection Services and the NHS were quite efficient, but they were also starting to get stretched beyond their limits.

"Well, Agent Kareem," said my boss, Commander Williams. "It seems that another baby has been abandoned at the NHS today. We need to get the parents back here as soon as possible to make an example of them. They need to know that there are consequences for their actions, even if they leave the country. We have the skill and the resources to track them down and bring them back."

I could see he was getting upset. Even though he was a crusty old bachelor, I had noticed the soft spot he had for little children. If a crime involved children, he would be quite troubled for a long time, although he tried to hide it from the team. He would make sure that his team caught the perpetrators. I knew that was just a front for a soft heart and a kind soul.

"I understand," I replied. "We do need to work in such a way that the guidelines and processes are streamlined and future offenders are stopped. We can only do that if we are strict about the law and can forge cooperative liaisons with the countries where the fugitives are hiding." I was worried about this continuing trend. My disquiet was also tempered by my worry about Sarah. That always was at the back of my mind. "You do know that the law is not very clear about relatives kidnapping their own children, but we still need to be the hope of these young people. They are British subjects and deserve their civil rights. By bringing their parents back and getting them justice, our voices will be that much louder to help others in the future."

"Absolutely," agreed Commander Williams. "Since most of the cases involve people from your former neck of the woods, I would like you and your team to take special interest in bringing the perpetrators to justice." He harumphed indicating that the meeting was over. I nodded and headed out to interview the Siddiquis, relatives of the most recent victim of abandonment. This meant I had to go to the hospital where Sarah worked. I hoped I would manage to see her, and maybe we could have lunch together. Even just getting a glimpse of her from afar always energized me and made my day much better.

When I got to the hospital, I was ushered into the main clinico-pathological conference room by a friendly nurse. And who did I see talking passionately in Urdu to the couple sitting there with anxious expressions on their faces? My Sarah! As usual, she was in the midst of things. I chuckled inwardly as she turned and looked at me in surprise.

"Tanya! They said that someone from Interpol was coming to interview the Siddiquis. I was hoping it would be you." She smiled that beautiful happy smile that she reserved only for me. Or for her little patients.

Sarah told me that she had tried to talk to the baby's

uncle and aunt. Unfortunately, the only positive outcome was that they had now signed the consent form for Amina's surgery and she was on her way to the operation theater. The Siddiquis looked terrified. More so since I walked into the room. I represented the law, and they were afraid that they would be arrested for their relatives' transgressions.

I sat across from them and looked pointedly at the couple. I think they were a bit disconcerted by my silent scrutiny. So they should be. That was the intention.

"Please, ma'am! We no know nothing. We just look after baby because she have nobody. Please, no punish us!" Mrs. Siddiqui was on the verge of a breakdown. The more agitated she got the more garbled her English became.

All of a sudden, Sarah stood up to come and whisper something in my ear. I looked at her speculatively and she just nodded. I had learned to trust her instincts and her intuition, so the next question that I wanted to ask the terrified couple had to be quite significant.

"Who lives in Gojra?" I asked quietly. The Siddiquis looked at me with startled expressions on their faces.

"Oh, Allah!" Mrs. Siddiqui said. "I know these English police clever! See they find out where your brother and his wife hide!"

Sarah looked at me with a pleased, almost smug expression on her face. She had hit the jackpot once again with her ESP. Now was the time to act fast. We didn't want the Siddiquis to alert the absconding parents. I strode determinedly to the door and opened it. Two constables were already there waiting for my orders.

"Would you please be so kind as to take Mr. and Mrs. Siddiqui home? See that they don't talk to anyone and don't use the telephone. Also, arrange for their children to stay with neighbors or any other relatives who live nearby. We don't want them to use their children as messengers."

I addressed the now distraught couple then. "Before you go home, I would like to have the contact information you have of Amina's parents, as well as any other relatives and friends that you know in Gojra. If you don't cooperate, it will be considered obstruction of justice and you could be prosecuted."

With a visibly shaking hand, Mr. Siddiqui reached into the inside pocket of his jacket and drew out a small well-worn notebook. He flipped a few pages and stopped when he came to what he was looking for. Noticing that he was looking around for something to write, Sarah gave him a sheet of paper and a pen. He wrote down a few numbers and an address on the paper. I watched him carefully and thought he looked too self-satisfied. I held out my hand for the notebook and he reluctantly handed it over to me. I gave him a stern look and leafed through the dog-eared pages. I was right—there were two other addresses and numbers that he hadn't added to the note. I wrote down the rest of the information, gave him his notebook back, and signaled to the constables to take the couple home.

The Siddiquis looked understandably upset. It wasn't their fault, but what their relatives had done was considered child abuse by the authorities and it wasn't taken lightly in England.

Now I just had to let my counterparts in Lahore know where Amina's parents were and they would hopefully handle them from there. Although keeping the Siddiquis under temporary custody was a gray area, we couldn't let them tell the parents that we knew where they were. There was a big chance that they would disappear once again and we needed them to take responsibility for their child.

After the constables left with the now contrite couple, I looked over at Sarah, who was writing her notes in Amina's file. I always thought that she was adorable when she was in her "doctor" mode. It's astonishing how time flies. We had known each other ten years, five of which we had been living together in England. I had something special custom made for her. When I was in Amsterdam for one of my official meetings, I found a jeweler in a quaint alley just off the main road from the Dam Square area. He was just putting a card in his window which advertised that he crafted custom-made jewelry. That sign caught my eyes immediately. The crystal-like tinkling bell on the door of the shop was like an omen that I had come to the right place. Mr. Vandergroot understood immediately what I wanted, and we spent a few hours discussing the pendant that I wanted him to design for Sarah. Now it was finally finished and in a small velvet box in my pocket. I wanted to give it to her that night, but I let my usual impatience take over and smiled as I watched her work on the file. The joy I felt being with her was something precious and couldn't be expressed with a small trinket.

"Sarah," I said in a soft voice, "Are you finished with your notes?"

"Just a minute. I need to sign them and then you have my complete attention," she said with a smile.

She signed her notes with her usual flourish, picked up the files, and walked around the table to come and sit next to me.

"What is it, Tanya? Do you want to give me my anniversary present already?" She laughed. She knew me so well. As if on its own volition, my hand went into my pocket and withdrew the small maroon velvet box.

"These years have been so precious to me. I don't think there is a way to express my love and gratitude, but I hope this serves as a token of what I feel for you today and every day." I handed the box to her.

Sarah was so touched with my words that she had tears in her eyes. Almost reverently, she opened the box and looked inside. Lying on a bed of red satin was the pendant that I had designed for her. It was a silver stethoscope that was entwined with little silver handcuffs. There was a small solitaire diamond embedded where both symbols met. It was twinkling with a fire that seemed to corroborate what I had just said to Sarah. She seemed spellbound as she looked at the pendant in what I could only describe as awe. I could see from her expression that she loved it. I just wondered if she would like it as much when I told her that there was a utilitarian aspect of the pendant as well...

"Tanya! This is beautiful! My stethoscope will now always be locked with your handcuffs. The diamond just makes it even more beautiful. Is it a symbol of light and strength? What better way to express our devotion to each other? I will always wear it and I promise that I will never take it off!"

"Well," I said sheepishly. "That is actually the idea."

"What do you mean?" asked Sarah. She seemed amused.

"Have a look at the clasp. It's an unusual one that can only be opened with a special key. Under the diamond is a small micro-homing device that only very few law enforcement agencies have at this point in time. I had heard about it when I went to the MI-6 laboratories, and I managed to get one after badgering my partner Andy at

Interpol. If you press the diamond, it will release a signal that can be tracked. The only drawback is that since it's a fairly new technology, the range is very short, but you could be tracked from at least a kilometer away."

"Oh, Tanya! Thank you! I know why you did this, so don't look so mortified. You have taken my misgivings about my family seriously, and for that I love you even more. You have gone out of your way to ensure that I am safe." She launched herself out of her chair and into my arms. "I won't kiss you here because anyone could walk in. We will continue this discussion in the evening."

"Oh, there is one more thing." I opened my briefcase and took out a small cardboard box. "I have had some visiting cards made for you." I couldn't wipe the smile off my face. Sarah would love these. I was sure.

Opening the box, she took out one of the cards. It was maroon on one side, and the other white side showed her relevant information as well as my office numbers. The most significant thing was that the card had a watermark of her pendant. "I want you to use these cards when you believe there is a threat and want to send a message to me." I was worried for Sarah. These were just small measures that could help if there was a situation where she was in danger.

"I want you to know how much I love you whenever you touch the pendant. There are times when my heart overflows with what I feel for you. I know I don't say it often enough, but I love you, Sarah Shah, and I promise I will try to keep you safe and follow you to the ends of the earth if I ever have to."

"That is the sweetest thing you have said to me in a long time. I love you, Tanya Kareem. So much!" Sarah reached out and entwined our fingers. She was usually very shy to show her emotions at work, and obviously I was also there in an official capacity. Yet we felt that we had to connect, even if it was just by holding hands.

Suddenly Sarah bent forward and engulfed me in a hug, laying her head momentarily on my shoulder. She had tears in her eyes when she turned her head and gave me a gentle kiss on my lips. It might just have been fleeting, but I saw her love for me in her eyes. I would swear on a stack of holy books that the sparks between us were even more wonderful than back when we first realized that we loved each other.

"Go now before I ravage you, you beautiful agent of mine. I don't want anyone to have a free show if they popped their heads in. After all, we can't lock the door of the conference room." She chuckled and gave me a saucy wink. I was a bit off kilter, but then that was what I always felt whenever I was near Sarah. It was a good feeling.

She hugged me once more and I smiled. "I need to go to the headquarters and inform our Lahore office that they need to send someone to Gojra as soon as they possibly can. I'll see you at home, love." I gently leaned forward and kissed her cheek, reluctant to leave her.

"And I need to go to the NICU." Sarah didn't let go of my hand at first. She held on tight. When she ultimately did, she had a sad smile on her face, as if she just had one of her ESP premonitions. I vowed at that very moment that I'd always protect and care for her as she deserved. I prayed with all of my heart that I would be able to do so.

CHAPTER 2

HELPLESS ANGELS

"Every child you encounter is a divine appointment."
~ Wes Stafford

Sarah

FINALLY, THE DAY HAD ARRIVED WHEN I WOULD BE taking the final examination to get my membership in the Royal College of Pediatricians, Child Health (MRCPCH). Once I passed, I could be considered a specialist in our country, and even other countries in the world, but in the UK there was a hierarchy that had to be climbed academically to reach the zenith of one's career. This was achieved through further study, research, and presenting a requisite number of publications in well-known medical journals. While I was pleased that I had reached my initial goal, I was also apprehensive. I felt a psychic shift in the atmosphere. I was afraid that my parents were going to try to get me back home after I received my membership. I had already been threatened by anonymous calls and letters from my family that had been sent to my place of work.

I know it sounds paranoid, but I thought I might have seen one of my brothers lurking outside the hospital. After all, I have always had felt a peculiar sensation when someone focuses on me—I can feel whether their intentions are negative or positive. He ducked into the shadows when he saw me looking around trying to find the person who was spying on me. I went so far as to tell Mr. Jones not to give any information about me to anyone, even if they said they were my family. Out of necessity, I had given our hospital porter a very abridged version of my history. He was a discreet soul and didn't ask many questions, and I always made it a point to give him a nice present and a tip for Christmas for helping me see the hospital as my sanctuary. But I had the sense this was soon going to change. My feelings of disquiet were increasing day by day. I had to focus on my studies and pass the exams. If and when I went back and see my family ever again, I wanted to hold my head up high and show them that I had achieved what they thought was unattainable for me while being with Tanya. We didn't really care if they liked us or not, but we wanted to live in peace—without fear and without looking over our shoulders all the time.

"Dr. Sarah Shah, roll number 55?" A smart looking woman walked towards me while looking at the clipboard in her hand.

"Yes, that's me." I hoped that she didn't hear the tremor in my voice, but then, she was probably used to nervous doctors coming in for their exams.

"Professor Grant is waiting for you in room number 25.

Best of luck." Giving me a brief smile, she indicated with the wave of her hand towards the room. I checked to see there were no unnecessary creases on my white coat and straightened my stethoscope around my neck before knocking on the door.

"Come in, Dr. Shah," said the professor. When I saw the kind smile on his face, half of my anxiety nearly melted away. I had met this gentleman before when he visited his patients at our hospital. He wasn't one of my teachers and that's why he was able to be my examiner.

"I have heard good things about you, and I hope to welcome you as a member of the Royal College of Pediatricians and Child Health at the end of today."

I smiled nervously and looked around. I saw that my patient was already waiting for me.

"Ah! I see you are eager to start." Grant pointed at to the baby who was sleeping peacefully in a cot nearby. "I would like you to examine this baby and tell me what you have observed."

I rubbed my hands together to warm them and approached the baby. I didn't want to startle her. She was a beautiful and chubby little girl with pink rosebud lips that were moving in her sleep as if she was dreaming of having her bottle. Her little fists were on either side of her head. She had a tousled head of blonde curls and looked almost angelic. What could possibly be wrong with such a beautiful child for her to be included in our exams?

While I gently opened the snaps of her onesie, I kept up a running commentary of my observations.

"Female baby, approximately nine months old. At first glance, I can see that she is sleeping peacefully with no apparent external malformations or signs of illness, and... Oh!"

Professor Grant smirked. "Yes, oh!"

As I gently drew the clothes off the sleeping baby, I saw that she had large black lesions all over her body. They weren't open or infected. I was nonplussed. What in the name of heaven was that? I had never seen such a thing before. My face fell and I was sure that I would have to repeat the exams. There was no way I could bluff my way out of this.

"Well, what is it?" Professor Grant still had an amused look on his face, as if he was thinking about a previous humorous incident.

I took a deep breath and thought it was better to be honest. Might as well rip the band aid off in one go. Then I could go home and feed my self-pity with pizza and ice cream. "My apologies, but I have never seen such a case in my life, sir." I looked despondently at the floor.

"That is the answer I've wanted to hear from the candidates since early this morning!" Grant jumped up and shook hands with me. I was bewildered. "To tell you the truth, Dr. Shah, I haven't seen such a case myself, and I wanted to see the candidates' reactions. What better way to gauge who would be honest with me and who would try to bluff their way through? You are the first person to admit that they have no clue, and I respect you for it."

Seeing that I was a bit shell shocked, he beckoned me to go once more near the baby. "Have a closer look at the lesions. What do you see?"

I pulled my torch out from my breast pocket and shone the beam over the black lesions. *Poor baby*, I thought. *What condition does she have, and how will it impact her life when she is older?* Then I saw what the professor meant!

"Professor Grant! These are massive moles!" I exclaimed. I was relieved that the lesions were more or less harmless. At least for now. Unless they became malignant when she is older. There was always that chance.

"Yes! I see that you have a good eye. Can you imagine the stress this poor little girl will have when she is older? Thank God there aren't any visible lesions on her face and hands."

After that hiccup, he grilled me on various aspects of the disease, or rather condition, as well as the baby's growth and development. I was surprised when he shook my hand and said, "Well done, doctor."

I was floating on air. My first thought was to call Tanya, but she was in Amsterdam, or was it Vienna? for a meeting with the top brass. I knew that the exam had gone well. If I had been paying better attention, I would have noticed the man who suddenly stood in front of me, blocking my way to the entrance of the railway station.

I looked up in surprise and saw that it wasn't a thug who was blocking my way, but my brother Adam. The same brother who had helped me escape from Pakistan five years before. I heaved a sigh of relief. I was convinced that my parents would send some dubious henchman after me. But the timing was a bit too convenient. After all, I had just walked out of the examination venue.

"What are you doing here?" I asked.

"Is that the way you greet your big brother, who you haven't seen for five years?" he said with a laugh.

I hugged him briefly and then stood back and looked at him. There was something that was not quite right. I could feel that he was very uncomfortable and was hiding something from me.

"I needed to see you, talk to you," he said hurriedly, looking around the street as if he was expecting someone to come and disturb us.

"Let's go back into the hospital. You can get a good cup of tea or coffee in the hospital cafeteria, and we can talk there uninterrupted." I took his arm and pulled him along. Maybe I was so happy to see my dear brother once again that I let my guard down. Even though my intuition was prickling at high speed, I made a choice at that point to ignore it. After all, Adam wouldn't hurt me. Would he?

I bought two cups of tea and a plate of scones at the cafeteria. Adam looked cold. We were desert rats after all, and when the temperature dropped even a bit, we would shiver. It took me a while to get used to the unpredictable English weather. No wonder that the people on this little isle have so much to say about the ever-changing climate.

Adam ate the scones as if he was starved. I looked at him in amusement. "Slow down; there are more where these came from."

He just grunted and continued to chew while washing the large bites down with his tea. Once he was done, he sat back and looked at me.

"How are you, little sister? You look well."

"I am. I have a good job and a good life here. Thanks to you."

A shadow crossed over his face. He looked almost guilty. I felt there was more to his visit. My intuition was pinging again.

"What's wrong, Adam? Is everything all right at home?" A frisson of fear ran up my spine.

"Ammi is not well," he blurted out. "She wants to see you before it's too late. Her words, not mine." He looked away. There was more to it. I was sure, but he still wouldn't look at me. "I have promised to bring you back home."

Seeing my distress at hearing that my mother was very ill, Adam misconstrued what I was feeling. "Don't worry, Sarah. It will be a short visit, and then you can come back here again."

"It's not that." I was appalled that Adam thought I was so shallow. "I am worried about Ammi. Why wasn't I told earlier that she was ill? Why tell me at such a late stage? I need to know what is wrong with her. Maybe we could bring her here to London for her treatment."

Adam seemed confused and couldn't understand that I needed details about Ammi's health concerns. I also didn't think it unusual that he didn't have details to offer because, not being medically trained, he wouldn't know. In my academic arrogance, I overlooked a lot of signs that pointed towards caution.

"We need to leave as soon as possible," he said. "Ammi is waiting for you. The doctors haven't given her much time."

"Can she come to the telephone? May I talk to her before we leave?"

"No. She is very weak. We need to go now."

"Hold your horses, bro. I need to go home and pack. I also need to let Tanya know that I am leaving." I smiled to soften the sharpness that had crept into my tone. Now I knew something wasn't right.

"You have your things at home, in Karachi. And if you are still as paranoid as you were before you left home, I know that you have your passport in your locker." Adam tried to smile, but it looked more like an uneasy grimace. "There isn't much time. I have already told you that Ammi is not well. We need to leave immediately!"

"Adam, be reasonable. I can't just get up and go like that. I need to let my boss know and leave a message for Tanya..." I broke off at the hard look on his face. Out of the corner of my eye I saw two men stand on either side of the cafeteria door. They looked familiar. Then it dawned on me. They were the same men I had seen around the station and the hospital spying on me!

"What is going on, Adam?" I was worried and scared, and also deeply disappointed that my brother was betraying me. My favorite brother. The one who had helped me before was now stabbing me in the back.

Adam firmly took my arm and walked me towards the hospital exit. I tried to free myself, but he was too strong. The timing was perfect for them because we were the only ones besides the catering staff in the cafeteria and they were too busy getting ready for the lunch crowd to bother about us. I felt a slight sting in my left arm, as if I had been stung by a bee. Then there was nothing. Just dark, velvety oblivion.

Tanya

AMSTERDAM IS ALWAYS beautiful in springtime. I knew Sarah would have loved the carpets of flowers there. We had visited Holland many times over the years, but we seemed to have missed the month of March, when the crocuses and daffodils start to push themselves out of the post winter soil. And then hyacinths and tulips follow, keeping the colors continuous till summer. The rainbow created by the flower fields is breathtaking. I was starting to sound like Sarah, but they say that happens when a couple lives together.

My meeting with the officials at the local Interpol office was difficult. There were more and more south Asian girls and even boys abducted every day. It was frustrating. There was talk of creating a monitoring cell, but all the red tape meant that it might take some time till anything concrete was implemented. Until then, local and international law enforcement agencies had to continue to work together.

The sad point was that many of the children and young adults abducted from the UK and the rest of Europe were forced by their own families to get married. There was no proper legislation, but I hoped forced marriages would soon be recognized in the UK and Europe as a form of domestic or child abuse and a serious abuse of human rights.

"Ah, there you are!" said my immediate supervisor, Mr. Thomas, as I walked into the conference room. "I hope you had a pleasant journey?"

I just nodded and smiled. He probably didn't want to know about the gull that had pooped on my jacket when I was on the ferry. Smiling inwardly, I set my briefcase and my files on the table. I nodded my greeting to the three other people who were sitting at the table. They were my peers and had also come over for the meeting from their respective countries. They were to present the data from their areas just like I had to.

"Have you compiled the statistics for the UK regarding abductions with special focus on forced marriages?" It always amazed me that Mr. Thomas was so pompous. Even condescending, I might say. I had a file as thick as a law book in front of me. Didn't that indicate that I had data?

I cleared my throat, sat down, and opened the massive file.

"Sir, the abductions seem to be increasing day by day. The most common nationalities are Pakistani, Indian, Bangladeshi, Somalian, and Arabic children along with young adults of British origin. The numbers of the unrecovered abductees are quite high while the ones recovered are extremely low. The respective governments are not very cooperative. They think that now that they are married, even if under duress, it is a family matter, and they are wary of interfering, which is quite frustrating."

"That is true, Agent Kareem." I wish the bureaucrats would get over the red tape and start working on the legislation for the prevention of kidnapping and forced marriages out there. It would not only help the UK, but also most of Europe, where there are immigrants with similar problems. Till then we will have to take things case by case."

My counterparts had similar reports. The only glimmer of hope was the up-and-coming non-governmental organizations that were willing to help in any possible way.

"Agent Kareem, I believe you told us the last time we met that you fear for the safety of your partner." Agent Meister from Germany was a good friend, but he always made it a point to act formally when we were attending meetings.

"Yes, I am worried. More so because she has been getting threatening letters at her hospital. She doesn't think that I know, but because of our concerns, I do have to ensure that she is safe and well taken care of." I had a bad feeling and wanted this meeting to be over soon so that I could hop back onto the ferry and head home.

There was a discreet knock on the door and a young

bespectacled woman walked in and came over to me. She bent down and said in a low voice, "Agent Kareem, you have a phone call. It's your London office. They said it was urgent."

I felt as if a cold hand had squeezed my heart. I hoped my feelings of disquiet were wrong and Sarah was all right

"If you would excuse me, I need to take this call. They said it was of utmost urgency." I gave everyone a terse smile and quietly left the room.

The secretary pointed to the phone on her desk and then moved away to the other room to give me privacy.

"Tanya Kareem here," I barked into the phone.

"Tanya! Thank God!" It was my work partner. Andy was a good agent and he always looked after Sarah, covertly, when I wasn't in town.

"What happened, Andy? Is everything all right?" I didn't want to ask the question that was hovering on the tip of my tongue. I was too scared to say anything.

"I am so sorry, but Sarah has been abducted by three men from the hospital just an hour ago. Mr. Jones tried to stop them, but he was pushed and hit his head on the pavement. He is now in the ER of the hospital with a concussion."

Feeling as if my legs had turned to jelly, I sat down on a nearby chair with a thump. I was in shock. I was barely aware of Andy's voice trying to get my attention through the speaker of the telephone.

"Are you all right, love?" The secretary had come back into the room when she heard the thump.

I realized that I was in all probability looking shell shocked, but I shook my head and picked up the phone once more.

"How did this happen? I thought you were keeping an eye out for her!"

"I did... I was..." Andy stuttered.

"Then what in heaven's name happened? How did anyone get close enough to Sarah to abduct her!" I was roaring into the phone by now. It wasn't fair on Andy, but I felt so impotent, so helpless. I needed to get Sarah back. As soon as possible.

"I am so, so sorry." Andy was beside himself with remorse. "I thought she was still at her exam. Mr. Jones, the porter, saw what had happened and he said that she was taken by three men from the hospital in a wheelchair and dumped in the back of a black nondescript car. To his untrained eye, it looked like Sarah was drugged because she was slumped in the chair. After she was pushed into the waiting car, the men then shoved the wheelchair onto the sidewalk and drove off."

Drawing energy from some inner strength that I wasn't even aware of; I wiped the tears off my face, composed myself and walked into the meeting room once more.

"Well, it's ironic that I am here trying to help the team to compile data to push legislature on kidnapping and forced marriages while my own partner has just been kidnapped. I would like to leave immediately to investigate and try to get her back. Hopefully, when she is back, we could use this first-hand experience to push harder." I tried to sound dispassionate and professional, but I couldn't keep the tremors from my voice.

I hardly heard the words of sympathy that my colleagues offered me. I just needed to go. I left my data file with Mr. Thomas and grabbed my briefcase.

Just as I was barreling down the corridor to the exit, I

heard Mr. Thomas call me. My first instinct was to ignore him, but I knew that if I was to be successful in getting Sarah back, I would need all the help that I could get.

"Agent Kareem! Tanya! Wait!" It was nearly comical to watch Mr. Thomas's portly frame trot along the corridor.

I stopped and waited for him to reach me. He had to take a few moments to catch his breath before he could talk. "The company helicopter is already on the helipad. I also need to go back to London immediately. Please, come with me. You will be there quicker than if you took the ferry."

I looked at him in surprise—not so pompous after all. There was a soft spot inside dear old Mr. Thomas. I nearly stepped forward to hug him, but I knew that wouldn't have been appreciated.

"Thank you, sir. That is very kind of you."

"Come along then. Time waits for no one. Let's go."

The helipad was on the roof of the building and as we stepped onto the tarmac the blades of the helicopter started to rotate. Mr. Thomas and I bent forward and ran to the aircraft's door. We pulled it open and tumbled into the cabin. Soon we were soaring over Amsterdam and the beautiful fields of flowers, but the spectacular views hardly registered with me. I was nearly in a trance. I prayed to God to keep Sarah safe and bring her back to me.

"I will bring you back to see these beautiful flowers, Sarah, my heart," I vowed.

CHAPTER 3

JOURNEY OF PAIN

"However difficult life may seem, there is always something you can do and succeed at." ~ Stephen Hawking

Sarah

THERE WAS A STRANGE VIBRATION SURROUNDING me. My whole body was vibrating. That was weird. My tongue felt like cotton wool, and I couldn't open my eyes. I started to panic. It was terrifying. I used all of my willpower to open my eyes a fraction, but the light made me flinch and I closed them again. Why was my seat vibrating? It still hadn't dawned on me where I was. Once more, I opened my eyes bit by bit while my brain caught up with my body and my senses. I was in an airplane! My body was scrunched and huddled in the seat and I was facing the window. I tried to stretch, but my muscles complained and I felt a cramp developing in my left calf. The person sitting next to me put a hand on my arm. Adam! Once my savior and now a veritable Judas!

"Well, well, look who decided to wake up," Adam mocked me just as he used to when we were children.

"This is not funny. You have brought me here against my will! How dare you!"

"I had to do it, Sarah. They were blackmailing me. They sent me because they thought you would trust me." He did look contrite, but it barely registered with me. I was furious and hurt.

I tried to stretch my aching muscles again. I also realized that I needed a drink of water and to use the facilities. I was a mess, but, thank God, the fuzziness in my brain was ebbing away and I was more alert. I was still dressed in the clothes I had worn to the hospital, but someone had placed my jacket on top of me to keep me warm.

The most important thing that I had to do was to get a message to Tanya. She would be devastated when she heard that I had been taken. But I knew her—she would find me, so I just needed to leave a trail of breadcrumbs for her to follow. Knowing my family, I was sure they had planned this abduction a long time before, and they wouldn't be happy simply with having me home. I shuddered to think what they had in store for me, and I prayed for God to help me get back to my life and my real home in England...back to my Tanya.

I looked at Adam with revulsion and he recoiled when he saw my expression. I was surprised to see that he had tears in his eyes.

"Crocodile tears, bro?" I sneered at him.

"I know you hate me and feel betrayed, but I didn't have any choice."

"Everyone has a choice, Adam Shah!" I nearly shouted.

"Listen, Sarah. Just listen to me. Please. Then judge me. For heaven's sake."

"I don't know what you could say that would make me feel differently. You are despicable."

Adam looked away, but not before I saw tears streaming down his cheeks that he tried to covertly wipe away.

"Please, Sarah. Just listen."

"First get me some water and then I will think about listening to your sob story." I couldn't stop sniping at him.

After the flight attendant brought me some water and I had drunk enough to soothe my parched throat, I turned to Adam.

"Speak! And it had better be good."

"Sarah, please..." I turned my head towards the window.

After taking a deep breath, he began to speak. "When you left things became very difficult for me since the family obviously blamed me for helping you escape. They wanted to bring you back immediately, but I convinced them to let you finish your studies. I had to argue with our parents and Azaan to leave you alone till you received your MRCPCH."

I didn't say anything. My lips were curled in a sneer as I looked pointedly at him waiting for more.

Adam sighed and continued. "Everyone ostracized me for helping you, and the tension nearly drove me crazy. The only solace I got was to go for walks on the beach at sunset. You know how the colors of the sun reflect from the clouds and create a medley of beautiful colors at sunset. You used to love walking with me at Clifton Beach."

I nodded, but I was puzzled. Where was this story of sunsets and phantasmagoria heading? What did that have to do with my being so brutally ripped away from my idyllic life?

"So?" I sneered.

"I met someone on the beach—a young woman who enjoys watching the sunset as much as I do. She is a doctor like you, but from a university up north. From Peshawar. She used to come to the beach to get away from her family. Like I did. Her parents had recently passed away, and her brother was now her guardian. He would harass her all the time, and he controlled what she should wear, or eat, or what specialization she should pursue. He used to poke his nose in every aspect of her life.

"Gulnaz is my soul mate. We fell deeply in love. When we were together, we talked about everything possible under the sun, and believe me when I say that we enjoyed each other's company immensely."

"Well, good for you!" I still wasn't sure where this story was going, so I was a bit snippety.

Adam started to look drained. He held up his hands to signal that there was more to come.

"We decided that we wanted to get married, so I asked Ammi and Baba to talk to her brother to get his permission. I was so in love with her that I hadn't even asked her who her brother was. Now, Khan is a very common name, as common as Smith is in the UK, you know that." He tried to smile but failed miserably.

"When we went to Gulnaz's house, we found out that her brother was Dr. Farooq Khan—the same Dr. Farooq you were engaged to before you left."

It was slowly dawning on me. Adam's marriage was probably dependent on my being there, although I still didn't understand why.

"Dr. Farooq agreed to us getting married as long as you came back and married him. There would be a double wedding or none at all."

I gasped at Farooq's audacity. How dare he!

"Why?" I spat out. "You know what a horrible person he is. You helped me once you saw how he behaved towards me and the other female doctors in the hospital."

"Yes, I did." Adam averted his gaze for a moment. "That is why I refused his condition. I told Ammi and Baba that I would not willingly let you marry a man who would make your life a living hell just for my own happiness."

"Then why all this drama?" I gestured towards myself and the plane.

"Gulnaz and I married in a secret ceremony two years ago and we lived together in a flat at Sea View. We hadn't told anyone where we were and what we had done. Dr. Farooq thought his sister was working in a hospital across town and was busy with night duties, so out of convenience she would stay in a room at the hospital's staff complex. Ammi and Baba knew that I had bought a flat and was living on my own. Or so they thought. We were very happy, and that happiness made me understand why you had risked everything to be with the love of your life. After all, I did the same thing, didn't I?"

I slowly started to empathize with Adam. I knew there was going to be a turning point in the story where he was forced to the situation at hand.

"Gulnaz became pregnant. We were ecstatic and yet, knowing Farooq's brutal nature, we were scared. I did the next best thing—I told our parents. Since the baby was well on its way, they softened their stance towards my marriage and welcomed Gulnaz into the family."

"Congratulations," I said tersely. "Then, what is the problem? Why are you making my life miserable now?" While I was happy for Adam, I still was upset.

"Farooq found us one day. He had gone to visit Gulnaz at the hospital and he was told that she didn't live there and never had. He was obviously livid. He followed Gulnaz home and barged into our flat shouting and screaming obscenities at us. He then dragged his sister by her arm and took her with him. I couldn't do anything because I didn't want to hurt Gulnaz. If he had pushed her or jostled her, either she or the baby could have been hurt. I have not seen her since, but Farooq has been in touch with us and has promised that I will get my wife back only if I exchange her for you. He has taken Gulnaz deep into the tribal area and no one knows where she is. The only news that I have recently received was that she has given birth to a baby boy. Farooq is using him as leverage as well. I was beside myself... I was devastated that I couldn't hold my baby boy when he was born. Sarah, only you can help me get my family back!" Adam started to sob. His story did touch my heart, but I still couldn't understand how he had agreed to sacrifice me for his happiness. Almost as if he could read my mind, he spoke again.

"I know Tanya is an excellent agent. I have followed her career, and she has been highly decorated and is well respected in Interpol. If anyone can find you, she can. But please, please, don't make things difficult for me. Gulnaz, my son, and my own life are at stake. I beg you."

I kept quiet. I had to think about all this, but the two thugs who turned out to be Farooq's men were sitting across the aisle from us. How could I send a message to Tanya if I was being watched so intently?

Suddenly, the plane PA system cackled to life. "Is there a doctor on board? Is there a doctor on board? Please, contact the closest flight attendant immediately. We have a pediatric emergency on board." The announcer sounded desperate. I stood up on wobbly legs to respond to the emergency request. One of the thugs across the aisle grabbed my arm to stop me and told me to sit down immediately. I shook off his grip. How dare he think that I, a qualified doctor, would refuse a cry for help? I ignored them and pressed the call button for the attendant.

"Are you a doctor, madam?" she asked.

"Yes, I am a pediatrician. You said there was a pediatric emergency, didn't you?"

"Oh, thank God, yes! Please come with me doctor!"

I followed her to the front of the aircraft, where there was a young mother who was holding a two-year-old baby. He was clearly having trouble breathing. His lips were blue and he was getting limp by the second.

"What's happened?" I asked the mother.

"I don't know. He was playing happily with some beads and then he suddenly started to choke and turned blue."

"Aha!" I thought to myself. "A classic case of choking on a small object." I had seen many young children and babies with suspected foreign-body aspirations. Of course, I commonly saw them in the emergency department, so I was very familiar with what was happening to the baby. He had the typical "sentinel event," which consisted of a sudden onset of choking, gasping, gagging, wheezing, stridor, difficulty in breathing, change in color, or difficulty in swallowing. The first thing a parent or doctor needs to think if they see something similar happening is that the baby could have aspirated something, most probably something small that he or she was playing with. That initial diagnosis may save lives.

I took the baby gently from his mother and sat down on a nearby seat. I looked into his mouth but didn't see anything. I didn't want to sweep my finger in blindly to try and find a foreign body, because that could accidently push it further in. Therefore, I started a series of back thumps alternating with chest compressions. After the second set, the baby gave a heave and, with a sharp cough, a little red bead shot out of his mouth and he started to cry. His color came back to normal quite soon, but just to be sure, I took my stethoscope out of my bag and listened to his chest. Yes, there was good air entry in both of his lungs. His mother looked relieved and hugged me, but I think the flight attendant was even happier that the calamity had been averted. Many of the passengers nearby started to clap as I walked shyly away. The flight attendant gratefully shook my hands and asked me to follow her—I was ushered into the first-class area and given a seat there. Wow! I knew that if I stayed there alone my captors would come looking for me and would in all probability cause a ruckus. I didn't want that to happen.

"Thank you so much, but I am on the flight with my brother. He might get upset if we are separated."

"That's understandable. The seat next to you is fortunately unoccupied and will be given to your brother," she said with a smile.

"I would like to ask for a favor," I said hesitantly. "Could you call the number on this card and tell Agent Tanya Kareem that I have been taken against my will to Pakistan? I need her to come and get me as soon as she can." I took one of the cards Tanya had made for me with our signature logo from my bag and I gave it to the attendant. "Please do that for me when you fly back to London."

The flight attendant, whose nametag said that she was called Sandra, looked suspiciously at the card, but she must have realized that my distress was genuine.

"Why do you want me to do that? You know that by law I need to report anything out of the ordinary, especially cases of kidnap or suspected slavery. I am sorry, but I will have to contact the authorities. However, since you are a respectable doctor, I will give you a chance to tell me your story."

I was on the verge of panicking and regretted saying anything. I didn't want the authorities alerted just yet, not now that I knew Adam's family was at stake. I told Sandra our story as briefly as possible. I also explained that I wasn't sure how honest the police in Pakistan were and whether they would betray us. I emphasized that lives were in danger.

"You said that your partner works for Interpol?"

"Yes, that is why I need to let her know where to look for us."

Knowing that Tanya was an agent of Interpol softened Sandra's stance towards alerting the authorities and she promised that she would try to help as much as she could. I heaved a sigh of relief when she nodded briefly and put the card in her pocket. "Please, don't forget. It's a matter of life and death. At least it is for me."

While bustling around in the cabin, Sandra covertly pressed a small piece of paper in my hand and told me to contact her if I needed to. She said that she had thought about my dilemma and she wouldn't mind acting as a liaison between Tanya and myself if it were possible. Thank God for kind and understanding people!

After a little while, Adam joined me and, even though

we were both still quite upset, we enjoyed the large leather seats and being pampered by Sandra in First Class. The thugs tried to come a couple of times to check on us, but Sandra didn't allow them to come near me citing airlines rules and regulations. I concluded that their IQ must be rock bottom. Where did they think we would run off to? Would we jump off the plane and skydive over Bulgaria?

"By the way, I have something of yours." Adam started to root through his pockets. He drew a shiny object from his inner coat pocket and slapped it into my hand. It was my pendant!

"I don't know what is wrong with this trinket, but whenever we went through security it would make the sensors and alarms go crazy, so I took it off. It was difficult because the clasp is strange, so we had to clip it off with wire cutters."

I was furious. They had damaged my pendant, my precious anniversary present from Tanya.

"How dare you even touch my things! Isn't it enough that you have violated me and my life in England? Now you have destroyed my pendant!"

"Calm down, Sarah, the pendant is not damaged; it's just the chain that has been cut. It can be fixed quite easily. I promise I will get that done once we are in Karachi."

"Just stay away from me and my things!" I turned away from Adam. I didn't want to talk to him anymore. At least for now.

I closed my eyes after our succulent meal and tried to send my thoughts, prayers, and affirmation of my love towards Tanya. I knew she would find me. She had the support of Interpol and, more importantly, she had a very sharp mind. In the meantime, I hoped I'd have the strength to fight whatever negativity was rushing towards me like a runaway train.

Tanya

THE FIRST PERSON I saw when we landed in London was Andrew... Andy. He had such a contrite look on his face, but my first instinct was to punch that expression off it. Whoa! Where were these violent thoughts coming from? Taking a deep breath, I thanked Mr. Thomas for the lift. While in the air, he had told me that I could take a long leave of absence to concentrate on getting Sarah back. He liked Sarah. She was their family pediatrician and his children adored her. Well, maybe they adored the stickers and lollipops she handed out after the consultations a bit more.

"Just bring your doctor back. And do let me know if there is anything we can do on our end if needed."

After taking my leave from Mr. Thomas, I turned to Andy. He flinched at the steely expression on my face. I didn't blame him and knew he felt guilty because Sarah had been taken on his watch.

I tried to smile to assure him that I was over my momentary anger, but it was difficult. How could one control these feelings? This mixture of hate, anger and sadness really put me off kilter. And I couldn't use Andy as a punching bag—it wasn't fair, and antagonizing him was not wise since I needed his help.

As my partner, he knew me very well, so he gently took my arm and steered me to a nearby café where I usually enjoyed a cappuccino. We found an empty table in the back and I settled there with my bags while Andy went to get our drinks. I looked around at the other patrons dispassionately, wondering how the world could still be turning while my life had been shaken to the core. I lifted my hand to sweep my bangs away from my eyes and noticed that it was shaking. I couldn't show any weakness to anyone. Sarah needed my strength.

Andy returned with our orders and we began to discuss what we knew so far and whether any of our agents could get any information regarding Sarah's whereabouts.

"She was taken to Heathrow Airport. The security cameras there showed her in one of those complimentary wheelchairs that you get at the terminal. The photos confirm that she was slumped in the seat indicating that she was either drugged or ill. We have already shown her picture to security as well as customs personnel at the airport and they recognized her. They said they were told that she was ill and needed to be fast tracked through. Somehow they had forged medical reports to prove that. She was on flight BA147 to Karachi with short stopovers in Dubai and Kuwait. We had people waiting in the transit areas of these cities but neither Sarah nor her brother disembarked from the plane like the other passengers."

"Her brother?" I was surprised. I thought she had been taken by some unknown thugs.

"Yes, according to the flight manifest, she was travelling with three other people, one of whom was Mr. Adam Shah. We found out that he is one of her twin brothers."

"Adam? How? Why?" I was confused. He had helped Sarah come to England five years before... What had happened? Why was he doing this? Sarah must be devastated!

"Our contacts have told us that Sarah helped a patient on

the flight and she and her brother were then bumped up to first class. We were also able to talk to the flight attendant, Sandra. Apparently, Sarah gave her one of her unique visiting cards and had asked her to contact you. So at least you know that she travelled comfortably." Andy tried to inject a modicum of humor into the situation, but I was in no mood to lighten up. I felt as if my brain was drowning in some dark fog. No matter what I thought about or tried to do, there was a wall surrounding me. I needed to focus. Panicking or losing my temper would not help Sarah in any way.

"What is their present status? What do our agents in Karachi say?"

"Sarah and her brother were met by a man called Dr. Farooq and then taken to their father's house in the Defense Society. They have security guards there and the walls and gates are very high. No way to take a look inside. Apparently, the guards are a new addition."

Dr. Farooq! Why wasn't I surprised? He was bound to raise his reptilian head sooner or later. He never forgave Sarah for jilting him. He was a scumbag then and it seemed that he hadn't changed at all. As a matter of fact, it looked like he had become worse.

I had to go to Karachi, but I needed to get into the city without anyone finding out. For influential people like Sarah's father, it was easy to know when a persona non grata arrived at the airport. I had often sought the customs and airport security personnel to get information. Maybe they would be more helpful to a colleague? I couldn't take that risk—I needed to go to Karachi incognito.

"Andy, could you arrange a Pakistani passport for me

with the relevant stamps and visas, please? Obviously, not in my name. I will give you a photograph later on."

"Right, I will start on that immediately." Andy looked relieved that he had something to do. "Would you like to me to come along?"

I smiled for the first time in the last few hours. Andy looked typically British with his fair hair and blue eyes, and he would stick out like a sore thumb if he went along with me. "I need you here. I have a few friends in Pakistan who I trust and will help me. But I do appreciate the offer."

I gathered our notes and my bags and we left the café. Andy reminded me to get my passport photos to him as soon as I could. He took my bags with him and promised to stow them in my locker at the office. He promised to bring them to the airport once my travel arrangements had been finalized. For now, I needed to visit Mr. Jones and see whether he remembered anything significant.

Mr. Jones was sitting up in bed watching television. He looked quite droll with the white bandage on his head. He was surprised to see me and switched the TV off immediately.

"I am so sorry, Ms. Kareem. I feel so guilty. Dr. Shah had warned me that there might be some unsavory characters after her, but I couldn't stop them." He started to get a bit agitated. I didn't want him to get upset, especially since he had a concussion, so I put my hand on his where it lay on top of the blanket and gave it a friendly squeeze.

"It's not your fault, Mr. Jones. These people are devious. You couldn't have stopped them. And I know you did try— that's why you are here in the ward, right? I have come to thank you."

"I just wish I could have done more."

"May I ask you a few questions? I need to know exactly what happened. Maybe there are a few clues that we can get from what you saw."

"There wasn't much. I just saw these three men wheeling Dr. Shah out of the hospital. She was slumped over in the chair as if she wasn't conscious or was drugged. I tried to stop them, but you know what happened next, and here I am."

"I would like you to think very carefully. Was there anything unusual about these men? Maybe you saw something that was out of the ordinary. Any small clue would help."

Mr. Jones leaned back and closed his eyes. He was still for such a long time that I thought he had fallen asleep. Just as I was going to tiptoe ruefully out of the room, he started to talk while still having his eyes shut, as if he was trying to relive the moment when Sarah was taken.

"Well, the men were obviously of Pakistani origin, but what struck me was that they were all very well dressed. All of them wore dark suits, and the car they were driving was expensive too. It was a black Bentley." Mr. Jones lapsed into silence once more. He took a deep sigh and went on. "I am quite good with remembering numbers and I like checking the number plates of the cars passing by. This car had quite unusual plates—DPL-058."

"That is a diplomatic number!" I exclaimed. At least I knew now where to start my search.

I thanked Mr. Jones for his help once again and left the hospital. I caught a taxi and asked to be dropped off at the Pakistani High Commission. I had a few friends who worked there, and the chief of security was a colleague from the time that I was Chief Inspector of Police in Karachi. I hoped he would be available to meet me.

The High Commission staff recognized me and I could pass through the security checks with ease. For inter-agency law enforcement officers it was more of a formality than anything.

I waited in one of the smaller conference rooms on the ground floor while one of the aides went to look for Inspector General Habib. I was impressed—he had been promoted quite quickly. But then, he was one of the good guys. I knew that he had impeccable integrity and if I ever needed him he would always be there for me. As a colleague and as a friend.

I had to wait for at least thirty minutes before Habib strode into the room. He was a big man with a loud booming voice, but I have seen him with his children, and he is one of the gentlest souls that I know. However, any felon who crossed his path would never get to know that side of him that he reserved only for close friends and family.

Even though this was a formal visit, Habib engulfed me in a bear hug.

"Are you all right, Tanya? You have upset quite a lot of influential people." He sniggered uneasily.

"So you do know why I am here to see you. I wouldn't expect anything less from you. I was wondering why I was being made to wait."

"I had to get whatever information there was available before I could meet you. That is why you're here, right?"

Habib was one of the few people who knew what Sarah meant to me. He was also one of the invitees at our commitment ceremony. I was touched that he had already compiled a folder with whatever information I could hopefully use.

"Sarah's father knows a lot of influential people," Habib said. "She was kidnapped with the help of some embassy staff. As a matter of fact, I just found out that whoever arranged the kidnapping was using our security staff to track her. I am so sorry I couldn't find out earlier, otherwise we could have stopped this nonsense from the beginning. I was in Washington for a high-powered meeting. You know how it is; we are not even aware of the outside world while we are working there. Most of the time we are incarcerated in the meeting rooms. You do know that the Americans are paranoid about leaking security secrets."

"It's not your fault, Habib. I appreciate what you have put together for me. You have already seen everything in the file. What do you think I should do?"

There was a knock on the door and Andy walked in with one of Habib's aides.

"Meet Abdullah, Tanya. I trust him explicitly. If you can't get hold of me, he has instructions to help you on a priority basis. He will be your liaison officer. Rest assured no information will be leaked or passed on to anyone else, no matter how high their security clearance is. That is the least I can do for you, my friend."

While I tried to express my gratitude to Habib, Andy handed me a sealed envelope. I ripped it open and saw that it contained a return ticket to Karachi and a new Pakistani passport. It already had British and European visas stamped in it. Just the photograph was missing.

"Abdullah, Take Agent Tanya into the photo studio in the basement and get the High Commission photographer to take her photo for the passport. Then get the seal affixed on it so that it looks authentic."

Habib hugged me once more, not caring that the other men were in the room. "Good luck. And do bring our girl home as soon as you can."

Wiping my eyes on the sleeve of my coat, I followed Abdullah to the basement. Andy waited discreetly for me in the conference room. He was aware of the protocols in foreign missions and didn't want to overstep his welcome here.

The embassy photo studio was interesting. It was small, but there was a collection of props in a corner where you could find anything from scarves to caps and all sorts of clothes. I chose a colorful scarf and twisted my hair into a tight braid.

I draped the scarf on my head and had my photo taken. It was developed within half an hour thanks to the new technology that they had acquired. I looked different. Nondescript. Like a regular young Pakistani woman. Abdullah affixed the photo onto the passport and stamped it with the embossing seal. Now it looked quite official.

Wishing me the best of luck, he handed the passport over to me. Andy and I decided that I would go to the airport immediately. I would read the folder and our papers on the flight, and I could buy essential toiletries and underwear from the airport. It was pure luck that I still had the bags that Andy had stowed away for me when I arrived from Amsterdam.

"Can we make a quick detour to Southhall before we go to the airport?"

"Of course." Andy sounded surprised and looked at me

curiously. "Do you want to get some ethnic clothes to wear for the journey?"

"Aren't you the bright spark today, Andy?" I mocked. I was trying to make light of a situation that was weighing heavy on my heart. I probably wasn't doing too well, because the look he gave me was full of compassion and sympathy.

We went to one of the popular Pakistani boutiques in Southhall where I was able to get two ethnic ladies' suits, *shalwar kameezes*, and a pair of matching leather sandals. Those were more than enough to blend in and enter the country without drawing any attention to myself. We were sure that they had people looking out for me, and they would report my entry into the country to Sarah's father or whoever else was involved. That was how the "Old Boy's" network's cogs rotated in Karachi—a person of interest would cough in one part of the city and the sound would reverberate and echo throughout all channels of communication. Faster than the speed of light.

Andy dropped me off at Heathrow, and after saying goodbye to him, I immediately went to the ladies' room to change into my new clothes. My hair was still in its tight braid and I had heavily outlined my eyes with kohl. I don't think I would have recognized my own self if I had tried. Satisfied with my appearance, I went through the routine security and immigration procedures with ease. No one looked twice at my passport. It was just stamped, and I was waved ahead.

Heaving a sigh of relief, after a short shopping spree for essentials, I settled down in one of the many restaurants at the airport. I realized that I hadn't had anything to eat since we heard that Sarah had been taken. My feckless stomach started to growl an indignant protest for having been ignored for the most part of nearly twenty-four hours. A sandwich and a cup of tea would be like manna from heaven, but I had cut the time a bit short. As soon as I was getting comfortable, they announced the boarding of my flight. The gate was still a short distance away, so I gathered my bags and literally galloped to the gate to board as one of the last passengers. I was so focused on getting ready for the journey that I hadn't realized Andy had booked me into Business Class. I heaved a grateful sigh of relief. At least my tall frame would be thankful for the extra leg room. Just as I was putting my passport and ticket back into my bag, I noticed a piece of paper sticking out of the passport. I hadn't seen it before. It was a note from Andy. He wrote: "Dear Tanya, I hope you have a pleasant journey (courtesy Business Class as advised by the boss) and bring Sarah back. We are all rooting for you." I was touched and sent a prayer heavenwards to help me get the love of my life back. We don't need this unprecedented negativity in our lives. After all we have been through, we do deserve some peace and quiet in our lives. I settled back in my comfortable seat and closed my eyes. I must have been half asleep because I felt Sarah next to me. I could even smell her perfume. Her presence was overwhelming. As if from far away, I heard her voice calling me. *"Help me, Tanya. Come find me. I need to be with you. I will always love you!"*

I opened my eyes with a jerk hoping that I would find Sarah sitting next to me. Unfortunately, there was no one there. I realized then that she was sending me telepathic messages. She had told me once that if one was open to such messages, one could actually communicate intuitively. I didn't completely believe her, but on this flight to Karachi, I became a firm believer.

CHAPTER 4

PATRIOTISM

"Breathes there the man with soul so dead,
Who never to himself hath said,
'This is my own, my native land!'
Whose heart hath ne'er within him burn'd
As home his footsteps he hath turn'd." ~ Sir Walter
Scott

Sarah

I WAS HAVING SUCH A NICE DREAM. IT WAS ABOUT the hiking holiday we had in the Cotswolds last year. It was such an idyllic break for both of us. The serenity of the area was captivating and so destressing. We would hike all over the rolling hills during the day and take picnic lunches with us. I also loved eating on the lawns of the stately Sudeley Castle. Tanya and I made up stories of the people who had lived for centuries there. Luck was on our side when we were able to get a comfortable room at a bed and breakfast in the town of Chipping Campden. I was also happily surprised that we were just in time for the arts and crafts fair that it was so famous for.

Suddenly, a raucous noise intruded my subconscious and rudely woke me up from my dream. No! I didn't want to leave Tanya. I didn't want to wake up!

"Ladies and gentlemen, we are about to land in Karachi, where the local time is 08:15am and the temperature is 32 degrees Celsius. As we start our descent, please make sure your seat backs and tray tables are in their full upright position. Fasten your seat belt securely and see that all carry-on luggage is stowed underneath the seat in front of you or in the overhead bins. Thank you."

I sat up, still irritated that my dream had been interrupted and I had to face my reality once more.

Looking out of the window as we circled Karachi, I realized that this wasn't the way I wanted to come home. The feeling of nostalgia and homesickness that I had willingly tamped down over the years started to bubble onto the surface while I tried to identify the landmarks as we flew over them. Malir cantonment was a carpet of greenery with the commercial vegetable gardens punctuated sporadically by a poultry farm here and there. As we approached the city, I saw the Mazar of the Quaid, and looking towards the horizon, I could just make out Clifton beach. My parents' house was nearby, in what was called the Defense Society. It was an upper middle-class area of the city and everyone who thought they were anyone tried to get a house in that massive housing colony, so much so that the prostitutes from the red-light areas in the city had covertly bought houses there to give the impression of being respectable.

After the plane landed and we disembarked, I was again surrounded by my unwanted escorts. When we got off the crowded terminal bus, they tried to hurry me along, but in my asinine way I shuffled my feet, slowing them down. Adam looked at me in exasperation. He knew what I was up to because that was how I used to avoid unpleasant situations as a child—delaying the inevitable. He tried to take me by my arm to hurry me up, but I abruptly pulled away.

"I don't have as long legs as you do, Adam." The initial irritation that I had felt towards him when I was kidnapped came back in full force. "I can't walk as fast as you do."

"If you don't hurry up, we will drug you again," growled one of the goons.

Holding up his hand, Adam told him to back off. At least he was doing that much. Both of my brothers knew my aversion to drugs, but I was surprised that he was defending me. It would have been easier and quicker if he had agreed with the goon to have me drugged.

"We got what we wanted. She is now in Pakistan. Leave her alone!" My brother literally barked at the men.

"But Dr. Farooq..."

"No, leave her alone. I will see that she gets home safely. She is my responsibility!" Adam was furious now. He had seen how they had treated me in London, and he was now not so sure that this whole situation was a good idea. I could see that he was already feeling bad about everything. And so he should, I thought petulantly.

We walked down the long corridor towards the immigration counters and then the luggage carousels. It was strange to hear predominantly Urdu spoken by the people around me after having been attuned to English for so long. There was a smattering of English, Pushto, Sindhi and Punjabi that occasionally pierced the linguistic wall of Urdu. The airport was small, much smaller than Heathrow, and the passengers seemed to jostle one another as they tried to outrun or outwalk each other to get to the counters, not realizing that they would only be able to leave the confines of the airport once they received their luggage.

As we moved along the corridor, I noticed a woman in ethnically Pathan clothes who seemed to be weaving and stumbling along towards the departure lounge. She had two small children with her and seemed oblivious to her surroundings. Moreover, she had a terrified expression on her face. Suddenly, she pitched forward and fell with a shrill cry. Curious bystanders flocked around her, watching but not trying to help. Probably they didn't know what to do since they weren't qualified to help at all. But I was.

Elbowing my way through the crowd, much to the chagrin of my escorts, I barked at the bystanders to move away to give the woman some air. I thanked all that was holy that I had my instruments in my bag. I shone my torch into the now unconscious woman's eyes and noticed that her pupils were pin pointed. Her breathing was almost imperceptible and shallow.

"The airport health services counter is next to the immigration counter. Please, alert them that there is an emergency here." I shouted as loud as I could. Adam heard me and set off at a run. I told the goons to be useful and see that no one would crowd around in curiosity. At least they did that well.

Loosening the woman's clothes, I kept an eye on her

breathing. She looked as if she had an overdose of a drug. If I was right in my assumption, it could be heroin. Her boarding card indicated that she was travelling on the same aircraft that we had arrived in, on its return journey to London.

I found a packet of gummy bears and two lollipops in my bag. I made the children sit on the chairs nearby and soon they were happily sucking on their treats.

Their mother, on the other hand, wasn't doing very well. Her breathing became even more shallow and her heartbeat was barely discernible. I started CPR and told one of the goons to find Adam and tell him to hurry up. He looked at me suspiciously.

"Oh, for God's sake! Where do you think I will run off to while this woman needs medical care?" I rolled my eyes at his utter stupidity. "Go, maybe you can for once save a life too?"

He lumbered slowly off while looking over his shoulder every few steps. "GO! HURRY!" I shouted. Thankfully, he sped up. In the meantime, I continued with CPR. I desperately needed Naloxone. That was the antidote of heroin and could save her life. I hoped the airport medical team would have that injection with them.

After a hectic fifteen minutes of CPR the team arrived. They were prepared for multiple situations at the airport and could give the woman the required injection immediately. Her eyes fluttered open after a few minutes and she tried to speak.

"My children..."

"They are safe, don't worry. Do you know what happened to you?"

"No, I don't. All of a sudden I felt ill and couldn't breathe very well. I felt that I would pass out, but I tried to remain conscious as long as I could for the sake of my children."

"Are you a heroin addict?" I asked bluntly. There was no time to beat around the bush. We were able to stabilize her for now, but she needed hospitalization.

"No..." There was a frisson of uncertainty in her voice.

"Then why are you having symptoms of heroin poisoning?" I wanted to shake her shoulders, but I knew that she would either get more agitated, or she wouldn't say anything at all. I had to keep a pleasant demeanor if I wanted relevant information from her.

She saw her children watching her with wide terrified eyes. However, her face relaxed when she realized that they were in good hands.

I had just learned how to heal with energy. The Japanese call the process reiki. I knew that to get this woman strong enough to tell her story I needed to send some reiki to her. She needed justice because, if my intuition was right, she was just a pawn in a large-scale nefarious scheme. Therefore, I closed my eyes and placed my hands on her shoulders as she spoke. Almost immediately, I felt the familiar warmth and electrical tingling seeping from my fingertips to the woman. She settled unconsciously into a more comfortable position. Then she looked up and spoke with a stronger voice now.

"I might as well tell you my story. After all, who is going to be there for my children if I am no more?"

I nodded in agreement but didn't want to interrupt her. I kept my hands on her shoulders and she seemed to be drawing comfort and strength from my touch.

"My husband took a loan from a man in our village. He wanted to expand our cultivated fields by planting in the fallow areas. He was supposed to pay him back within a year, but our crops were attacked by swarms of locusts, so unfortunately we lost everything. The same man bullied us almost every day and asked to pay back the money with a 25% interest. The longer we took to pay back the loan, the higher the interest rose.

One day, he came to my husband and told him that he wanted to buy me from him. If he had agreed, his loan would be wiped off. My husband may be poor, but he is an honorable man. Obviously, he refused. As a result, he was beaten up quite badly and was hospitalized for nearly a month." She took a deep shuddering breath. I asked if she wanted to take a break.

"No, I need to tell you everything. I don't know how long I have. Or whether I will survive or not."

I put my water bottle to her lips and let her take only a few small sips. I didn't want her to choke or throw up.

Taking a deep breath, she indicated that she wanted to continue her narrative.

"On the day that my husband was discharged from the hospital, the same man came to visit us with his henchmen. He said he would stop harassing us if I carried some heroin for him to England."

She closed her eyes. I took out my stethoscope once more to see whether she was breathing properly. For now she was. The airport team wanted to take her away, and the police had also arrived and were trying to elbow their way in. Adam asked them to wait until I could get her whole story.

"I was forced to swallow twelve condoms filled with heroin. It was exceedingly difficult, but I did it for the sake of my husband and children. It was a dangerous chance to take, but I thought that maybe they would leave us alone and we could live in peace after that?"

One of the condoms must have burst in her gastrointestinal tract. That was why she had such toxic symptoms of heroin poisoning. Once she stopped talking, the medics transferred her onto a stretcher and took her away. Now we had to deal with the police.

Someone put their hand on my shoulder. It was different from Adam's touch. I abruptly turned around to see who had invaded my space. I hated it when people I didn't know touched me.

"Whoa! Slow down!" said a distinctly feminine voice. It was Inspector Razia! I was so relieved to see her. She pulled me into a hug and I felt comforted for the first time in twenty-four hours. She was a friend of mine and Tanya's, and I was pleased to be with someone who loved me unconditionally for who I was.

"Razia! I am so glad to see you! How are the twins? Your family?" I had to keep up the pretense of normality until I could let her know what had happened. Razia knew about our concerns and problems regarding my family, and she had assured me she would help us whenever she could. Now I just needed her to know what was going on.

She understood the reason of my inane chatter immediately. She turned to Adam and said, "Why don't you go through immigration and get your baggage? In the meantime, I need to get a statement from your sister. We will be at the airport police station. It's just down the road. Sarah, please give me your passport and I will fast-track you through immigration."

The goons had expressions on their faces that bordered between rage and nausea. It would have been comical if the situation weren't so serious. They couldn't argue with the law, could they?

Razia took me to the head of the line and had my passport stamped immediately. Then she escorted me out of the airport through a staff exit. She winked at me when we did so. I knew it was because she didn't want me to be seen by whoever was picking us up.

Once we reached her office, the first thing she did was ring for her stenographer to come and record my statement and for the office boy to order tea for both of us. Then she listened to what I had to say about the woman who I had resuscitated. She let me speak and only added a question in between if she needed further clarification. Once that was over, she dismissed her stenographer and looked at me seriously.

"What happened, Sarah? Tanya is frantic. She is looking for you and is understandably worried and upset."

Knowing that whatever I said to Razia would get back to Tanya, I told her what had happened and Adam's role in the whole fiasco. I wished I could have allowed Razia to spirit me away like she suggested, but then Adam would be in trouble again. I told Razia that I would try to stay in touch with her. Adam had told me that he was confident Tanya would find me and so was I.

"Please, tell Tanya that I love her. She will always be in my heart, but I need to see how this plays out. For the sake of my brother's happiness, even though he's acted like an imbecile instead of talking directly to me."

Once we finished our tea, I stood up and smiled. "I think we have let them wait long enough."

Razia walked around her desk and gave me a big hug. "I will try to have my men and women look out for you. Wherever you go. However, I know that not all of them will be loyal to me. We need to agree upon a sign so that you know the person you meet is trustworthy."

That was a clever idea. But how would we do that? Then I remembered the special cards that I had in my bag. I pulled them out and gave a small pile to Razia. "If anyone shows me one of these cards, I will know that they came directly from you and are therefore trustworthy."

Razia took the cards with a smile and put them in her uniform pocket. "I will keep these hidden so that they are confidential, and no one will have any inclination what they will be used for."

I was so blessed with good friends... Look out, Farooq, I thought to myself. If you have friends in high places, well, so do I.

"I will ask my sergeant to take you to your brother now. Adam knows me, but the less we are seen together the better it will be for you." I agreed and reluctantly said goodbye to her. It was so nice to reconnect once more. Deep within one of the side pockets of my bag was Razia's card with all of the relevant phone numbers to contact her. It was my good luck charm. My safety anchor. I felt so much better now that fate had sent Razia to me. I don't believe in coincidences—they are answers to our prayers and we should be grateful for them. There was one chance in a million that a woman would literally fall at my feet with an overdose and that Razia would be the policewoman on duty. Thank you, God. You're the best.

Trying to look demure and nonchalant, I met Adam and the goons outside the airport. The police sergeant stopped just long enough to let me hop off the jeep and hand me my passport.

"You took your time," growled one of the goons.

"What do you expect? Tell the police that your "goonship" is waiting?"

"Huh?!? Who is that?"

"You, of course. You are a goon and I shall continue to call you that because I do not want to know your name. You don't deserve my knowing your name. Hence in my mind you are nothing but a goon with a low IQ." I turned my back to him while he blustered indignantly and asked Adam who was picking us up.

"I don't know," he said ruefully. "I was told that we would be picked up, but no one seems to be here yet. Let's wait another ten minutes and then get a taxi if no one comes."

Just then, a reconditioned Jeep Wrangler stopped in front of us. It was Farooq's pride and joy. He had bought it in a junk yard and had restored it with his father. I groaned inwardly. As if I didn't have enough on my plate, I had to meet this idiot as well.

"Hey, Sarah!" he yelled at the top of his voice. It grated on my ears. Every single thing about this man irritated me. I ground my teeth in frustration with the effort to hold my tongue. I didn't want to start a shouting match in public.

The goons stepped forward and flung Adam's luggage on the back of the jeep. Just as they tried to climb in, Farooq dismissed them disdainfully and told Adam to sit in the front with him. Apparently, I was supposed to squeeze myself into the back with the haphazardly thrown bags.

I sighed and climbed in. I was too tired for any further drama. I just wanted to go home and sleep. Maybe even get to resume my dream. But I knew what the next hurdle would be—my parents.

Tanya

FINALLY, the plane landed in Karachi. I needed to act as fast as possible. I didn't have any checked in luggage and would get out of the airport as soon as I could get through the immigration procedures. The moment the doors of the aircraft opened, I hurried out and made my way towards the passport control counters. Despite my low-key appearance, I was worried that I might be recognized and information of my arrival would then be passed on to Sarah's kidnappers.

I needed to talk to Razia. She was one of my best friends and the one person in the police force that I liked and trusted explicitly. The last time I had talked to her she told me that she was posted at the airport precinct, which was walking distance from the terminal. I hoped she would be there because I didn't want to waste time waiting for her. I needed an ally—a trustworthy ally. I also hoped that Andy had managed to get through to her while I was on the flight.

I fought my way through the crowds who had come to welcome their long-lost relatives and friends at the airport. Seriously, these people needed to get a life. Coming to the airport was like a party or a picnic for them and they dressed for the occasion as well. Yes, I was grumpy. Any signs of hilarity or happiness just annoyed me at this moment in time.

I turned towards the precinct, which I could see in the distance. The border of the building was painted in the distinctive navy blue and red stripes that indicated it was a police station. I could also see that a few official jeeps were parked under the trees outside the compound. Keeping my fingers crossed that I would be able to catch Razia before she left for her rounds or whatever she did at the airport, I walked at a steady pace towards the building.

Since I was in disguise, I knew that I wouldn't be allowed entry into the office easily, but I didn't want to identify myself as a law enforcement officer just yet. Therefore, I went to the visitor's counter and asked the policeman on duty whether Inspector Razia was available. He looked me up and down in a very disdainful and lecherous manner. I was furious, but I held my temper in check.

"I need to talk to Inspector Razia, please," I repeated and tried my best to sound nice, but I couldn't help grinding my teeth in frustration as I spoke.

"And why would you want to speak to her? What business do you have with her?" The man was trying to stonewall me and annoy me at the same time. I wondered if it was because he didn't like desk duty. Or was he just his usual incompetent self? Whatever the case, I just wanted to see my friend.

"Will you tell me whether Inspector Razia is available or not!" I raised my voice in irritation and the man had the cheek to just smirk at me.

"What is going on, Sergeant?" I heard a familiar voice ask behind me. "Why are you upsetting this woman? Our job is to help people. Or have you forgotten our motto? 'Proud to serve'?" Razia sounded disgusted with her colleague. Rightfully so.

Hearing the reprimand from his superior officer, the man looked down shamefacedly and started to shuffle some papers on his counter. Razia hadn't recognized me yet. I was pleased that my disguise was holding up. I slowly turned around to look at her. She gasped when she saw me and silently signaled that I should follow her into her office.

Once inside she closed the door firmly behind her and pulled me into a hug.

"Tanya! Oh, thank God! I was wondering when I would see you! I knew that once Sarah arrived in Karachi, you wouldn't be far behind. I also received a garbled phone call from Andy saying that you were upset and were looking for Sarah. The only thing I clearly understood was that you were on your way here."

"Sarah! Have you seen her? Do you know about her kidnapping?"

"Yes, she was here earlier this morning. I had to take her statement regarding a woman she had treated at the airport. She told me everything."

"Was she all right? They didn't hurt her, did they?"

"She seemed okay. She was with her brother and two other men. Adam encouraged her to treat the sick woman, but the other two tried to interfere. I was told she was quite stern with them. You know how she is where a sick person is concerned—she goes all out and fights for them."

We shared a smile at that. Both of us had seen Sarah in medical action. It was always impressive.

"She asked me to tell you that she's fine. Apparently, her brother is being blackmailed by a man called Dr. Farooq. He is behind this kidnapping drama. I wanted to detain her, but she was worried for her brother's wife and his son's safety."

That was news for me. Razia brought me up to speed on Sarah's story. I was resentful that Razia hadn't detained her, but I understood why Sarah had to go along with her brother's plan. At least for now. She was a person of integrity and if she knew that her brother's wife and her nephew were in danger, she would try to help as much as she possibly could.

With a deep sigh of frustration, I asked Razia what we should do.

"Let us stake out her parents' house for now. I am sure you have already received the information that she is there, and that they have guards outside the house now. No one can go in or out without them knowing it. We need to know what their plans are and how they will be moving forward. But we have to hurry up because I have been told that the household is preparing for a wedding. My men have informed me that the caterers are already setting up marquees, chairs, and tables for the event." Razia sounded worried. There was a feeling of dread in the pit of my stomach. How would we get Sarah out of there?

"She loves you, Tanya, but she needs to see how this plays out." Looking at me speculatively, she suddenly got up as if something had occurred to her just then. "Where are you staying while you are in town?"

"I was hoping to stay with you." I gave a small, embarrassed laugh. I hadn't told her in advance that I was coming and I wasn't sure that I was welcome.

"You know you are always welcome in my home," said Razia as if she was reading my mind. "The twins will love to get to spend some time with their Aunty Tanya."

She stood up and put on her peaked uniform cap and left the room. I followed her meekly, trying to stay within my disguise persona. We still weren't sure who to trust. We climbed into her jeep and drove the short distance to her house. It was a nice, simple one-story house that was clearly a government issued accommodation. The front lawn was a riot of color with flowers and *champa* (plumeria) trees. The fragrance of jasmine was almost overpowering. Razia had always been a keen gardener and everyone used to fight to get her house when she changed her postings.

A servant girl came out of the house as soon as she heard the jeep. She reached out and took my bags without asking. "Shall I put these in the guest room?"

"Yes, do that, and bring us something cold to drink afterwards."

It was nice and cool in the house. There was an air of serenity there. I told Razia as much and she chuckled. "Yes, it is peaceful now, but wait till the twins come home from school. Then serenity panics and flies out of the window."

Razia hurried to change out of her uniform. After drinking the fresh lemonade served to us by her maid, we left the house, this time in her private car.

"We need to see what is happening at Sarah's parents' house. Everything that we do needs to be planned meticulously. The most important thing that we must do for now is to get a message to Sarah to let her know we are nearby and will try to help her in every way we can. It's an extremely strange situation. If we pull her out too early, her brother might not see his family for a long time, and if we are too late, she could be forcibly married to Dr. Farooq."

We reached the large house in the Defense Society. As Razia had told me, there was a lot of activity going on. Trucks were offloading foldable tables and chairs while men wearing shirts with the logos of one of the top caterers in town were taking bins filled with cutlery and crockery from vans to wash in large tubs of soap water that were set down in the driveway near the gates. Electricians were crawling over the roof of the house installing fairy lights. It looked just like a normal house getting ready for a wedding. I bit my thumb in frustration and looked at Razia with indignant tears in my eyes.

There were angry voices coming from the house and we edged nearer to hear what was going on. A woman's voice was complaining that the woman who applied bridal henna hadn't arrived yet.

Razia looked on speculatively. I could literally sense her mind churning every possibility and discarding them as she thought of and subsequently rejected the ideas. Suddenly, she perked up. "I think I know what we can do. I have a colleague who is amazing at applying henna. I am going to call her and tell her to come and act as if she did that professionally. Through her, we will be able to send Sarah a message. My colleague will also be able to let us know what is happening inside the house."

It was sheer luck that we heard about the no-show of the henna woman. We drove to the nearby police station and phoned Razia's colleague, Tehmina. She came within twenty minutes because she lived nearby. As a disguise, especially to convince Sarah's mother that she was the henna woman, she wore faded cotton clothes and had a crumbled plastic bag with henna cones and lemons in it.

"You were lucky that I was at home and that I had all this stuff with me. It has saved us time."

We were happy that Tehmina had agreed to help so readily. We briefed her on the situation and told her what we wanted her to do. Her eyes sparkled as she found the situation amusing. She was known to always be up for an adventure.

We dropped her around the corner of the house, and she walked the rest of the way. We kept an eye on the gate of the house and we were relieved when we saw that she was readily welcomed inside.

I had given her one of Sarah's cards so that when Sarah saw it, she would know that she could trust Tehmina, and know that she came from me and Razia.

Now we just had to wait. We needed to know how and when we could rescue Sarah without jeopardizing her and her brother. We were walking a very fine line.

CHAPTER 5

EVASIVE NUPTIALS

"I loved them so much that I used to drive myself crazy trying to figure out why they were hurting... Why they betrayed me so easily... What was happening in their life that would lead them to treat me so abusively... Then, in a moment of clarity, I realized that I am not the "Narcissist Whisperer" and freed myself from that toxic behaviour." – Steve Maraboli

Sarah

I WAS JOSTLED AND BUMPED AROUND IN THE BACK of the jeep along with the luggage. It was extremely uncomfortable. I was sure I would have impressive bruises when we reached our destination. I wouldn't call it home—it hadn't been a home ever since I left under a dark cloud. The canvas cover of the jeep didn't have any windows, so I had to lean forward to look out or have a whiff of fresh air, but I was reluctant to do so because it brought me nearer to Farooq, whose cheap cologne had already polluted the interior of the vehicle. I was on the verge of feeling claustrophobic. We hadn't eaten anything since the dinner on the plane, so, on top of everything else, I was feeling lightheaded and hypoglycaemic. Even though I wanted the ride to be over as quickly as possible, I was dreading my reunion with my parents. I had a very uneasy feeling. As we got closer to their house, my hair started to stand on end, and I was shivering despite the oppressive heat in the jeep. My intuition was buzzing at full speed. I was certain that this was not going to be a happy homecoming.

To distract myself, I opted for the lesser evil and leaned forward to look out of the jeep from the windshield in front. Adam and Farooq were talking with each other, but I didn't register what they were saying. The noise of the diesel engine was too loud, and I just didn't care at this point. Farooq tried to include me in the conversation by looking over his shoulder and shouting something or the other at me, but I didn't answer him. I could see that my indifference was making him angry. I know it was petty, but that pleased me —knowing that my silence bothered him was a bonus point in my book. Idiot!

The cacophony of the traffic added to the sound of the diesel engine, so I was even more disinclined to converse with anyone. I entertained myself by looking at the familiar painted minibuses that were trying to stuff as many commuters as possible within their bowels while rushing off, hardly giving anyone a proper chance to hop on or hop off. For them it was always a race against time. The scariest sights were the families settled like Tetris blocks onto motorcycles with the driver weaving his precious cargo in and out of the traffic with undeterred sangfroid. I would mostly be afraid for the infants in the mother's arms. Since they were riding side-saddle, I was always worried that the baby would jerk or slip, and both the mother and the baby would be traffic fodder.

Finally, we turned into the lane leading to my parents' house. It was usually a very quiet cul-de-sac, but that day there seemed to be a flurry of activity going on. There were preparations for a celebration underway and many people were rushing in and out of the open gates to get on with their tasks. Farooq turned his head to look back at me when he stopped the car. He didn't say anything, but he raised his eyebrows suggestively and gave me a lecherous smirk. I sneered at him and tried to get off the jeep before he could say anything. As I was struggling to get by him, he suddenly reached out and pulled my arm roughly towards him. He was hurting me, but I didn't give him the satisfaction of showing that it bothered me. I could smell his fetid body odour mixed with his noxious cologne and the garlic on his putrid breath that he had probably had for his last meal.

"You can't escape me this time, Sarah! I will make you pay for the humiliation I had to endure when you went away all those years ago. And don't try to say anything to your family. I still have my sister and nephew hidden away. They will do as I say! I have them all in the palm of my hands." With that he gave me a hard shove that almost made me fall onto the road. If this was a sample of what Farooq had in mind for me, I could look forward to a life of utter misery. Why would my parents hate me so much that they were willing to let me live a life of pain? I wouldn't cry. I refused to show any weakness to anyone. Nobody was my friend here. Everyone had an ulterior motive or an agenda, but I would be strong. For myself, for Tanya, and also for Gulnaz.

Oblivious to our little altercation, Adam strode ahead into the house. He seemed eager to meet someone, but if it was his immediate family, he would be disappointed. Farooq had not honoured his side of the bargain.

As I stepped into the gateway, Farooq revved his jeep's engine and drove away with a screech of his tires like a juvenile teenager shouting, "See you later, alligator!"

I rolled my eyes in disgust and then looked around. Serious preparations were taking place for the sham wedding. I had to think fast to get myself out of this predicament. I doubted I would have Adam's help this time because I was sure he would be worried about his family. I knew Farooq would try to marry me this evening and still not let Adam see his wife and son. I needed to get someone to listen to me or we were all doomed.

My father was waiting for me when I traversed the lawn, which was already being set up with tables. When I walked up the three steps leading to the front door, he took a step towards me and raised his arms as if he wanted to hug me, but my mother's stern voice stopped any gesture of welcome or affection.

"You can hug her all you want when she is married and your honor is restored. For now, Sarah, go and greet your grandmother and then have a shower. You don't smell very nice."

Of course, I didn't smell very nice—I had been wearing the same clothes for twenty-four hours and being stuffed at the back of Farooq's oily jeep didn't help either. I was sad that I wasn't acknowledged by my parents. Even after a period of five years. But then what did I expect?

One happy thing about this whole situation was that my grandmother was here. I had missed her. She had always doted on me, not only because I was the youngest in the family, but also because I was the only girl in a long line of boys. I thought and hoped that she would help me.

"Which room is Dadi staying in?" I asked my mother.

"In your old room. Just go up and stay there for a while. You will be out of the way, and knowing you, I don't want you to sabotage anything before the ceremony tonight." With that, she turned her back on me and walked stiffly away. I looked at her retreating back in sorrow. I would have loved a hug or a soft word of affection from her, but it was not to be.

I knocked politely on the door before I entered. I didn't want to disturb Dadi if she was resting.

"Come in!" my grandmother's hearty voice called out. "Sarah! Oh, thank God you are here! I was getting worried. Your parents have told me all sorts of rubbish about you."

I hugged her and then sighed and sat down next to her. I laid my head on her shoulder and felt instantly comforted. My shoulders were slumped in defeat, and yet there was, as always, a glimmer of hope. I prayed that Tanya would be able to get me out of this predicament against all odds.

"Why are you looking so sad on your wedding day, sweetie? Don't you like the groom?"

"I hate him. He is cruel and inconsiderate. I have been kidnapped from England by Adam because Farooq has in turn kidnapped Adam's family."

Dadi looked at me with a shocked expression on her face while I told her what had happened in the previous twenty-four hours and also about my life in England.

"I am so sorry, not only for what you had to suffer, but

also for the idiotic behavior of your parents. Farooq sounds despicable. What do we do now? How can I help you?"

"Dadi, I love you, but why are you so willing to help me?"

"Because this is all so wrong! Even though some people mistakenly say that the parents have the last word about marriage in Islam, it is not true at all. Forcing someone to marry is absolutely un-Islamic and was very much discouraged by the Holy Prophet. Peace be upon Him."

We were quiet for a short while. Ideas and thoughts were processed and discarded. Suddenly, my grandmother sat up and said, "I have an idea that will beat all ideas!"

I had always loved Dadi's cheerful outlook, but I was not overly optimistic about my chances.

"Is your friend Professor Jahan Ara still at the government hospital?"

"Ye-e-es!" I said drawing the single word out while looking at Dadi as if she had lost her mind. How could Jahan help us out of our predicament?

"What if I fake a heart attack or a stroke? Then you would have to call an ambulance and send me to the hospital. You can insist that I am taken to your friend because you trust her. Also, I will insist that you and Adam come with me in the ambulance. Once in the hospital, we can persuade your friend to admit me in the critical care ward. At least for a day or two."

That was brilliant! I knew that Jahan would help me. She knew what a creep Farooq was and had seen his shenanigans firsthand when he did his residency at her hospital. I hugged Dadi. The plan just might work. And if I could find a way to call Razia from the hospital it would be perfect. That way Tanya would know where to find me and we could plan our next moves.

There was a phone in my room. Unfortunately, it was an extension of the main house phone, but we could take a chance that no one would pick up the other phone downstairs. I would try to call Jahan. Maybe the noise of all of the activity in the house would drown out the tinkling of the bells on the main phone as I dialed the hospital number. Taking a deep breath, I crossed my fingers and dialed the familiar number. I didn't say much to Jahan because I was still worried that someone might listen in, but I did tell her that I needed a favor. A medical favor. She was an associate professor at the hospital and was in a position to help me out. Therefore, she agreed without any hesitation whatsoever.

Step one completed. Now I had to brief Dadi on the symptoms to make her "heart attack" look realistic.

Once she had rehearsed for a while, Dadi demonstrated her fake attack to me. I went to the little fridge in the room and emptied a tray of ice into a small cloth and wiped her face and hands with it.

Dadi finally signaled that she was ready. "Let the drama begin!" She could be quite a sport and hilarious when she wanted to be, and moreover, she would do anything for her loved ones.

"Baba! Baba!" I yelled at the top of my voice. "Something is wrong with Dadi!"

Since my father's study was next door to my room he came immediately. He saw his mother's face contorted in pain. He took her hands in his and said, "By Allah, you are freezing! Bring a blanket, Sarah!"

I stuck my head once more out of the room, this time

calling for Adam. He helped me get Dadi settled. I asked my father if her hands were warmer now. I knew they wouldn't be because Dadi had hidden the cold towel with ice under the blanket and she kept on rubbing it over her hands.

Trying to suppress the giggles that wanted to burst out of me, I peered at Dadi and looked studiously at her. I checked her heart rate and her blood pressure knowing that they were normal, but I told my father that I was worried for her.

"Let's not procrastinate here!" I said firmly. "I am taking Dadi to see my friend Jahan Ara. She is the one physician that I trust with Dadi's care."

My father had his head bowed over his mother's hands and just nodded his consent. I dialed the same number as before and told Jahan that we were on the way.

Dadi was in her element. She weakly gestured to me to come nearer. I put my head near her so that I could hear what she had to say. "Get an ambulance. It will be more convincing." I bit my lips to stop myself from smiling. By now a crowd had gathered in our room, curious to see what the commotion was all about.

I got everyone except my parents and brothers to leave the room and then called Jahan again. She promised that she would send a private ambulance with all the bells and whistles. I was feeling a bit guilty for all the drama, but we were paying for the private ambulance, so the feeling of disquiet left me as soon as it flickered in my thoughts. Dadi and I should have been actors. Still feeling a slight twinge of guilt, I decided that I would apologize to my father later on, when we were safe and far away from all the wedding travesty that was happening around us.

The ambulance arrived within fifteen minutes and Dadi

was quickly loaded into it. The paramedics had been given instructions to listen to me regarding her treatment, so they waited for me to say something, but they started giving my grandmother some oxygen through a face mask. It couldn't get more authentic than that. I was surprised when my father insisted that I accompany my grandmother to the hospital. I thought I would have to fight to do that, but luckily, things were smoothly falling into place.

"Come back as soon as you have settled your grandmother. You need to get ready for this evening, Sarah!" My mother was unbelievable. My grandmother was suffering from a "heart attack" and she still wanted the wedding to go on.

"Not now!" My father was irritated. For once he was standing up to my mother. "Have you no compassion? My mother is having a heart attack and is on her way to the hospital, and you are only concerned about a wedding that Sarah never wanted in the first place!" He was now roaring with anger. For a heartbeat, my mother looked quite taken aback, but then she just scoffed and walked back into the house.

Just as I was about to climb into the back of the ambulance a nondescript woman approached me. "I have come to apply henna on your hands and feet for the celebration tonight."

"Can't you see that I am on the way to the hospital?" I was surprised how people were not even concerned about human suffering. They just wanted their work done, be paid, and go happily along with their lives. I shook my head in disgust.

"No, no, you misunderstand me, doctor. I just want to give you my card in case you need me in the future." She shoved a card into my hand. I gave it a perfunctory glance and then gave it another startled look. My heart started to beat like a drum. It was one of my cards and that meant Tanya was nearby.

"Please, tell whoever gave you this card to come to the government hospital, to Dr. Jahan Ara's ward. I will meet them there," I whispered to her. She didn't show that she had heard me, but she walked out of the gate to let the ambulance be on its way. She had found me! My heart was nearly bursting with happiness. But for the sake of the "non-playing" bystanders I needed to have a serious demeanor. Till we were alone.

Dadi winked at me. "Well, that was easy."

"Shhhh! Don't talk. You need to be strong!" I had to say something mundane to convince my brother, who was sitting in the front of the ambulance. We needed to get far away from the house before I could let him into the scam.

Jahan was waiting for us with a big grin on her face. She had arranged a bed for Dadi in her special care unit. It was nearly empty because renovations were going to start in the ward within a week, so it was convenient to admit Dadi there for a couple of days.

Once all the paperwork was completed, we sat down next to Dadi's bed. Adam was puzzled that nobody was attending to Dadi.

Jahan gave Dadi a perfunctory examination. "Well, you are just as healthy as you were a month ago when you came to me for a check-up, but I am going to take this opportunity to do some routine tests." Dadi hated needles, but she knew that Jahan had told her to get these tests done before and she had ignored her instructions. "You are caught now, Dadi; no way out." Jahan laughed at the disgusted look on Dadi's face.

Adam still didn't know what was going on. Dadi sat up in the bed and laughed. "I am all right, Adam. This was a scheme Sarah and I hatched to get the two of you away from the house. We don't have much time because your father will be here soon. I don't think your mother will come though. I am amazed that she is so persistent and still wants to go on with the wedding tonight."

Adam stared at us open mouthed. "What are you both doing? Why are you jeopardizing my family?" He was beside himself.

I put my hand on his arm to calm him down and explained that Farooq had not been inclined to bring Gulnaz and the baby to Karachi. They were still hidden in the mountains.

"What! How can you be so sure?" Adam was starting to get quite upset with me.

I rolled up the sleeve of my shirt and showed Adam the deep bruises on my arm in the shape of Farooq's hand. "He told me that he would make me pay for his 'humiliation,' and also that Gulnaz wasn't in Karachi as he had promised. She was still hidden in an unknown location in the mountains. He wanted us to get married tonight without honoring his side of the agreement so that he could torture you as well as me. He is not trustworthy, Adam. This was our only way to escape. I promise you that Tanya and I will help you in any possible way to get your family back."

Adam was horrified as he realized Farooq's treachery had not only hurt him but Tanya and myself as well. He tried to apologize, but I waved his apologies aside. After all, he was as much a victim of Farooq as I was. Now we just had to wait for Tanya and Razia to come to us. Then we needed to decide what we would do.

Tanya

JUST AS WE watched Tehmina enter the gate, an ambulance came careening around the corner and stopped in front of it. Almost at once, sensing the urgency, the catering trucks moved away and the ambulance started to back up into the driveway. What had happened? Was Sarah all right? Adrenaline kicked in and my heart started to beat very fast. What did Sarah call it... yes, tachycardia? I needed to know what was happening. I put my hand on the door to open it and get out, but Razia stopped me by putting a cautionary hand on my shoulder. "Calm down, Tanya, Tehmina will tell us what is happening. Then we will act accordingly."

She was right. We waited for not more than twenty minutes. Then, as soon as the ambulance drove away, Tehmina jogged over to our car. She opened the door and sat in the back trying to catch her breath before she spoke to us.

"Well?" I was impatient. Razia put a hand on my thigh to calm me, but my frustration made me push the border of rudeness.

"It seems that Sarah's grandmother has had a heart attack. She told me to tell you that they were going to the government hospital and that you should meet her there. In Dr. Jahan Ara's ward." Tehmina gasped.

As she was talking to us, Razia had already started the car and made a sharp U turn go onto the main road. She was a good driver and navigated skillfully through the dense rush hour traffic with ease. We were at the hospital just a few moments after the ambulance had reached it.

The information counter at the hospital reception directed us towards Medical Ward One, where Dr. Jahan was the head of the department. The nurse at the ward counter had been told that we were expected and showed us the way to Sarah's grandmother's room. Razia and I stood in front of the closed door for a few seconds composing ourselves. We didn't want to barge in looking for Sarah if her grandmother was really sick.

I knocked tentatively on the door and was surprised as the voice I longed to hear in the last twenty four hours cheerfully bid us to enter. Sarah jumped up from where she was sitting and hugged me tight. Out of respect for the others in the room, she just kissed me on my cheek, but I felt her love in the pressure she applied with that one kiss. Holding my hand, she led me to the bed, where a cheerful, ruddy faced octogenarian was sitting. She looked quite healthy. Not what I would have imagined a person would look like if they were supposed to be in the throes of a heart attack.

"Dadi, this is my Tanya. My soulmate."

Dadi looked at me with quizzical interest. "So you are the person who enticed our Sarah away from us." She smiled and extended her hand to me. I took it and held it for a while. I didn't know what to say, but I knew in my heart that this magnificent old lady was our ally and I was so grateful to be in her presence. There was a lump in my throat when I realized that everyone in the room was a friend and I was sure they would help us unconditionally in any situation. All except Adam. He had betrayed Sarah. Razia had told me why, but I still harbored a deep resentment towards him. I gave him an angry look and he noticeably recoiled and went to sit in a chair furthermost from me.

"Don't blame Adam." Sarah smiled as she saw my expression and Adam's reaction to it. "He realizes what he has done, but the blame for this whole fiasco is Farooq's. He played on my parents' and my brother's feelings. He wants revenge, and he wants to hurt the whole family by getting it." She showed me the bruises that Farooq had inflicted on her. I was livid. If I hadn't been aware of the risks, I would have stormed out of there and hunted Farooq down right then. Razia had one of those new compact cameras in her pocket and used it to take some photographs of the bruises. We would use these photos as evidence if we needed to prove his cruelty and abuse later on.

We hardly heard the soft knock on the door and were surprised when Sarah's father walked into the room. He stood in the doorway in shock when he saw the almost party atmosphere in the room.

"What is the meaning of this?" he blustered.

Sarah looked scared for a fraction of a moment, but then she squared her shoulders and spoke up. "Baba, you do know that it's wrong to force me to marry someone I can't stand. Farooq is not a nice person. You should have realized that when he kidnapped your daughter-in-law and grandson. And yet, you go ahead with condemning me to a life of torture and grief?"

Mr. Shah was quiet for a while. He looked at his mother, who had an expression of disgust on her face. "Do I understand that your heart attack was a scam? That you are helping Sarah and Adam?"

"Yes, and so what if I am? I have more love for them in my pinky finger than you have in your whole being. You are their father, but you aren't there for them when they need you."

"What do you want me to do?" he said harshly.

"Just love them. They are part of you. Don't throw them towards despair. Sarah has Tanya in her life. Accept it and get to know Tanya. Adam needs whatever help he can get to have his family back with him once again. Can you do that?" Dadi sounded extremely annoyed with Baba.

Mr. Shah gave his mother a sad look. She indicated with her chin towards Sarah, who was standing there with her arms crossed and her chin raised defiantly. I was so proud of her. Slowly, he turned to Sarah, opened his arms, and enveloped her in a hug. "I am so sorry, my darling daughter. I have never stopped loving you. Please forgive me." Sarah hugged her father back and started to sob almost uncontrollably. All the grief and sense of abandonment from her family that she had bottled up all these years came bubbling out. It was like witnessing a catharsis. Mr. Shah just held her and stroked her back comfortingly. Once she had calmed down, she held her hand out to me.

" Baba, please, welcome Tanya into the family. She is and always will be my partner. I love her. I mean I am in love with her."

Mr. Shah hesitated, and then looked at me with an apologetic expression. He held out one arm and hugged me and Sarah together. Something clicked within me. All of a sudden, I felt whole once more. Even though we had hardly talked about it, there was always the feeling of loss and deprivation that I could see in Sarah's eyes when we talked of home. My biggest failure was that I couldn't give her the satisfaction of seeing her family all these years, but now I was sure that I wouldn't see that sad expression in her eyes anymore. She was at peace, surrounded by love. She deserved that. Actually, I deserved that as well.

We all settled down on the chairs around Dadi's bed. "So, Ma, you are also part of all this." Mr. Shah gestured with a smile towards Sarah and Adam, who were whispering in a corner.

"Sarah, Adam, come here! What are you planning to do? Come join us. Let us all know so that we can help you." Dadi looked at her son with pride. Finally, he was behaving like a loving father should. Without prejudice and without unnecessary acrimony.

"At least my fake heart attack worked. Now we need to plan our next moves. We need to get Gulnaz and the little one back... by the way Adam, what is your son's name?"

"His name is Daniyal. He is our little prince." Adam was preening with pride, till it occurred to him that his family still wasn't with him. He momentarily looked as if the air had gone out of a deflated balloon.

"Don't worry, we will get them back for you. I can't wait to hold my nephew in my arms." Sarah hugged her brother. That is another one of her traits that I love. She is so forgiving.

"We need to act fast, before Farooq or Mrs. Shah know that they were deceived. Let's seriously think about our next move." I tried to bring everyone to order. I was anxious and needed action. I was anticipating a backlash from Farooq. I don't think it would even matter to him that Dadi was still in the hospital, because he seemed to have no empathy and I was sure that he would still try to push having the wedding in the evening.

"I will stay in the hospital as long as I can. Dr. Jahan said that she could keep me here up to three days without anyone asking any questions." After the requisite tests were done, Jahan had promised to pamper Dadi for a couple of days. She was looking forward to that.

"And I will come every day to visit my mother," said Mr. Shah. "Just remember this, if I knock three times on the door, that means someone is with me. Then you stop what you are doing and act sick again." We all laughed at that. Dadi thought it was a great idea in case we wanted to prolong the deception for a few more days.

"Farooq's family is from a small town called Parachinar, deep within the Tribal Areas on the Afghan border. I am sure he has taken Gulnaz and Daniyal there. Nearly every adult male in the region has an AK47 rifle and they love using them randomly. I do know that they always start feuds on insignificant matters... It will take all of our resources to find them and spirit them out." I looked at Razia, who nodded at me. "We will get as much help as possible from the local police, courtesy of Razia and my Interpol colleagues. I am confident that we will not fail. We cannot. All of our lives are at stake!"

"Our goals are to get Adam's family back home and you two back to England," said Razia.

"Why don't we take Adam, Gulnaz, and Daniyal with us to England? They can stay with us until things calm down here." Sarah jumped up in her exuberance. She was sure that her brother and his family would be safe with us, and I actually agreed with her plan. Farooq was not to be trusted. What guarantee did we have that he would leave us all in peace once we got away?

"Baba, our passports are in my bedroom, in the bedside table drawer. There is also a photo of Daniyal there. Could you ask your friends at the Passport Office to get an urgent passport for the baby?" Since passports were manually generated, getting one within a few hours wasn't impossible. I was glad that Adam was coming out of his funk and was finally planning ahead.

"After I get the baby's passport, I will take all three to the British High Commission and get visas for them," Mr. Shah said. I gave him my official Interpol card and my bosses' names. If he had problems getting the visas without Adam being there, he was to ask to speak to the High Commissioner and give him those names as references.

"Now I know that if Farooq even suspected that we are going to travel up north, he would have people looking out for us at the airports and the railway stations. I have a friend who is an army pilot and he happens to be flying a C-130 Hercules supply plane to Kohat tonight. I have arranged that we will all go to the air force base and meet Captain Zafar at 1600 hours. He has agreed to let us hitch a ride." Razia was all business. Bless her, while we were having our family reunion, she had already planned ahead. We were lucky to have her as a friend.

"That is just in two hours! We need to get our things together! Everything is at home!" Sarah was starting to panic.

"We don't need anything, Sarah," I said. "We will buy what we need on the way."

"Where have I heard that before?" She sighed and rolled her eyes.

"Well, Tanya has a point." Razia sounded amused at our repartee. "The aircraft, though large, will be loaded with supplies for the air base in Kohat. We have permission to fly only if we keep what we bring to a minimum. Extra weight would just overburden it."

"But it's going to be cold in the mountains! How will we

survive?" Sarah insisted.

Razia held up her hands in a conciliatory gesture and laughed. "When I arranged for our flight, I asked Tehmina to go to the market and buy us some sturdy shoes, sweaters, and warm coats. She also found thermals and a few aluminum insulation blankets. We will get other supplies from Kohat if we need them. Don't worry."

"I suggested to Razia that we parachute over Parachinar. It would save time." I said that with a straight face. I knew that Sarah was afraid of heights, and she would never even think of doing anything like that. It was so good to be with her and to tease her.

Sarah pulled a horrible face and stuck out her tongue at me. Everyone started to laugh. I think it was more out of relief that we were together again because it wasn't really that funny.

Razia pointed at her watch. It was time to go so we said goodbye to Dadi and Mr. Shah and piled into Razia's car. It was a tight fit with all of us in it, but the drive to the air force base was thankfully short. My long legs were beginning to cramp and I couldn't wait to stretch them again. Razia said that she would leave her car at the base and Tehmina would try to pick it up later and take it home.

Sarah seemed calmer and happier now that she was with us, but even though I didn't show it, my anxiety level was still quite high. If it were up to me, I would just grab Sarah and take her back home to England, but I understood her empathy and sense of duty to her brother, and we all had pledged that we would be there for Gulnaz and Daniyal and bring them home. Thank God one of their parents was on our side. I would have loved to see Mrs. Shah's face when she realized that Dadi's heart attack was just a sham.

CHAPTER 6

ROUND THE MOUNTAIN PASS WE GO

"Courage is the most important of all virtues because without courage, you can't practice any other virtue consistently." ~ Maya Angelou

Sarah

NONE OF US SPOKE WHILE WE DROVE TO THE AIR force base. Everyone seemed lost in their thoughts. Occasionally, Razia and Tanya would confer with each other in low voices. Their law enforcement training was kicking in and they wanted our impromptu excursion into the mountains to be as perfect as possible, so they were discussing every possible scenario. We had a ridiculously small window where we could get Gulnaz out of Farooq's house, and every possibility had to be taken into consideration.

We reached the guard house at the air force base and stopped at the barrier but were immediately waved through once Razia flashed her police ID to the soldier standing there. She parked the car in the now nearly empty parking lot and we all got out. I could see that Tanya was relieved that she could now stretch her long legs—poor dear must have had a cramp because the seat was pushed forward to accommodate all of us in the car.

Tehmina was already waiting for us in the terminal, and she had four bulging backpacks and sleeping bags along with light weight collapsible tents ready for us. I was grateful that we would have a change of clothes and be more or less comfortable and warm if we ended up at the mercy of the elements.

Just as I was looking around trying to orient myself, I noticed a shadow lurking near the entrance door. It wasn't moving and seemed quite ominous... As usual, my hair started to stand on end. I quickly moved closer to Tanya, drawing strength by her just being there. "Who are you? Come out!" I shouted. Everyone started at my loud voice since no one had noticed anyone else there.

A figure detached itself from the shadows and walked slowly towards us. It was one of the goons who had kidnapped me and I feared that we had been caught. My heart was beating so fast that I thought it would jump out of my chest. I didn't want to admit defeat—we had come too far to fail. I edged even closer to Tanya.

The goon silently held up one of his hands to indicate that he came in peace. I was horrified to see that his hand was covered in blood. His arm was injured, and he was trying to staunch the bleeding by pressing a filthy cloth over it. He took three faltering steps and then collapsed onto one of the chairs that were in the waiting area of the terminal.

"Please help me, Dr. Sarah!" he said in a faint voice.

My medical training instincts kicked in. I just couldn't let him suffer or die. "Help me lay him down and get some of these sofa cushions under his legs to elevate them. We need to get as much blood to his head as possible." I started to order everyone around me to assist. He was one of my kidnappers, but he was also a human being. How could I ignore Hippocrates's directive to do no harm?

Razia brought me a basin filled with warm water along with a box of tissues and a handful of clean rags. I borrowed Tanya's Swiss army knife and sliced the man's sleeve off. The dark powder stains surrounding the wound meant that he had been shot at close range.

I cleansed the wound as much as I could, packed it with the clean rags, and applied a pressure bandage. That was the best we could do with the limited resources we had.

"What is your name? I can't keep calling you 'Goon,' can I?"

Even though he was in pain, he smiled. "My name is Tariq. Farooq flew into a nasty rage when he heard that you had escaped. He blamed me for it and shot me. As soon as I could get away from there I came to warn you. Please, hurry and board the plane. Don't worry about me!"

Tariq was right—we didn't have enough time. Farooq could get there any minute. "How did you know that we were at the air force base?" asked Tanya.

"I work at the High Commission for Pakistan in London. I am a junior diplomat, so I was allowed to look at the official logs and saw that there was a plane leaving for

Kohat. I put two and two together and thought I should take a chance to see if you were on the flight. Farooq thinks you have gone to the civilian air terminal. You still have some time before he comes here."

"We won't leave you like this. You need proper treatment and monitoring. Moreover, the bullet needs to be taken out or you might get an infection and the wound won't heal well. You are lucky it's just a flesh wound and the bullet has just missed your humerus bone, but the huge amount of bleeding indicates that a major blood vessel might have been damaged. We are taking you with us."

Tariq, who was visibly fading, just weakly nodded his consent.

Tanya and Adam helped Tariq stand by supporting him under his armpits. Somehow Razia found a wheelchair at the first aid station and they helped him sit in it. He was then wheeled to the waiting aircraft while we gathered our bags and followed as fast as we could. I was glad that the pilot had already started the engines because I heard a commotion behind us just as we exited the terminal. Tanya took me by my arm and we started to run. Razia and Adam picked Tariq up and ran with him up the stairs and into the aircraft. In the distance, we saw a livid Farooq being detained by the airport security staff. We all flew up the steps into the plane. I only breathed a sigh of relief when we sat down and the pilot started to taxi down the runway. I watched from the window how a security guard was trying to stop Farooq from running after the plane. His face was contorted horribly while he shook in anger and punched the air with his fists in frustration.

The aircraft was a stripped-down cargo plane. There were bucket seats with harnesses on them which were extremely basic and uncomfortable. Once the plane had taken off, we looked around to see how we could make Tariq more comfortable. He would not last the two-hour flight by sitting in one of those seats. I was worried for him and hoped that the wound wouldn't start bleeding again. We found some sacks in a corner that Razia spread on the floor in the main cargo area. We lay him down there with one of our backpacks as support for his head and another one under his legs to have them elevated. Although Tehmina had bought small First Aid kits for everyone, there were no strong pain killers in them. I had some paracetamol with me and made Tariq take the tablets with small sips of water, hoping they would take off the edge off the pain.

After about twenty minutes into the flight, Tariq asked to talk to me. I had to sit very close to him because his voice was weak and the plane was very noisy. "I am so sorry about everything. Dr. Farooq has friends in the High Commission, and we were asked to help him. I didn't like this from the beginning, but we were under orders from one of the senior staff there. I don't think that even they were aware of what Dr. Farooq wanted to do."

I patted his shoulder and told him not to talk too much. We had decided that we would leave him at the military hospital in Kohat, where he would be well taken care of.

"No, Dr. Sarah, let me speak. Then I will rest. You have only shown kindness to me. You could have turned me away." I made a noncommittal noise, but I let him speak.

"I come from the same town as Farooq. We grew up together. That was one of the reasons that he could compel me to help him. I know how to get there, and I can help you. Gulnaz is hidden in her parents' house with her child."

"You are injured and we can't ask you to be our guide." I

was a bit touched that Tariq wanted to help me, but I still wasn't sure that we could trust him.

Tariq must have seen the uncertainty in my face. "I understand that you are concerned about my sincerity, but let me tell you that I am not a 'goon,' as you kept insisting on calling me. I am a respected government servant who was forced by his superior officer to do things that go against my principles and ethics. I would like to atone for what has been done to all of you—to you Dr. Sarah, and to Adam." He started to cough. Razia put the water bottle to his lips, taking care that he just took small sips.

"Rest now, Tariq. We can talk later." Realizing that he was shivering, I took one of the aluminum blankets from my backpack and covered him.

"No, listen, you don't understand! Farooq will follow you. He will catch up with you because even though he's not an expert, he is to some extent familiar with the area. Before I came to the terminal, I called my younger brother. He will meet us at Kohat. I have asked him to take you to Parachinar over the mountains. You will get there well before Farooq, but that route is difficult and treacherous in some places."

"We can handle it," said Tanya. "Now rest. We will talk again when we meet your brother." Nodding gratefully, Tariq closed his eyes and fell into a restless sleep.

The loud engines made it difficult for us to talk to each other, so we tried to make ourselves as comfortable as we could. A nap was definitely needed if we were to start our journey into the mountains almost immediately. I put my head on Tanya's shoulder and she pulled me close. Even though we didn't know where this adventure would take us, I felt safe by just having her near me. She smiled and wrapped her arms around my shoulders before she closed her eyes and fell asleep. My safe haven. My love. In all of the turmoil and chaos, she was my focus of sanity. I thanked God from the bottom of my heart for giving me Tanya back in my life.

Tanya

THE DRONE of the airplane had lulled me to sleep. It seemed that I was much more tired that I was willing to admit. When I woke up, Sarah was cuddled next to me and the others were asleep in various poses. Adam had his head on the seat and his legs were draped over the side. He appeared to be folded over just like a pretzel. He looked uncomfortable and really hilarious. I was so grateful that Sarah was beside me. The quiet time we had at the moment let me look at her as she slept. We had been together for a while, but it still amazed me that she could look so innocent while she slept. Every time I looked at her, I would fall even more in love with her. There was no doubt in my mind at all that she completed me.

I heard Tariq groan with pain, and I gently disentangled myself from Sarah and went to see whether he was all right. He was asleep. Or maybe unconscious. He was sweating and restless, and his forehead was burning hot. Much as I didn't like to, I had to wake Sarah up. Tariq needed her medical skills.

"Sarah, wake up." I gently caressed her cheek until she opened her eyes and smiled.

"You are here! I knew it wasn't just a lovely dream."

I kissed her quickly on her lips and told her about Tariq's condition.

"It seems that he has an infection. We need to get the bullet out as soon as possible." Sarah looked concerned as she examined Tariq. "Can you ask the pilot how much longer our flight will be? In the meantime, I will try to bring Tariq's fever down by wiping him with some damp cloths."

The cockpit was open, unlike in regular passenger aircrafts. I put my head in the doorway and signaled the co-pilot. He got up and came to me.

"When are we landing in Kohat?" I asked.

"In another fifteen minutes. Is there a problem?"

"The man who was shot is having a fever and is not doing too good. Would it be possible to radio ahead for an ambulance to pick him up once we have landed?"

"Sure, I shall do that immediately." The copilot gave me a thumbs up sign and went back into the cockpit.

Sarah was relieved that the flight would soon be over. She stayed with Tariq until the plane was ready to land and we had to sit down and strap on our seat belts. He was still semi-conscious, but he seemed to be settling down under her ministrations.

As promised, a lumbering military ambulance was waiting for us. The medics came aboard before we could get off, and they took Tariq away once Sarah briefed them about his condition in detail.

We gathered our belongings and walked down the stairs of the plane, glad to be on terra firma after the rough plane ride. Before she walked down the steps Razia thanked the pilot and co-pilot for their help.

"We are coming back in two days, so if you are here, we

can offer you a ride back home," Captain Zafar was kind enough to offer.

"Thank you," Razia and I said in unison. "We hope to be here by then. Hopefully, even earlier," I added.

"I wish you all the best then and consider this an open-ended offer." With a nearly imperceptible tip of his hat, Captain Zafar turned to go into the office to hand in his inventory and logs.

We hefted our backpacks and tents and made our way into the small terminal building. There was a man who resembled Tariq sitting on one of the chairs there. He stood up and walked to Adam, since he was the only male in the group. In this male dominated society, that was considered a sign of respect.

"Salam, I am Khalid. Tariq's brother." He shook hands with Adam and nodded in greeting to the rest of us. "Tariq told me that you would like to fetch Dr. Gulnaz from Parachinar. He wanted me to take you there on the shortest possible route. That would be partly by jeep and partly on foot. Are you all up to it?" He swept a calculating gaze over us.

Sarah was standing next to me, and I could feel her anxiety. "Do you think we should trust this man?" she whispered.

"I don't think we have any other option, but he should know that he will be taking law enforcement officers deep into the mountains. We won't let our guard down since there are many areas where there is no population whatsoever."

"Well, I for one am ready to trust him. I just want to bring my wife and child back home." Adam was getting loud, agitated and wanted to commence the journey as soon as possible.

Tariq looked startled. "Dr. Gulnaz is your wife? Her son is your child?"

"Yes, I thought you knew that. Why would you help us otherwise?" Adam was confused.

"I am so sorry, sir. Farooq told us that you were going to kidnap Dr. Gulnaz to dishonor her and our tribe. He paid me to take you deep into the tribal area and leave you there. It was only when Tariq told me what he did that I agreed to guide you to Parachinar, but I still wasn't completely convinced that you were innocent. I believed Farooq because he is from the same village as us, but it seems his behavior hasn't changed, and he still is a pain in the neck as he used to be when he was younger."

Sarah's intuition had won once again. The vibes she got from Khalid had made her nervous.

"I married Gulnaz two years ago. Daniyal is my son." Adam was now getting flustered.

"Do you have any proof that you are married?" asked Khalid.

Adam fumbled in his wallet and took out a well-thumbed photograph and showed it to Khalid. It was of him and Gulnaz in their wedding finery.

"Thank you for the verification. I am ashamed that I listened to Farooq. I have also seen how kind you all were to my brother. Because of you, he will be well taken care of in the military hospital. You can rely on my loyalty. Everyone likes Dr. Gulnaz in our village. She has saved many lives with her medical skills. We would rather help her than her brother, who is always bullying or blackmailing us to do his dirty work. I apologize for my earlier behavior."

I looked towards Sarah. She knew what I was silently asking her. She nodded—the uncomfortable feeling that she had earlier was gone. She smiled at Khalid and said, "Then let us start our journey. I know it's dark now, but we will get there earlier if we set out now."

"You are right, doctor. The route is 179 kilometers if we go by the proper road, but if we go halfway by road and the rest of the way over the mountains, the distance is 127 kilometers. We need to leave now if we are to reach Parachinar before Farooq gets here."

I realized that Razia had been missing for a while. I peered out of the windows of the waiting room and saw her talking to Captain Zafar and another officer. They were discussing something quite intensely and nodding. Finally, Razia shook their hands and came back inside.

"Captain Zafar suggests that we use one of their helicopters to get as close to Parachinar as possible. We can walk to the town from there and no one would be any wiser. We can then get Gulnaz and the baby out and, even if we have to walk back to Kohat, we could hide in caves and gulleys if Farooq tries to find us." Razia was her usual efficient self. I was grateful for her connections—sometimes you can't get things done in Pakistan unless you have solid contacts willing to help.

We went back out onto the tarmac. At the far end we saw a Bell AH-1 Cobra twin engine helicopter starting its rotor blades. I was glad that it was one of the larger ones because it could seat at least six passengers comfortably.

Sarah held onto my hand almost convulsively. It was one thing to fly in an airplane, but a helicopter reminded her of her fear of heights. I would have to distract her along the way. Thankfully, the flight would only last twenty minutes and then we would be walking for another half an hour until we reached Parachinar. I only hoped that Gulnaz could leave with us immediately since any delay might tip the scales either way. We needed to be as diligent as possible, almost commando-like.

Khalid had a clever idea. He suggested that he would travel with his jeep on the route we were planning to take on our way back and drop some supplies and our bags in a cave halfway there. He would then be waiting for us to guide us over the mountains back to Kohat. Since he was now going to be alone and not burdened down by passengers, he would reach the cave quicker because he could go over rougher terrain with his four-wheel drive. One we reached the cave we would travel back to Kohat in the jeep. It was a relief to know that our escape from the area would be smooth and swift.

"Are you sure that Farooq doesn't know about this cave?" asked Sarah.

"Even though Farooq is from this area, he never liked wandering in the mountains like other children from our town. He always wanted to leave for the big cities. He hardly played with anyone and kept mostly to himself, so I doubt that he knows about the cave." He drew a rough map on a piece of paper to show where the cave was, and how we could reach it from Parachinar without being seen by anyone. He explained the route to us in detail and then handed the paper over to Razia, who he seemed to acknowledge as the leader of our group.

Khalid left as soon as we boarded the helicopter. It was a surreal experience flying over the dark mountains just by the light of the full moon that had risen an hour before. We could see where we were going, but the black and gray tones were disconcerting—I liked my landscapes in full technicolor.

The noise of the blades made conversation difficult. The pilot had only two headphones, and Razia, who was sitting next to him, wore the other pair. Sarah relaxed her near death grip on my hands once we were up in the air. I thought that she wasn't as scared as she thought she would be simply because she couldn't see how high we were. If I didn't know any better, I would say that she was starting to enjoy the ride.

After a short while, Razia signaled with her hands that we were going to land soon. The pilot was quite good and found a flat plateau where he landed easily. We were close enough that we could trek into town but far enough that no one was alerted to the sound of the helicopter. From the peak of the mountain where we were, we saw the lights of Parachinar twinkling in the distance. We said our farewells to the pilot and picked up the bags that we had kept with us. They were the smaller bags with our money and passports in them. Adam and Sarah still had to get their passports from their Baba, but Razia and I wanted to keep ours nearby. We couldn't risk losing them right now.

We all silently thanked Tehmina while we quickly changed into the clothes and shoes that she had bought for us. Without them we wouldn't have survived the chilly weather that was still prevalent at the end of March and the beginning of April in the mountains. I was sure that when the sun rose and we could see our surroundings clearly, we would notice that there was still some snow on the higher peaks.

Adam took the lead and followed a path that was probably made by the mountain goats that were indigenous of the area. The moon lit the way, so we didn't need to use our flashlights, which was fine because we didn't want to alert anyone that we were on the way. I was happy that we had quite a good head start and was confident that we would manage to rescue Gulnaz and Daniyal before Farooq got there. I couldn't wait for us to be on our way back home to England.

CHAPTER 7

(WO)MAN PROPOSES; GOD DISPOSES

"Life is what happens to us when we are making other plans." ~ Allen Saunders

Sarah

I AM NOT THE MOST GRACEFUL GAZELLE IN THE best of times, but I think I did quite well on the uneven mountain paths. After walking and stumbling in the dark, we finally reached the outskirts of Parachinar. Adam knew the address because he had visited with his wife many times before when Farooq wasn't there. He told us that Gulnaz's family home was on the outskirts of town, on a hill looking over the valley. I am sure that if we had visited in a friendlier time, we would have enjoyed the panoramic views and the mountain air, but we were all tense and just focused on completing our mission—to fetch Gulnaz and Daniyal and go back home as soon as possible without being caught by Farooq or his goons.

Taking advantage of the night, we stealthily crept from one building's shadow to the other trying to avoid the streetlights as much as possible. We wanted to be sure that no one could see or identify us, although what we were doing wasn't illegal since the person we were "kidnapping" was a willing participant. However, the tribal areas had their own laws and we didn't want to waste time untangling ourselves from unnecessary obstacles.

Adam came to a sudden stop and we had to hold onto each other to stop ourselves from falling as we bumped into him. I was about to tell him off when he pointed at a building on the hillside above. "I think that's the place!" he whispered.

The house was impressive. The architect who had designed it had made sure that the side overlooking the valley was made predominantly of plate glass. The rest of the house was constructed with local river stones and lots of polished walnut wood. The prominent decorative rafters had been carved by local artisans with flowers and wildlife. I imagined having breakfast in the room that overlooked the valley. It would have been nice to look down at the river Kurram making its way to merge with the river Swat. I knew from previous visits with my family to the area that the view rivaled the vistas of Switzerland and Austria. There was sheer beauty in its undeveloped rawness.

Tanya and Razia motioned us to go ahead while they looked around for any threat that might harm or delay us. I loved it when Tanya got into cop mode...simply adorable.

"How will we get in?" I asked Adam. "Does Gulnaz know that we are coming?"

"We had discussed that if it ever happened that she was taken away by her brother, and if I had to follow them to get her back, then we would have a secret knock on the door. That way she would know it's me or someone that I have sent to get her." Adam still looked worried. "I hope she remembers the code. If she is fast asleep it's sometimes quite difficult to wake her up."

"Well, we will get to that when it happens. Let's go and try to signal her. We can't loiter here for long."

Adam went to an almost hidden gate that was built in a fence surrounding the back garden. It was fortunately just latched but not locked. He opened the gate and motioned me to hurry up and follow him.

We walked stealthily across a cultivated lawn that was surrounded by lush flower beds. Even in the faint light from the streetlamps they looked pretty. There was a plain wooden door just ahead where Adam stopped and took a deep breath. "This is the door from where Gulnaz said she would be able to hear if anyone knocked at night. Her room is conveniently just nearby."

Adam started to knock on the door. It sounded like SOS in morse code. Three long, three short, and then three long knocks. Good idea. It was different and most probably none of the inhabitants of the town would think to knock like that in any case.

Almost immediately, the door was flung open and a slim young woman about my height flung herself without any hesitation into Adam's arms. They kissed and hugged as if they were drowning and couldn't get enough of each other. I gently cleared my throat, making them aware that they were not alone.

Adam had a happy look on his face, but Gulnaz was

blushing a deep red. "I am so sorry! You must be Sarah, Adam's sister. You do resemble him. It's so great to finally meet you!" Gulnaz, who was quite pretty with hazel eyes and light brown wavy hair that cascaded down her back, was rambling to hide her embarrassment. "Please come in. I just have to get Daniyal ready. My bags are already packed. Actually, I never unpacked properly since the day I arrived here. I knew that one way or another, Adam would get me." She grinned at Adam. I saw how much they loved each other in just that one glance. I knew that Adam had spoken the truth when he said that he had finally found his soulmate.

We followed Gulnaz into the house. She spoke normally and didn't take care to muffle any noise that her footsteps or voice was making.

"Isn't anyone home?" asked Adam.

"My uncle and aunt, who live here with us, have gone to Mingora. One of my mother's cousins has died, so they went to express their condolences personally. They will be back by tomorrow evening." Gulnaz had a happy lilt in her voice. "Only the servants are here. They are probably sleeping by now, as it's quite late for these mountain folk to be up at this time. However, I do have Marjan, one of the midwives, in my room. She has come to talk to me about a case."

Adam walked immediately to the crib where his son lay. He had this look of incredulous awe on his face. He gestured with his hands as if he wanted to pick up his son, and then drew them back again. It seemed as if he didn't know what to do. He was so overwhelmed. He couldn't stop the tears cascading unashamedly down his cheeks. He was stunned, surprised, and in love with the little human lying there looking up at him with such trusting eyes. I'm sure he inwardly cursed Farooq at that moment for keeping his child away from him for the past six months. There was so much that he had missed. He looked helplessly at Gulnaz, who at once knew what he wanted so she lifted Daniyal out of the crib and gently placed him in his father's arms.

"Look at you, Adam! A father! And I am an aunty! That's wonderful!" I had to say something, even though it was a commonplace statement, or I would have started to cry because of the beauty of the moment. I knew from the expression of both my brother and my sister in laws faces as they looked down at their son together, that they would prove to be exceptionally good parents to little Daniyal.

"Why don't you go and tell Razia and Tanya to come inside while I help Gulnaz with Daniyal?" I finally told Adam, breaking the spell.

Gulnaz followed him out as if she couldn't bear to keep him out of her sight, and I went to tell Tanya that we would be a short while and then went back to Gulnaz's room to help get her things together. There I saw a tall, statuesque woman who was standing with her back to us. She was looking down at Daniyal's crib and was talking the usual baby nonsense that adults seem to think appeal to babies. Daniyal must have liked it because I heard his cute baby giggles.

The woman turned towards us and smiled. She was absolutely gorgeous. Her features were typical of the women seen in the northern Himalayan areas, from her unblemished skin to her long, luxuriant hair, but her amber eyes were sad, as if she had most of the weight of the world on her shoulders. The most shocking thing, however, was the convoluted horn that grew from the middle of her forehead!

Seeing that Gulnaz wasn't alone, she self-consciously covered her head and her forehead with a large shawl.

"Don't worry, Marjan, my sister-in-law, Sarah, is also a doctor. She might be able to help you with your problem."

Marjan and I looked first at each other, then at Gulnaz, who just laughed at the puzzled looks on our faces.

"While I get Daniyal ready, why don't you tell Sarah your story, Marjan?" She nodded and turned to me. Marjan looked embarrassed. I didn't blame her—after all, I was a stranger to her, and it must have been difficult to talk to someone she had just met just a few seconds before, but after looking speculatively at me, she gave a small shrug, cleared her throat, and began to speak.

"I am the village midwife and have delivered many babies here in the town and also in the outlying villages. Unfortunately, I started to get this unusual bump on my forehead. Its consistency is like the keratin of human fingernails. I have tried all sorts of medicines and lotions, but it doesn't go away. Slowly and gradually, it increased in size till it developed into this ugly horn that I have on my forehead today. I was and still am respected here in this town, and many people don't even bother about this aberration of mine, but then a new Mullah was appointed for the main town mosque. He was impressed by the doctrines of the Taliban and has tried to influence the townsfolk with his fire and brimstone sermons. Most of the people here are Shia Muslims, so they are not very receptive to the Taliban dogma, but that didn't stop that cleric from trying to reign in terror." Marjan stopped to take a deep shuddering breath. She poured herself a glass of water from the silver jug on the table and took a few sips to moisten her mouth before she continued to talk.

"One day, I went to the Mullah's house to deliver his wife's baby. Instead of being grateful that I helped her with an extremely difficult delivery, he started to malign me in his Friday sermons, calling me the spawn of Satan because of my "horn." He told the people to keep me away from their wives and children or they would bear the mark of Satan as well." A silent tear trickled down her cheek. "He was convinced that his wife's difficulties at the time were because of my evil influence. I am at my wit's end. I need to have this aberration removed so that I can live a normal life once more." Marjan started to sob piteously.

Alarmed, I looked towards Gulnaz for help, but she was busy puttering around to get her and Daniyal's things together. I did the next best thing... I hugged Marjan and promised her that we would try our best to help her. She clung to me desperately while her sobs slowly receded into hiccups. I continued to pat her awkwardly on her back, hoping that she would calm down since we were on a time schedule and needed to go as soon as we could.

Once I managed to untangle myself from the hug, I picked up a piece of paper and a pen from a nearby table, wrote something on it, and handed the note to Marjan.

"Who is this note for?" she asked while turning it around and around, trying to decipher my doctor's handwriting, which was in English and not Urdu.

"This is the address and a reference for you to meet my friend, Dr. Gohar Sarfaraz. She is a well-known plastic surgeon in Mingora, Swat. She knows me well and will help you get rid of your..." I indicated awkwardly with my hand towards her forehead.

Marjan looked surprised and then grabbed my hand and kissed the back of it reverentially. "Thank you, thank you!" Just for a moment, a troubled look flitted across her face, and then she dipped her head forward as if she came to a resolute conclusion, shook her head, and smiled once more.

"What is it?" I was curious to know what was going on in that head of hers.

"Nothing much, really. I was just wondering how much the whole procedure will cost, but then I thought that I would sell my gold bangles to pay for the operation."

"No, you won't have to do that!" I exclaimed. "Gohar works in a government hospital; therefore, she will operate on you for free." Marjan looked delighted. I was happy that I was able to help someone on this trip, even if it was vicariously.

Thanking me once again, she started to leave the room. I realized that it was suddenly noticeably quiet and I looked around for Gulnaz. Her bag was missing, and Daniyal wasn't in his crib. I thought that she must have joined the others and Adam, so I walked to the door. There was a whisper of air as I felt rather than heard the curtains move, and for a moment, I felt the hair on the nape of my neck stand on end. Danger! A cloth with a sickly-sweet smell was clamped over my nose and mouth. Before I fell into deep dark oblivion, I heard Marjan's voice shout out in dismay, "What are you doing!?"

Tanya

RAZIA and I stayed out of the house, even if it would have been interesting to see how it looked from the inside. I was always interested in unusual as well as ethnical architecture. That's why I loved visiting old mansions and castles in Europe and England. I was glad that Sarah shared my hobby as well. We had a lot of fun exploring in our free time, but little does the world know about the hidden natural and architectural gems that were around this country, especially in the remote mountainous areas. We walked the periphery a few times and made sure that there were no undesirable people around. We especially kept a vigilant look out on the main road, since we were sure that Farooq would be barreling down that road in his perceived self-righteous rage.

Even though it was still cold for March, the air was crisp and invigorating. Parachinar would have been nice to visit for a holiday, but for now, the moonlit beauty surrounding us didn't quite register that well because we were all on tenterhooks wanting to leave before we had to face Farooq.

After a short while, Adam came and joined Razia and I. There were a few benches and chairs on the lawn and even though it was a bit chilly, the three of us sat down.

"Gulnaz is getting the baby ready, and Sarah is talking with a midwife who was visiting her."

"Sarah always seems to find someone with whom she interacts with her medical skills." I laughed, but I was proud of my doctor.

Adam looked impatiently at his watch. "I wish I had been able to send word to Gulnaz earlier, then we wouldn't have had to wait while she prepared herself for the journey. I know it's different travelling with an infant, but we might have had a bit of a head start."

Razia and I looked at each other and smiled. Adam was new to the requirements of young women and children. "It will be easier once you are married a bit longer." I smiled, patting him on the shoulder.

Adam grinned ruefully. "I would like to apologize for all the trouble I have caused you and Sarah. Moreover, I really appreciate that you came along to help me rescue my family. You didn't have to do that; you could have just gone home."

"You are Sarah's brother. I love her more than life, and I would do anything for her. Therefore, being here for you was a no brainer. You are family and we value that. We will always be there for each other. Or at least I hope so." Adam looked gratefully at me and nodded in acknowledgement. We had laid our animosity to rest. We were friends once more.

"Also, even though you did act like a moron, we do appreciate what you did for us five years ago." I laughed, while Razia laughed with me as well.

We heard a rustle in the bushes, and I quickly stood up to see what had caused it. As I didn't see anyone at the time, I thought it might have been some nocturnal animals foraging for food, so I didn't give it much thought. After another five-minute wait, Gulnaz walked out with Daniyal in a carrier and with an overstuffed backpack on her shoulder.

"Adam, you can strap Daniyal's carrier onto your back. He will be easier to carry that way when we walk over the mountains."

"Where is Sarah?" I asked. All of a sudden, I felt that something was wrong, but I was too afraid to put it into words. For the past few hours, if Sarah was out of my sight, I would get mild palpitations or bouts of anxiety that only abated when I knew where she was or if she was near me.

"She was talking to Marjan; she will be here in a minute." Gulnaz seemed unconcerned and quite nonchalant, so I tried to tamp down my feelings of dread. We waited for another ten minutes, but there still was no sign of Sarah. Everyone was getting worried by now. We didn't want to delay our journey back. We needed to move as soon as possible.

"I'll go and see where she is," I finally said as I abruptly stood up. I didn't want to wait anymore. I wanted Sarah near me immediately. My feeling of disquiet just wouldn't go away!

The entrance lobby and the corridors in the house were empty. I looked in all of the rooms, but no one was there. It was like a haunted house with hints of past inhabitants permeating the atmosphere. I became more and more agitated as I opened the doors and only saw darkness. At the end of the corridor, I found a door under which a faint light was seen. I opened that door hoping that I had found Sarah, but instead, there was a woman leaning against the wall sobbing as if her heart would break. She turned her tear-stained face towards me and I nearly recoiled when I saw a horn in the middle of her forehead. I had already thought the empty house felt haunted. Was this a ghost or a banshee that had revealed herself to torture me? Had she taken my Sarah away from me once more? Oh God! Was Sarah even alive?

As I stood there in shock, the woman spoke. "He has taken Dr. Sarah! He has taken her! I am so sorry!"

Realizing that she was a human being and not a figment of my imagination, I shook myself out of my terrified haze and went forward to shake her gently by the shoulders. She continued to cry and rant, but I couldn't get anything intelligible or useful out of her. Since I was scared that the only clue to where Sarah had gone would disappear into thin air, I took her firmly by the arm and led her out to the garden where everyone else was waiting for us.

"What has happened, Marjan?" asked Gulnaz, looking concerned when she saw that her friend had been crying.

"Hasnain crept into the room while Sarah and I were talking. He drugged her with chloroform that I think he had stolen from the clinic and has taken her with him. He left me behind to tell you that he has kidnapped the 'big doctor from London.' His wife is extremely ill, and he wants Sarah to treat her. He has this weird idea in his mind that someone 'foreign' would be better than local doctors. It's just the mentality of the people here. God help us if anything would go haywire. These people then bay for blood."

"This is unacceptable!" I roared my frustration. Knowing Sarah, she would have anyway had a look at his wife if only he had asked. Now his idiotic behavior was putting us all at risk.

"In the first place, how did he know that we would be here? We were very careful, and I don't think that anyone saw us coming." Razia was as flabbergasted as we all were.

"He was on his way to get Gulnaz and when he peeked into the window, he heard Sarah speak English with her, and you know that she doesn't look typically Pakistani, so he mistook her for a foreigner." Marjan was pacing on the garden path and wringing her shawl in despair.

"Do you know where Hasnain has taken Sarah?" asked Gulnaz. Marjan was reluctant at first to tell us anything. She had been instructed to delay the search for Sarah until she had time to deal with Hasnain's wife's illness. He had threatened her and her son, so she was very scared to say anything at all.

"Tanya and I are law enforcement officers." Razia said. "She works for the international police, and I work for them here in Pakistan. I promise you that we can and we will take care of you. No one will harm you if you cooperate."

Haltingly and still visibly afraid, Marjan told us where to go. Hasnain had a house high up beyond the Kishan Gul Mountain trail. It was a difficult trail to walk up. There was no doubt that he must have had some help to carry an unconscious Sarah up the mountain.

We quickly gathered our gear and started towards the trail. Gulnaz stopped for a few minutes at her makeshift clinic in the town, where she picked up surgical instruments, masks, and gloves. She added the rest of the chloroform, IV glucose, and antibiotic injections to her bag as well. "I believe Hasnain's wife might need a caesarian section. She was due to deliver ten days ago and I had told him to take her into town for the delivery because I didn't have the facilities for major surgery in the clinic. I also don't have any drugs for anesthesia except the chloroform and just the basics that I am now taking with me. We can save time this way. And if Marjan and I help Sarah, we could be on our way earlier. Hopefully, before my brother makes an appearance."

I tried to remain calm, but God knows I was a bundle of nerves. I was imagining the terror Sarah would be feeling when she woke up in an unknown place after being drugged, but now, as we knew where to go, I focused on the task ahead. We all needed clear heads if we were to get Sarah back unharmed. These volatile locals were sometimes not to be trusted, and they could just injure her or worse on a whim or a fit of temper if things didn't go their way.

"Don't hurry; just walk at a steady pace and you won't get tired very soon," Gulnaz instructed us. "The air gets thinner the higher we go, so you will need to take deep breaths."

We walked silently along in a single file. The track was in some places not wide enough for anyone to walk abreast with each other, and there were parts of the path that were also precariously near the edge. Thankfully, when the sun rose we were able to see clearly where we were going. No doubt it would have been treacherous for us uninitiated "mountaineers" to have hiked the trail in the dark.

After walking for about three hours and meeting no one on the way except a few scrawny surefooted mountain goats, I checked the receiver that was connected with Sarah's tracking device, which was embedded in her pendant. I was relieved when I heard the steady pinging sound that meant she was nearby. We continued up the mountain path and after walking for a few more minutes we reached a cottage that was built on a cliff. There were thick planks and beams of wood that supported the base of the structure to prevent it from sliding into the valley below. It looked quite sturdy, but anyone who didn't know whether it would hold their weight would be nervous to set foot in there.

Marjan walked confidently to the front door and knocked. A worried looking old woman opened the door and pulled her in while talking rapidly in the local dialect. Marjan gently disentangled her arm from the woman and spoke to her in a soothing voice. She then looked over her shoulder and gestured to Gulnaz. I didn't understand a word, but it was evident that she was trying to reassure the woman that we were here to help her daughter-in-law.

"Ask her if Sarah is here?" I was impatient.

"Is the London doctor here?" asked Marjan in a language we all understood.

"Yes. She is here. Hasnain just brought her in." The old woman was clearly upset. I gathered that she didn't like the way that Sarah was brought to the house. "She is sleeping in the back room. I will take you to her."

I pushed my way in front and followed her down a dark corridor and into a room that had a large window overlooking the valley. But I had no time to look at the breathtaking view as the morning sun had started to add color to the beautiful surroundings; I just wanted to see how Sarah was. She was lying on the single cot in the room, covered by a colorful quilt. Her hair was tousled, and her breathing was even. I was relieved. "Could you please bring some hot tea? I will try to wake her up." I asked the old woman, who eagerly left the room happy to do something productive. I had the feeling that she did not like her son's way of getting medical help for her daughter-in-law.

I found a jug of cold water on the table nearby. I dipped my handkerchief in it and started to wipe Sarah's face. She grimaced when she felt the damp cold cloth and her eyelids began to flutter, but she stubbornly kept them closed. Encouraged, I continued to wipe her face until she pushed my hand away in irritation. "What are you doing, Tanya? Let me sleep! I was having such a nice dream."

I smiled and continued trying to get her to wake up. Her protestations became more and more frequent until she abruptly sat up. "Oh, God! I am going to be sick!"

I found a wastepaper basket behind the door and put it in front of her. She obliged by hurling her stomach contents into it as soon as it was placed on the floor. I could just jump out of the way in time. Gulnaz walked in with a tray that had a large teapot and cups on it. She hastily put the tray on the table and came forward to examine Sarah.

"We should be thankful that he made her inhale the chloroform. If the idiot had made her drink it, she could have been poisoned with dire consequences." She sounded relieved. "I was angry with Marjan. She should have kept the dangerous drugs in the clinic under lock and key!"

Sarah slowly and gradually started to become more alert after drinking the extra strong tea that Gulnaz had brought her. "What happened? Where are we?" She was still visibly confused.

I told her what had happened. For a moment, one could see that she was livid, but then I was surprised when she said in a quiet voice, "Poor guy must have been desperate to kidnap me. The least we can do is see what's wrong with his wife. Gulnaz, you need to help as well because I am a pediatrician, not a gynecologist. He should know that had he just asked, we would have helped anyway."

That's my Sarah. Always thinking of others. Always putting her patients first. How could I ever find fault with that?

CHAPTER 8

"The physician must be able to tell the antecedents, know the present, and foretell the future – must mediate these things, and have two special objects in view with regard to disease, namely, to do good and to do no harm." ~ Hippocrates

Sarah

EVEN AFTER DRINKING COUNTLESS CUPS OF TEA, I was still a bit groggy. I swear that if I stood up and started to walk around, I would slosh with all the liquid that had been forced inside of me. Tanya was looking at me with concern while Razia was impatient and wanted to leave as soon as we could. At this point, I wasn't in good shape to either maneuver the precarious mountain path or assess the needs of my patient, who was in the other room. I tried my level best to shake the fog from my brain. I was succeeding more or less, but not as quick as I wanted.

I slowly stood up and, with Tanya's help, made it in one

piece to the bathroom. After using the facilities, I felt a bit better.

"This is going to be difficult. I don't yet know what is wrong with Hasnain's wife, but since he felt he had to kidnap me, I am sure it's not good. I wish he hadn't been so foolish as to drug me. Thank goodness I am able to think a bit clearer now."

"I will try to help you to the best of my limited ability." Tanya smiled as she held me close.

"Just your caring presence is reassuring for me. I love you, Tanya. Thank you for coming after me so quickly."

There was a bang on the door. "Who is it?" Tanya was irritated that someone (though unknowingly) had the audacity to disturb a tender moment between us. Since I had left London, we hadn't had any time alone with each other. I think it was weighing heavily on both of us.

"Come on out, Sarah. Hasnain's wife, Mina, is not doing too well. You have to come and examine her. Gulnaz is not happy with the way she is at the moment." One could hear the panic in Razia's voice.

I went to the room where Mina was laid out on her bed and stopped in horror. Her abdomen was enormous with almost black veins branching out from the umbilicus. Due to the pressure on her lungs, she wasn't able to breathe very well. She looked toxic and a noxious smell of putrefaction was coming from her. If we didn't act fast, she would in all certainty die.

Gulnaz had already examined Mina, but just to be sure I did so as well. After all, if we were to work as a team, I needed to know what medical challenges we had to pit our knowledge against.

"Gulnaz, Marjan, I can see that Mina will be needing surgery. Can you get the room with the large table ready for that? It needs to be cleaned as much as possible. Also, ask Hasnain's mother to heat water. We will need a lot." I started to fire instructions at everyone. I realized that the weird fog following the dose of chloroform that I had inhaled was now gone and I was back in my element. Probably due to sheer willpower.

Turning back to Mina, I peeled back the covers from her rigid body. The putrid smell increased as I uncovered her. On palpating her abdomen, I felt that it was very hard and rigid. Just like a patient with peritonitis. That is an inflammation of the peritoneum — a silk-like membrane that lines the inner abdominal wall and covers the organs within the abdomen. I hoped it wasn't that. Additionally, she had a dark and pungent vaginal discharge that did not bode well. Something was putrefying inside her! Marjan had said that she had been due to deliver ten days before. It would seem that the baby had died in utero and had started to putrefy. Mina was in danger of toxic poisoning from her own baby.

Hasnain's asinine behavior worried me. My premonitions were going haywire. I was sure that if we performed the surgery we would be in danger from him, but if we didn't do anything Mina would die. It was a strange situation.

Tanya and Razia were both waiting for me in the other room. They were anxious to know what I had decided.

"She's going to die if she doesn't have surgery. I have done a few caesarian sections in the past, but not many. Thankfully, Gulnaz is experienced in obstetrics and gynecology. We will try to save her life. We are fortunate that

Marjan is also an experienced midwife. I just hope that we aren't too late."

"Why are you looking so worried, sweetheart?" Tanya could read me like a book and I smiled at her even though my heart was full of dread.

"We might have to remove her uterus and maybe some other organs as well. Her abdomen is so taut, and I am certain that the putrefaction has spread so far that she might have had one of her intestines perforated and I fear that peritonitis has already set in."

"You have your team together; I am sure you will do well. Take a deep breath, say a prayer, and work your magic." Even though her words were to reassure me, I was still worried for Mina. Not only that, but I was also afraid of what Hasnain might do when we told him that his wife wouldn't be able to bear his children anymore. It was such a male ego issue in these areas.

Tanya started to confer with Razia while I went to talk to Marjan and Gulnaz. We all agreed that the surgery would be difficult and extremely dangerous.

"Gulnaz, can you and Marjan talk to Hasnain before we start the surgery? He needs to know beforehand what we might find and that we will do everything possible to save Mina's life, but he also needs to know that her condition is due to his neglect—he didn't take Mina to the main hospital when he was advised that she needed a caesarian section."

Tanya and Razia came back into the room. They were still quietly arguing with each other, but when they saw that we had noticed them they abruptly stopped and turned their attention to us.

Looking at Razia for confirmation, Tanya cleared her throat and asked, "Don't you need some sort of written permission or declaration before you perform procedures in hospitals?"

"Yes, of course," said Gulnaz. "You are a genius, Tanya!"

"Yes!" Marjan chimed in. "We will write a consent declaration in Pushto and English and make Hasnain sign it. Instead of one or two witnesses, I suggest every one of us sign the document so that he can't go back on his word."

"Though it is a good idea, I am still worried about the volatile nature of the people who live in this area. Tanya and I are law enforcement officers, so the document could be considered legal till such time we get it notarized by an officer of the court if necessary. But Sarah, please hurry up. I don't want to stay here longer than we need to." I shared Razia's anxiety. Gulnaz and Marjan were already at the table drafting the discussed document. It was a promising idea and a safety net in civilized areas, but would it work here in the tribal area?

We argued, wrote, and rewrote the consent document, and once it was to all of our satisfaction, we called Hasnain into the room. He was taken aback that all of us were there to talk to him, but it was necessary since he needed to realize the gravity of the situation.

Gulnaz and Marjan quickly told him our observations regarding Mina's condition and how we were going to treat her. He needed to know that the surgery we had decided to perform was crucial to save her life and we couldn't guarantee what the outcome would be.

"Just save her life! I love her and I want her to live! But I have just one condition..."

We looked at each other in dread. We had an inkling what he would say next.

"Please, ensure that Mina is able to have more children in the future!" Hasnain went on to say.

Gulnaz explained what we had thought we might have to do once we opened Mina up. She spoke in Pushto so that there was no reason for him to say that he had not understood. He made a weird keening sound and started to cry. I was getting impatient. We were losing time here, time that was of the essence if we wanted to save Mina's life.

"Tell him we will let him know what we have decided once we start the operation and have seen what the actual condition inside is." Everyone looked startled at my tone of voice. I was rarely so sharp, but we needed to get started immediately.

After Hasnain reluctantly signed the document and all of us countersigned it, even his mother, the medical "team" hurried to where Marjan had prepared the room for the surgery. Everything looked very clean and a white sheet was draped over the table. Hasnain carried Mina in and laid her tenderly on it.

"Gulnaz, once you and Marjan have scrubbed for the surgery, please put on two pairs of gloves and two masks. We cannot risk getting an infection ourselves."

We didn't have any scrubs to wear, but we took some clean sheets and draped them toga-like over ourselves and fastened them with safety pins. That was the best we could do. Hasnain's mother had some garishly colored plastic tablecloths that we also tied around our waists with duct tape that Adam had in his backpack.

The only disinfectant that we had with us was Dettol, which was available in a gallon bottle. We poured it liberally over our patient's abdomen and scrubbed her. Marjan had ripped a brand-new sheet into sponge like pieces and had soaked them in boiling hot water laced with Dettol. They were now in small ceramic bowls placed conveniently near the table.

Thank God Gulnaz had had the foresight to pick up chloroform and some surgical instruments before they all followed me here. After we were certain that Mina had enough chloroform to render her unconscious, we cut into the abdomen. The fumes and stench rapidly became worse. The still-born baby inside her uterus was nearly liquid in its putrefied state. There was no way that we could save the uterus—we had to remove it to get rid of the toxins that were permeating the whole of Mina's body.

"What do we do now?" Gulnaz looked worried.

"Well, the only thing that we can do is show Hasnain. He needs to see for himself that saving the uterus is not an option."

Not moving from her position near Mina, Gulnaz called Adam. He peeped inside and instantly recoiled at the foul smell. I was surprised that I managed to still stand there giving my history of throwing up whenever I had been in similar situations in the past.

"Adam! Bring Hasnain in here! We need to show him Mina's condition. Please hurry!"

Hasnain must have been standing right there because he came into the room almost immediately. He had wisely covered his nose and mouth with a wet cloth.

"Hasnain, come closer." He inched forward furtively, his face a study in revulsion and fear.

"Gulnaz, please explain to Hasnain what we have seen and what we need to do."

As Hasnain listened, his agitation increased. We guided him to the "operating table" and showed him the uterus and

the baby and yet he wailed in a wretched voice...
"Nooooooooooo!!!!!"

Tanya and Adam came to take him out of the room, but he fought them. He shook his finger at me and shouted, "You will see to it that her uterus is saved. I don't know or care how you do it, but you will or I'll shoot you and everyone else here!"

Once he was taken out of the room, we continued with the surgery. These delays were dangerous for our patient and we had to hurry.

Even though we knew that Hasnain was against it, we made an informed medical decision. We did take out the uterus. Mina's life was at risk and we couldn't leave the now vile organ in her body no matter what her husband said. As I had suspected, a small part of the intestine had also putrefied and then ruptured. That was why she was having symptoms of peritonitis. Thankfully, we found two healthy sections of the intestine that we were able to anastomose together. After we finished, we flushed the abdomen out with plenty of water and soaked up the moisture with the clean rags. Gulnaz found some new bicycle tires' inner tubes that we cut up into strips to make drains so that the rest of the infected fluid in the abdomen could drain out, Mina was still stable, but now the difficult part started. We had to pump in as much intravenous fluid and as many antibiotics as possible or she would die of infection. She was already looking toxic. Ideally, I would have liked her to have a blood transfusion as well, but given our circumstances, it wasn't possible.

Gulnaz had brought along with her some IV glucose bags and vials of antibiotics, but they were not enough. We needed more. Much more.

"Are there any pharmacies nearby?" I asked Gulnaz.

"Not up here, no. There is a pharmacy that sells only basic medicine in Parachinar. Half the time, I'm not even sure whether the medicine that they are selling is quality stuff." She looked worried. What should we do now? We were supposed to be on our way. There wasn't time for us to stay with Mina. Farooq would definitely catch us, and Lord knows what trouble he would cause us.

We were thankful that we had Marjan, who would take care of Mina post surgically. That was in itself a great relief.

"Is there anyone that we can send down to the town for medicines?" I asked.

"I believe Hasnain has a younger brother, Abbas. Let's see if he can go and get the medicine for us."

I wrote a prescription and gave it to Marjan, who left the room to look for Abbas. In the meantime, I also wrote down detailed instructions for Mina's care. Gulnaz had assured me that Marjan was more than capable of looking after our patient.

Within a few minutes, Marjan rushed into the room with a worried expression on her face. "Dr. Sarah, Dr. Gulnaz, you need to leave! Farooq has been spotted coming up the hiking track!"

Gulnaz quickly instructed Marjan on the final after care instructions for Mina while I went to look for the rest of our team. They were in the next room drinking strong milky tea that Hasnain's mother had prepared for them. Hasnain himself was sullenly sitting in a chair with his hands tied in front of him.

I looked at the constraints and then at Tanya. "We are going to take him to the police station when we go back into town. He needs to be punished for kidnapping you."

"There is no time. Farooq is on his way up the path. We need to leave and see how we can avoid him."

"Hasnain, is there another way down the mountain?" asked Adam, who had been mostly quiet till now.

"Yes, there is, but it's too dangerous for you weak city people," he sneered.

"If you guide us down the mountain away from Farooq, we will drop the charges against you," Razia said in her sternest voice. "As it is, you should be grateful to Dr. Sarah and Dr. Gulnaz that they saved your wife's life."

"Hah!" he scoffed. "Saved her life? She is now useless to me. It would have been better if she had died!" He spat on the floor in disgust.

"Well, whatever you feel, you repulsive worm, that is beside the point. A human life has been saved by the grace of God. You will help us or the police will make your life miserable."

"The police are in my pocket; they are all my friends. There is nothing that you can do to scare me!" he exclaimed disdainfully.

"The local police might be, but the army, air force, and Interpol know where we are, and they will track us down and then you will definitely be in trouble."

The blood drained from Hasnain's face when he heard Tanya speak. He nervously gulped a few times and wiped the sweat from his forehead before he answered her.

"Oh, all right. I will help you, but we need to go now. If it gets dark the path will be even more dangerous. I can't guarantee your safety then."

He turned to me and said, "Dr. Sarah, I am not a bad man. I was just worried for Mina. I listened to the advice of different people about her treatment and delayed taking her to the hospital as Dr. Gulnaz had advised me to." He looked down, visible embarrassed. "Please, accept my apologies. I never meant to hurt you or talk bad about Mina as well. I love her. May I see her before we go?"

"Hurry up then, Hasnain. We all accept your apology because we realize that you were out of your mind with worry."

Razia accompanied Hasnain to his wife's room, concerned that he might run away from there. He was our only means of escape out of the area and we definitely didn't want to have an altercation with Farooq. I also followed them. I wanted to reassure myself that Hasnain would treat his wife with kindness and the love he professed to have for her.

Hasnain looked down at his sleeping wife. He kissed her forehead tenderly and quietly said, "I am so sorry, Mina." Then he started to cry. Razia stood there awkwardly looking around for some tissues to hand him. Not finding any, she handed him one of the clean rags that hadn't been used for the surgery.

"We have to go." Razia tugged at his sleeve. He looked at her with a dazed expression on his face as if he had just woken up from a bad dream. He nodded and wiped the tears off his face. Then walked resolutely out of the room.

Tanya

HASNAIN WAS VERY ANGRY. It was difficult to calm him down. I had a feeling that his anger was not so much at us but at himself, because Mina's condition was due to his unnecessary delay and neglect, but he had to blame someone and was therefore trying to direct his ire at the doctors who were in the other room valiantly trying to save his wife's life.

It came to a point that I became so fed up with him fighting to go in and disturb the doctors that I tied his hands together and made him sit in a chair, only allowing him to go with Adam to the restroom if he required it.

We were all worried. Time was passing by, and even though we were out of Parachinar, this little unnamed mountain hamlet was easy to reach if one knew the hiking trail. Obviously, having lived here most of his life, Farooq would know about it, and there would be many willing voices to tell him where we had gone if he bullied them enough.

After more than an hour and a half, Marjan finally came out of the room looking for Hasnain's younger brother. She went to the outer door, and at her call a teenaged version of Hasnain walked in.

"Marjan, Farooq is halfway up the hiking trail. You asked me to keep a look out for him. I was just told by one of my friends that he could be here within an hour." He then laughed. "Farooq has become soft; he used to be able to hike here much faster. I will try to distract him, but you will have to leave as soon as you can!"

Sarah had by now convinced Hasnain to guide us down another path. She always amazes me with her knack to calm down and communicate with people—another one of the countless reasons why I admire and love her. Recently I seemed to be counting the ways I loved her—very Shakespearean, I dare say. I couldn't hold back a little giggle. Razia looked at me in surprise, but I just shook my head at her indicating that it was not of any importance. At least not for her.

We left the house from the back door and followed a path that was extremely steep. We had to be careful—just one slip and one could fall down the deep ravine. Gulnaz had strapped Daniyal to her front because he was fussing, and she wanted to feed him as we walked along. He soon fell asleep with the sway of his mother's gait. I was thankful for that. We didn't want to alert our pursuers with a baby's cry if we had to hide from them.

When we were halfway down the mountain, we heard a faint roar of anger. I turned around and saw Farooq pointing at us and trying to run down the path. We could see that someone was trying to hold him back. If he wasn't careful he would slip and plummet down to the ravine below if he tried to rush down blinded by his angry temper.

We watched in fascinated horror as Farooq jerked away from the man who was trying to reason with him and hold him back. He started to trot down the path and suddenly his foot slipped and we watched in horror as he fell over the side. I heard someone shriek. It was Gulnaz; after all, no matter how badly he behaved, he was still her brother.

"Farooq! Oh, please Adam, we need to help him!"

Farooq's men were already moving cautiously down the path to assist him. Our dilemma was whether we should also go back up and lend a hand or continue our journey. Gulnaz was frantic and was shaking Adam and urging him to do something.

"Stop shaking my arm. The path is very narrow and I can also fall down if I lose my balance. Please, let go!" Thankfully, Gulnaz realized what she was doing and let go of Adam.

Farooq was still hanging from the ledge, but his men had reached where he was and were pulling him up. He looked shaken, but that didn't stop him from sending us a poisonous look.

He stood there for a short while and then shouted, "Go ahead; run away. I will catch you. Never doubt that. You have won the battle for now but remember... Farooq never loses!"

Heaving a collective sigh of relief that he was safe, we continued down the mountain. It was unanimously decided that we didn't want to go back up and face our nemesis. At least not for now.

The path was treacherous, but the view was breathtaking. The mountains in the distance were still snowcapped and looked magnificent. Wildflowers had popped up all over the slopes heralding spring, and we encountered many little waterfalls that were ice cold, numbing our fingers when we tried to cup our hands to drink from them.

When we reached the main path, we sent Hasnain back home. He was anxious to leave us because he was worried about his wife and wanted to be near in case Marjan required him to get more medicines for Mina. Razia and I told him that if he gave anyone any information about us or the direction to where we were heading, we would make sure that he was arrested for kidnapping and endangerment. I doubt that he would have given us away, because before he left us to go back up the mountain he thanked both of the doctors many times and reverentially kissed the back of their hands. Even though he was an idiot, he wouldn't betray the persons who had saved his wife's life.

As the path widened and we circumvented Parachinar, Sarah joined me and we unashamedly held hands, not only to support each other on the uneven terrain, but also because of the emotional toll the last few days had had on us. We needed to have some contact with each other. All of us were extremely tired and I hoped that Khalid and his jeep were waiting as promised at the caves.

As we neared the rendezvous point, I was happy to see that Khalid was already there. His jeep was covered by green foliage to camouflage it, but the prominent bumpers were still discernable. I pointed them out to Sarah and she laughed in relief and turned to the others to let them know.

Khalid was waiting for us inside the cave. It was enormous, nearly as big as a football field. There was an opening in the high cavernous roof which was quite convenient as it acted like a natural vent for the fire that was merrily crackling right in the middle of the cave. On the fire was a pot bubbling on an iron grate with something that was wafting delicious aromas. A stack of naans was set on a flat stone nearby to keep warm.

"It's about time you all arrived. I was going to go look for you if you had taken any longer."

The cave was big enough for us to pitch our tents. They would add to the insulation to keep us warm at night when it got really cold. We were all exhausted and were looking forward to having a well-deserved rest.

"You are sure that no one knows about this cave? What I mean is, no one of Farooq's people?" I was still apprehensive and didn't want us to be ambushed while we slept.

"I can assure you that you are safe here. There is a small pool fed by a waterfall just outside the cave. It will be cold, but at least you will be able to wash your faces and hands. I will warm some water in the morning before breakfast for everyone to use. For now, just tolerate the cold." He smirked at me. I was sure he thought we were soft city people.

We pitched our tents around the fire and had our dinner. It was a surprisingly delicious lamb stew cooked with tomatoes and potatoes. Khalid had also made a salad with onions and tomatoes to accompany it.

Once we had tidied up everything and stoked the fire, Khalid called me over.

"It is better that we keep watch while everyone sleeps. Even though I am sure that this cave is not very well known, we still don't want any surprises. Since I know that you are as tired as your friends, I will take the first watch and will wake you up at midnight for your turn." I nodded in agreement and told Razia about our plan. "Wake me up at 4am and I will take my turn then as well."

Sarah and I shared a two-person tent. It was comfortable and we needed the close proximity at that time. Though we weren't alone, just touching each other gave us some respite of the tension that was coursing through our veins. Our sleeping bags were warm, and the radiant heat of the fire lulled us to sleep almost immediately. I felt as if I had just put my head on the surprisingly comfortable inflatable pillow when I felt Khalid shaking me awake.

"Wake up! It's your turn to keep a look out," he whispered.

Quietly slipping out of the tent, I went to add some more wood to the dying fire. It started to crackle and send off sparks that lit up the cave. The warmth was enjoyable, but I kept going to the entrance to look at the path leading to it in case we had any unwanted guests. The vegetation around the cave hid it from the road, but we had a clear view in case anyone approached. I was impressed that Khalid had swept away the tracks of the jeep with branches. No one would be able to find us there. After about an hour, it started to rain, and gradually, the torrents started mini flash floods on the path. Any further signs that we were hiding there were erased as well. I started to relax. The sound of the rain and thunder were comforting, but I was alert and didn't fall asleep. At 4am, I woke Razia for her shift. I hoped that I could at least get another couple of hours of sleep before we left for Kohat.

I crawled back into the tent and settled down for a short nap. Sensing me near, Sarah turned to me and cuddled into my back. Even when she was fast asleep, she knew when I was there and took comfort in the knowledge that I would always protect her. And I knew that she would always be there for me as well.

CHAPTER 9

"While we are talking, envious time is fleeing: pluck the day, put no trust in the future." ~ Horace

Sarah

THE SWAY OF THE JEEP AS IT DROVE OVER THE uneven ground finally lulled me to sleep. I noticed that Tanya looked extremely tired and I saw her nod off a few times, but she stoically tried to remain awake. I was worried about her. I was certain that she was exhausted since she had been up half the night taking her turn in guarding the camp.

After we drove along for a while, Khalid looked at us over his shoulder. "Would you all like to stop for a short break? It's better if we do that now since it will take us another hour to reach Kohat."

Gulnaz woke with a start when she heard him. She

nodded and stretched. "I need to change Daniyal's nappy; he doesn't smell very nice at the moment," she said with a laugh.

Khalid stopped the jeep near some huge boulders by the river. They were high enough to hide us in case we wanted to relieve ourselves, which everyone promptly did. One by one.

Gulnaz found a large flat boulder on which she spread Daniyal's blanket and lay him down on it. It was convenient since she was able to wash and change him with ease. After that, she gathered all of the baby's paraphernalia and packed it once again into her colorful nappy bag. Then she took the clean, smiling Daniyal, who smelled strongly of baby powder, to wait for us in the jeep while she fed him.

The river rapids were evidence that the glaciers had started to melt, but they weren't as swift as they usually are in summer. Therefore, I braved the fast-moving water by wading on the pebbles near the shore. It was freezing! Like pure ice water. I quickly jumped out before my toes turned blue.

After we had refreshed ourselves and Gulnaz had finished seeing to Daniyal, we resumed our bumpy journey. In spite of the jostling, I promptly fell asleep with my head on Tanya's shoulder again, only waking up when the jeep hit potholes causing it to bump quite severely. We even hit our heads on the canvas roof a few times.

As we neared Kohat, we started to see signs of civilization. Children herding goats and sheep would try to race the jeep as it drove along. We had by then reached a proper road and soon entered the town limits of Kohat. Khalid drove to the Air Force officers mess as Captain Zafar had instructed him before we headed out to Parachinar.

All of a sudden, as we all piled out of the jeep, I felt a wave of despair and severe pain in my lower back. It was so severe that I doubled over in pain. Where was that coming from? My periods were not due for another week. There was no reason whatsoever for me to feel this way. Unless... I was picking up the pain from someone else. But who?

"I don't think I will be going back to Karachi with all of you," I said while trying to breathe through the pain.

Tanya noticed my distress and told me to sit down in the passenger seat of the jeep until I felt I could move again. The pain waxed and waned, thus giving me some respite in between intervals. It was excruciating and mysterious, but I knew that I couldn't leave until I had taken care of what was psychically attacking me.

While Tanya and I stayed by the jeep, the rest of our group entered the officers' mess. Gulnaz and Adam wanted to see to Daniyal's comfort and get something to eat for themselves, and I was sure that Razia wanted to call her twins.

Captain Zafar saw us arrive from the window of the airport office and came out to greet us. He looked worried and it seemed as if he wanted to say something to me but wasn't sure how to.

"What is it, Captain? Why are you looking so worried?" asked Tanya. I still wasn't able to articulate properly as the cramps kept squeezing my innards.

"I just got word from our Air Commodore that his daughter has been in labor for the past ten hours. It's a difficult case and the gynecologist has decided to do a caesarian section."

We looked at him intently with puzzled looks on our faces.

"The neonatologist had to suddenly go to Peshawar because her mother fell and broke a hip. There is no one to receive the baby. It is in distress, and that is why the doctor wants to operate immediately."

"And you want me to be there and resuscitate the baby if that is required?" I asked him.

Captain Zafar nodded. "I know you all have been through a lot these past couple of days, but this is a matter of life and death for the mother as well as the baby. This baby is precious because the mother has already lost three babies before."

Now I understood my pain and misery. As soon as I agreed to accompany the captain to the Military Hospital, the pain melted away as if by magic. I knew now that I was supposed to be here.

"Tanya, why don't you ask Adam, Gulnaz, and Razia to leave with the Captain for Karachi? We can follow later on."

She looked at me with an expression that was a mixture of affection and exasperation. She knew that once I had my 'feelings,' there was no stopping me. I had to follow them if it was to help someone. After making sure that I was feeling better, she left to talk to the others. In the meantime, Captain Zafar was getting impatient. "We need to leave for the hospital. The gynecologist is waiting for you."

"We are waiting for Tanya. As soon as she is back, I will go with you."

"You need to come with me now!" he said in a stern voice. "I will send a car for Tanya later."

I was torn. I knew time was of the essence if we wanted to save the life of both mother and child, and yet, after all we had gone through those past few days, I didn't want to leave Tanya.

Seeing my hesitation, Captain Zafar said, "I will instruct

my batman to wait for Tanya and bring her to the hospital. Don't worry; she will be all right."

As I walked towards the Military Hospital surgery, I saw they were already rolling the gurney with the patient into the operation theater. The gynecologist saw me with the captain and came to greet me with relief on her face. "Salam, I am Dr. Mahnoor. Thank you so much for agreeing to come. I was getting worried. The baby is in distress. The heartbeats are decelerating and there is evidence of meconium in the mother's vaginal discharge. My nurses wouldn't be able to manage the baby. It's at a great risk."

"Do you have all the equipment needed for neonatal resuscitation?" I asked.

"Yes, we do. Nurse Tabassum will take you to the resuscitation warmer. If there is anything you need, let us know."

"I will go and change into scrubs. In the meantime, I would like the warmer to be shifted as near to the operation theater as possible. I would actually prefer that it is inside the theater. That way we waste minimum precious time."

Dr. Mahnoor agreed and I wasted no time getting changed. As soon as I was ready, I went to inspect the resuscitation warmer and the instruments as well as the medicines that I would need in case intensive resuscitation was needed.

I was impressed with the speed and the efficiency of the surgery. When the baby was extracted from the uterus, it was limp and not breathing. Moreover, it was covered with greenish black meconium. My heart skipped a beat. I was worried. The baby had aspirated its own meconium in its distress. "Please, don't try to stimulate the baby!" I yelled at the operating team. "I don't want him to further inhale anything else. Just give him to me as he is. I will do what I can."

I took the baby and used a meconium extractor to suck out as much of the thick noxious substance from his mouth and trachea as I could. Then I intubated him and suctioned a bit more. The nurse continued to give him oxygen with an ambu-bag while I gave him cardiac compressions. We worked in synchronized tandem and within a minute, he started to whimper and move on his own. We didn't have to use any medication, which was remarkable. I took out the endotracheal tube and he let out a big cry. Everyone had smiles on their faces. It is truly a miracle when a baby takes its first breath and begins to cry lustily. More so when babies are born limp with faint heartbeats and no respiration like our little trouper there.

I stayed with the baby for over an hour because I wanted to be sure that he was stable. There was some mild respiratory distress which was to be expected, but I could leave him in the care of the pediatric nurse. He still had to have oxygen, but his neonatologist was on her way back from Peshawar, and she would be able to manage him easily. To add to his recovery, I gave him a few doses of reiki which I had planned to continue long distance for at least another twenty-four hours.

I went to change back into my clothes and give a detailed report to Dr. Mahnoor. I also wrote my findings and procedures in the baby's chart. Satisfied that I had done all that I could at that time, I went to look for Tanya.

I found her in the doctor's lounge. She was fast asleep on one of the leather couches there. I let her sleep for a short while. She was exhausted, but in sleep her face relaxed and she looked almost childlike. She was beautiful, and she was mine. I thanked God that I was blessed with such a loving and kind life partner who not only loved me but also tolerated my quirks and foibles.

Tanya

SARAH WAS off to another one of her medical adventures. I was certain that she would have already left given the urgency of the case. I went to look for Adam and found everyone, even Khalid, drinking tea in one of the lounges.

"Adam, you and Gulnaz will have to go to Karachi on your own. We will follow later."

"Why? We can't be separated now!" he almost shouted. "Farooq might be close and could catch you once again."

"Sarah has to help with a baby in the Military Hospital. It is the Air Commodore's daughter who is in difficult labor, and they need her to receive the baby. Maybe even resuscitate it if required." Adam started to grumble. He said he was tired of Sarah's medical side trips. "How do you tolerate her?" He sounded irritated, but also amused.

"There is no time to argue now," I said trying to suppress a smile. "Go to Abba and get your passports. Try to get a flight to London as soon as you can." I took a key from my key chain and handed it to him. "This is our house key. We have an alarm that you have to disarm before you can enter. The code is Sarah's birthday."

I turned to Razia. "I can't thank you enough for your help. You are a true friend, but now you need to go home to your boys. Although, since you have already been to our place in England, it would be ideal if you accompanied Adam there."

"My UK visa is still valid," said Razia. "I will go home and say hello to my boys, and then I'll pack a bag and meet Adam and his family at the airport."

I didn't want to impose on Razia, but she offered, actually she insisted, and it was a relief because Adam was not exactly sure where we lived.

"Adam, could you be so kind as to buy my ticket as well?" asked Razia. "I will pay you when I meet you at the airport."

With that decided, we all hugged each other and said our goodbyes. Captain Zafar, who was politely waiting on the sidelines, came forward and guided me to his car and his batman drove me to meet Sarah at the hospital.

I stalked around the waiting room, reading the notice boards and occasionally talking with the nurses. I wondered how long it would take and hoped that everything was all right. I looked at my watch and realized that three hours had already passed by.

I heard a phone ringing and saw the nurse pick it up.

"Are you Agent Tanya?" She called over to me.

"Yes, I am," I answered simply. I was dreading what she had to tell me, but she was smiling, so I thought it couldn't be bad news.

"It's for you. Long distance from Karachi." She handed the receiver to me with a smile.

"Hello," I said, wondering who it could be.

"Tanya! Thank God! I need to update you on our journey. I have news about Farooq!" Razia spoke very fast and in a high-pitched voice, a sign she was stressing out.

"Slow down," I said, raising my voice to make Razia listen to me. "Tell me what happened from the beginning."

"We reached the airport just in time to catch the C-180

flight to Karachi. I was worried because I didn't want to leave you and Sarah in Kohat, but I know she wouldn't leave anyone if they needed her medical skills."

"Right," I said, wondering where this was all going.

"We strapped ourselves into our seats and waited for the plane to take off, but there seemed to be a delay, so I got up and went to the cockpit to find out what the problem was." Razia took a deep breath. I could sense that she was trying to calm herself down.

"The pilot told me that the local political liaison officer had requested that we take along one of his people and we had to wait for him. After over half an hour, we heard someone walk up the stairs into the plane. To our horror, it was Farooq! I signaled to the others not to say anything, but I don't think they could have anyway because they had utterly flabbergasted expressions on their faces."

"Farooq again... I'm now glad Sarah and I didn't go back to Karachi with you. Did he behave himself on the flight?" I asked.

"He was his usual arrogant self, and he kept asking about you and Sarah, but none of us told him that you are in Kohat. We pretty much ignored him, and he just slumped down in his seat with a petulant look on his face."

"Farooq likes being the center of attention and I bet he didn't like being ignored. It's a shame he was on the plane with you all," I said.

"No, I was actually glad about that. I had no authority in Kohat to arrest him for his misdemeanors, but once we arrived in Karachi, there would be no holding back. I spent the whole flight thinking of ways to hold him long enough so that everyone could leave the country before his bail was posted."

"What happened then?" I asked cautiously.

"Once the flight was in the air, I went to talk with the pilot and asked him to radio ahead to Police Headquarters in Karachi so they had a police team ready for us when we landed. I had to show him my badge so that he could see I was authorized to request for backup. He was surprised that the passenger of the political liaison officer was a criminal who would be arrested as soon as we arrived."

"I am glad you had the means for a backup," I said. I was relieved that Sarah and I wouldn't be running into Farooq, but we still had to keep a lookout for his henchmen and goons.

"Well, a police squad was waiting at the foot of the stairs leading to the aircraft, and the sergeant entered the plane before everyone disembarked and presented Farooq with a warrant for his arrest. However..."

"Wasn't he arrested on the spot? There are plenty of charges against him—kidnapping, assault, attempted murder..." I feared Farooq had somehow avoided being taken into custody.

"He was clearly expecting the police to confront him, Tanya. He took out a piece of official looking paper from his inside pocket and flung it insolently into my face—it was a pre-arrest bail. It was surreal, and there was nothing I could do about it."

I was dumbstruck! Farooq was in Karachi and there was nothing that the authorities could do because of that pre-arrest bail.

"Adam is justifiably worried," Razia added. "If the police can't hold Farooq down, then he and Sarah are still in danger. How can they live in peace knowing that there is very little we can do to restrain Farooq?"

I was quiet for a few seconds, and then started thinking out loud. "The thing is that a pre-arrest bail is a legal relief in anticipation of a possible arrest, right? Simply put, if someone anticipates that there is a move to get him arrested on false or trumped up charges, or due to enmity with someone, or fears that a false case is likely to be built up against him, he has the right to move the court for grant of bail in the event of his arrest, and the court may direct, if it thinks fit, that he shall be released on bail." Of course Razia knew that, but I had to revise it in my mind so that I was absolutely sure about it. What a dire situation.

"You are right." Razia sounded worried. Adam had to be reassured that in spite of this pre-arrest warrant, Farooq couldn't touch him or his family or said warrant would be null and void.

"Where are you now?" I asked.

"At my place. We came here from the airport and plan to call Mr. Shah shortly."

"Good. The best thing that you can do at this moment is leave immediately for England just like I told you to. As soon as we finish here and can get Sarah's passport, we will follow you all. At least this pre-arrest bail ensures that he can't follow us there, since he has to be available for police interrogation whenever they require his presence." I urged Razia to make their travel arrangements a priority and we ended the call.

I was exhausted. While I continued to wait for Sarah to finish what she had to do, I tried to keep my eyes open. There was a newspaper in the lounge that was a day old, but I still tried to read it to stay awake. My body betrayed me and before I knew it, I was fast asleep on the comfortable couch, oblivious to what was going on around me.

CHAPTER 10

"There is no hospitality like understanding."
~ Vanna Bonta, Flight: A Quantum Fiction Novel.

Sarah

I was so tired. I could feel my fatigue nearly bogging me down making it almost impossible to lift one foot in front of the other. I really don't know how I made it to the doctor's lounge. It probably was because I knew that Tanya was waiting for me. Poor dear must be just as tired as I was, if not more. When I entered the lounge, I saw her sleeping quite comfortably on the wide leather couch which seemed to be the standard in all military institutions.

Just as I was going to mimic her and lie down on the couch next to Tanya, Air Commodore Rahman's wife came bustling in.

"What do you think you are doing here? This is not on! I

have told the maid to prepare a room for you to rest before you travel again. Please wake her up. You are leaving with me immediately!"

Her staccato voice in unapologetic loud decibels woke Tanya up before I could do so. She looked around in a daze. She must have really been in a deep sleep.

"Come love, Mrs. Rahman has invited us to stay and rest in her home. Let's go with her. She is right, for the two of us to sleep in the lounge wouldn't be seen fit." I laughed at the thought. Just imagine if some army or air force doctors walked in and saw two young women sleeping on the couches. I was sure that their expressions would have been priceless.

We gathered our bags and followed Mrs. Rahman to the official sedan that bore the air force flag on one side and the Pakistani flag on the other. We were to be escorted in style! What fun!

Once we reached the large bungalow, we were immediately shown into a large airy guest room. It had twin beds whose headboards were made of walnut wood with the unique wood carving of flowers and birds that the region is known for. They were covered with pristine, fluffy white bedcovers. In contrast the starkness of the room was broken down with the colorful curtains that were wafting gently in the breeze. It was a pleasant room to lay one's head down. I really wanted to do that immediately, but Mrs. Rahman had other ideas.

"Doctor, I have put fresh towels in the en-suite bathroom. Please go there for a shower, I am going to take your friend to the other bathroom to do the same. After you are finished, please come to the room two doors down to your left. We will have something to eat and then both of you can rest."

She resolutely took Tanya by the arm and marched her out of the room. I had to giggle when Tanya looked back with a mock frightened look on her face. I wiggled my fingers at her in farewell, and she started to giggle as well.

The shower was hot and refreshing. I felt as if I could go another few kilometers. But my treacherous tummy started to make weird animalistic noises indicating that I should give it some attention as well.

I was glad that we had a change of clean clothes in our bags. I had noticed that the laundry fairy of the house had taken our dirty laundry, and a clean cotton *shalwar kameez* of mine was ironed and laid down on the bed for me to wear. That is the efficiency of a military household I thought to myself. We used to have the same efficient service, and may I say pampering when I was younger, and Baba was a senior officer in the army.

Mrs. Rahman and Tanya had already started to eat by the time I found the dining room. The table was laden with all sorts of savory as well as sweet dishes. All of them smelt heavenly, and I was sure that they would be just as delicious. There was no doubt that the food tasted good because Tanya was tucking in without saying a word. That was typical of her when she liked what she was eating. She wanted to savor each bite. Not like me. Because of my medical lifestyle, I tended to gobble my food, sometimes even while standing if it happened that I was paged and I wanted to get as much in my stomach as possible knowing that some time would pass before I would be able to get some sustenance into myself once more. It's a wonder I didn't suffer from gastrointestinal problems.

"Ah there you are!" Mrs. Rahman indicated with her hand to a vacant seat next to Tanya. "Sit down, sit down, you must be hungry!" I wanted to politely say that I was fine, but my stomach betrayed me once more with its growl of despair. Tanya and Mrs. Rahman started to laugh. I think that was when the ice broke, and we were able to chat with each other without being too formal or shy.

"You are a miracle worker Doctor! I was so worried about my daughter and the baby. Bless you!"

"I was glad I was there in time to help." I said trying to be modest but pleased that I was able to add value to someone's life. Hey! I am human after all. I like a kind word of appreciation occasionally!

"Don't you worry, we will arrange your safe passage out of Kohat. But first you need to finish eating and then rest a while. Anyone can see that both of you would fall over if you were poked."

We finally finished the well-cooked meal and having said good night to the chatty Mrs. Rahman, we made our way to the guest room where we simply flung ourselves on the beds and fell into a deep asleep almost immediately.

It only seemed as if I had just shut my eyes when I was woken up by a knock on the door. I looked with half open eyes toward Tanya and saw to my surprise that she was still asleep. Groaning and mumbling a medley of choiciest curses under my breath, I reluctantly got up, padded barefoot towards the door and opened it. A maid was standing there with a tray that had two steaming mugs of tea on them. I took the tray from her with a smile and thanked her.

"Doctor ji, I will bring your laundry in a little while." She said and hurried off.

I could get used to being pampered like this. Imagine

getting an early morning cup of tea or coffee delivered to your door every day?

According to my watch, we had slept nearly 8 hours and it was already 7 o'clock in the morning!

"Tanya! Wake up! It's already quite late and we need to go." A frisson of fear bordering on panic started somewhere in the pit of my stomach. While I knew that we were safe here in the Air Commodore's house, I was worried what or who we would encounter today.

Tanya was just as disoriented as I was when she finally woke up, but she looked much better than she had the last few days. She looked rested, and moreover, you could see that she was happy once again.

Reaching out for a mug of tea, she inhaled the steam. "Now *this* is a good cup of tea!"

"Do you mean I don't make good tea?" I said pretending to be annoyed.

"No, no, sweetheart, you make the best tea in the world." I started to laugh because I really wasn't the best person to ask for a cup of tea.

"Hurry up and get ready, I am sure we will get breakfast soon. I am anxious to know what has been arranged for our departure."

Both of us got ready in record time and went to look for our hosts. We found them having breakfast in the dining room. Mrs. Rahman was pouring tea for her husband while he was half hidden behind a newspaper. I had to stop for a moment at the door, because the domestic scene reminded me of my parents. I felt a touch of melancholy when I entered the room. But once Mrs. Rahman started to talk in her distinctive manner, it melted away. Oh, I am going to have so much fun mimicking her when we were alone.

"Come in! I want you girls to eat something before you go. You can't travel on an empty stomach." We sat down at the same places we had the night before. Almost like magic, plates laden with eggs and potatoes appeared in front of us. The potatoes were cooked with some spices that I couldn't identify, but the smell and taste was delicious.

"It must be the mountain air and the organic food because everything tastes so delicious here. Even the water." I was gushing, I knew that, but I wanted to convey my appreciation for the substantial spread.

Tanya tried to hide her smile at my gregariousness as she ate. But I could see that she was enjoying her meal as much as I was.

Once we had finished another cup of tea, we sat back and waited for our hosts to let us know what they had planned for us.

Mrs. Rahman beckoned to her maid who brought a colorful bundle to her. She looked into it carefully, nodded her head and handed it to me. I was taken aback.

"What is this Mrs. Rahman?" I asked.

"Nothing much. Just some Chinese silk we bought from traders on the Karakoram Highway, and some gold bangles. They are for you. As thank you for what you did for our grandson yesterday. You went out of your way for us and delayed your journey. You could have refused, but we are grateful that you were there."

"But this is too much!" I exclaimed. Tanya gave me a pointed look. I knew that in the culture of the northern areas if you refuse a gift, it is considered an insult. But this was too much!

"I love the silk, it's amazing! But the bangles are..."

"Don't you like them dear?"

"They are lovely!" Mrs. Rahman picked them up and slipped them on the wrist of my right hand. "There. They suit you. I had already set these aside for the neonatologist. Since you were there for the baby it's only fair that you get the gifts. Please accept them with our sincere thanks."

Her husband peeked from behind the newspaper and nodded his head then ducked back again.

I didn't expect anything for what I did, but the gifts were beautiful, and Mrs. Rahman was happy that I had accepted them graciously.

"Oh yes, one more thing!" exclaimed the kind lady. "Women in these areas wear a chaddar when they travel. It has a dual purpose. Besides modesty, where you can hide behind it, and no one would dare to touch you. It's an unwritten code of ethics here. They also ward off the dust and grime of the road and you can reach your destination not looking very bedraggled." She handed me two pristine white chaddars that were immense. But if required could cover a person from top to bottom. She waved off my thanks and gave both of us a hug before we followed her husband out of the house.

Tanya

I WAS GETTING IMPATIENT. All this socializing and polite chit chat was slowly getting on my nerves. Maybe we have lived too long in the west because I saw a glimmer of my irritation mirrored in Sarah's eyes. She knew I wanted to leave as soon as possible, and she was actually doing a good job in trying to extricate herself from our hostess. No doubt we had to accept the hospitality graciously, but we needed to leave, and soon.

I turned my attention to the Air Commodore. He was still hiding behind his newspaper. Maybe so many women in one room was unsettling him? I smiled to myself thinking of many scenarios where we could frighten the man with our overt "femaleness". If the truth be told, the men in this area aren't very comfortable in the presence of women. There is a wariness which usually stems from the fact that they didn't want to offend the women or the men of their family. Feuds can occur at the drop of a hat. The nature of the mountain men was very volatile. And yet I was uneasy with his distance. It seemed a bit too much for a man who was supposed to be educated and a member of the Armed Forces.

"Sir, please could you let me know what plans you had for our travel today?"

"Hmph! Yes," He cleared his throat, folded the newspaper, and looked at me. "Where exactly do you want to go?"

"I'm sorry, I thought you knew." My disquiet suddenly went up a few notches. What was going on? "We would like to go to Karachi."

"There is no flight out of Kohat for the next few days, but I will ask my driver to take you to Peshawar. You can catch a commercial flight to Karachi from there."

It took all of my willpower not to scream. "I was told there is a C-180 flight out of Kohat today."

"Yes, you have heard right, but it is carrying some military paraphernalia that could be volatile, so we decided that we won't risk civilians going on that flight."

While I understood their precautions it was still irritating. Now what do we do?

"How far is it to Peshawar Sir?" I asked.

"Not very far, just about seventy-four kilometers. You could reach there within one and a half hour if you don't stop on the way." He was quite unconcerned. As far as he knew, we needed a ride out of town, and he was providing it for us. Maybe not the type of ride we wanted, but it seemed that in our case beggars couldn't be choosers.

"Then I think we need to hurry if we are to reach Peshawar in time to get a flight to Karachi," I said standing up.

"Sarah, we need to go. We will be travelling by car to Peshawar." She felt my irritation and tried to give me a conciliatory look. I waved her off impatiently. She came back within 10 minutes with both of our bags.

Mrs. Rahman pressed a basket of snacks and drinks in our hands for the way. She was generous and a good hostess. It would have been nice to spend more time with her if the situation was different. As it is I think she was staying with us out of politeness. I was sure that she wanted to go and be with her daughter and new grandson at the hospital.

We said our goodbyes to Mrs. Rahman and I was relieved that it wasn't one of the notorious long winded farewells that are sometimes seen in Pakistani society. That was even more proof that she wanted to leave for the hospital as soon as she could without giving the impression of being rude.

The Air Commodore took us to the driveway of his house where a battered Toyota was parked.

"I apologize for the transportation, but the official car will be used by myself and my wife since I foresee many trips to and from the hospital. This car belongs to my son in law. Though it looks like a jalopy, it is reliable. My driver will take you to Peshawar. He has instructions to see that you get on a flight to Karachi, and if you don't get one today, he is to arrange for your accommodations for the night."

As he spoke, tall a young man with a short haircut and a thick well-trimmed moustache walked towards us and greeted us politely. Even though he was wearing civilian clothes, you could see from the way he walked and from his posture that he had a military background.

"This is Saleem. He is a responsible person and will see that you are properly taken of."

Nodding our greetings to him, I gestured to Sarah to get into the car. I sat in front while she stretched out in the back. Sarah loved to sleep on long journeys, and I was certain that she would fall asleep as soon as we were on the road. Finally, we were on our way.

The day was bright and clear, while the air was crisp and clean with a slight chill. There was just a hint of the smell of woodsmoke from the fires that had cooked the breakfasts of the people living in the area.

The journey so far was uneventful, and I enjoyed the drive on the winding road around the mountain. There was no doubt that the scenery around us was beautiful. After a while I realized that none of us had said a word. There was an uncomfortable silence in the car. Sarah of course had dropped off as soon as the car started to move, and I could hear her gentle snores coming from the back seat. She had put one of the backpacks under her head like a pillow and had stretched out on the seat.

"Saleem, thank you for volunteering to take us to Peshawar," I said. I wanted to start a conversation to assess the person who was for now given the responsibility of our safety.

"I always obey an order," he said sullenly. Fair enough, he was after all a soldier. And he was driving someone else's decrepit car. It probably wasn't very nice for him.

But still I persisted. "What part of this area are you from?"

He looked furtively at me and then said again quite reluctantly, "Parachinar". That made me sit up. Everyone knew each other in that small town, and I was sure that he knew Farooq. Maybe that was why he was so sullen?

I didn't say anything further and we drove for an hour till we reached a town called Darra Adamkhel. Though small, this was the main town of the Frontier Region of Kohat. From what I remembered it was a hotbed of gun manufacturers. I had heard that the gunsmiths there could copy an AK 47 down till the last screw. And the efficiency of the weapon was supposedly even better than the Russian one it was copied from. Driving through the bazaar was eerie because all of the shops were predominantly selling weapons of all sizes and shapes.

"They even have guns that look like pens," said Saleem. He had noticed my interest in the bustling bazaar. "Would you like to stop and have a look around?"

"No, thank you. We want to reach Peshawar as soon as we can. We need to be in Karachi earliest by this evening."

"Well, I would like to have a cup of tea before we go on." He was firm and even belligerent in his insistence of stopping. I couldn't say much because in theory he was doing us a favor. It was just unfortunate that he was one of those people who are addicted to their mid-morning cuppa.

He parked the car in front of a tea house that had an

enormous steaming cauldron of tea bubbling away on the elevated wood stove right in front of the building. Leaving the keys in the car, he went out to talk to the man who was doling out the many cups of tea for his customers. I was glad that I was looking in the direction where he was going because I saw him shake hands and talk to a man who looked vaguely familiar. Suddenly it struck me where I had seen him. He was the other goon! Not the one who helped us, Tariq, but the one whose name we didn't know. Here he was friendly and chummy with the person who was taking us to Peshawar!

"Sarah! Wake up! Please." I was worried. This did not look good. I looked at the men and they were seated at a small table near the tea shop sipping their tea. They were talking quite animatedly and gesturing towards the car. I was now sure that they were talking about us, and that we were about to be "kidnapped" once more.

Out of the corner of my eye I saw a bus stop to the left of the car. The signs on it indicated that it was going to Peshawar. I signaled to Sarah, bent over, and slid out of the door with my head held low. She did the same and we swiftly made our way to the bus. Looking over my shoulder I was happy to see that the two men were still deep in conversation and hadn't noticed that we had exited the car. I realized that the chaddars we wore were now going to be our disguises.

We quickly made our way to the front of the bus and were able to hop on just as the driver was putting it into gear.

"Where do you want to?" He asked politely but in a rough dialect.

"Pekhawar," said Sarah. She said the name of the town with a harsh inflection just as the locals said it. That was clever. If anyone would ask around, they wouldn't be able to track us immediately since we didn't stand out.

We sat on the two front seats that were usually reserved for women. I just had enough Pakistani Rupees to pay for our tickets. We would have to go to a bank to exchange my pounds for rupees as soon as we had the opportunity to do so. The bus driver was in a hurry so he started off immediately. He navigated the twists and turns at high speed with the expertise of a person who had done that many times, but it still was disconcerting. Sarah draped the chaddar around her head, covered her face and promptly went to sleep once more. On the other hand, I kept counting the kilometers by reading the milestones as we passed them. I couldn't even think of closing my eyes at this point. I was sure that we would be followed. There were a few buses at the bus stop when we caught this one. Therefore, if they thought that we had boarded a bus, they wouldn't know which one. I was sure that it would be some time before our pursuers would find us. But I still wasn't able to relax.

There were a few Toyotas passing us as we drove along, Thankfully, they weren't the one we were looking out for. I hoped that I would be able to identify the right car when it came near since I realized that cars of that make and color were quite popular.

Maybe it was a miracle, or God listened to my prayers, but we soon entered the outskirts of Peshawar. On a hunch I leaned over and tapped the driver on the shoulder.

"Where does the bus stop?" I asked.

"We stop and pick up passengers to go back to Kohat and Parachinar from the main bus station in the middle of town."

"Could you stop the bus elsewhere and let us get out?"

Apparently it wasn't an unusual request because sometimes passengers did ask to be dropped off on the roadside if it was near where they lived or where they had to be at the time. Therefore, the driver just nodded his head. "Tell me when you want to get off, and I will stop."

"Can you stop a kilometer down the road near Green's Hotel please?" I had remembered the colonial hotel built in 1940. Not only would that be a place to stay in case we couldn't get a flight tonight, but they also took traveler's checks and foreign currency. I also remembered that they arranged car rentals as well. I wanted to be prepared in every way.

The bus stopped with a lurch in front of the main gate of Green's Hotel. I thanked the bus driver and we quickly got off and walked down the sweeping driveway to the reception. It was a beautiful building, constructed in the distinctive colonial style by the British. There were already a few people sitting in the shady verandas relaxing and having a mid-day drink or in all probability waiting for lunch to be served.

We were lucky to get a room and were checked in immediately. I asked the bell boy who escorted us to our room whether the concierge of the hotel was able to help us with flight bookings. He nodded in the affirmative, so I told Sarah to get settled and wait for me in the room while I followed the boy once more to arrange our tickets.

The concierge was an overweight old worldly man in a uniform that was pristine, but the style looked as dated as he was. Maybe they wanted to keep the historical/colonial ambience? He was very polite, though he had a puzzled look on his face when he heard my request. But he did promise to find us the *first available* flight to Karachi. Strange that he kept stressing on the availability. Normally there shouldn't be any trouble. And why was he looking at me as if I had lost my mind. His expression of incredulity did give me the impression that maybe I actually had.

"Why don't you rest in your room, and I will let you know when everything has been arranged." His tone was placating, even patronizing. I didn't like it, but I had to tolerate it, or go myself out into town to get the tickets and I obviously didn't want that for now. Thanking him, I slipped a hundred rupees into his hand and requested him not to tell anyone who asked about us, that we were at the hotel. I gave a larger tip than was usual to the bell boy with the same request. I knew that the front desk wouldn't give us away, because confidentiality was part of the hotel's mandate. Those were the last of our rupees.

Remembering that I had to call Razia, I asked the hotel operator to connect me to her through one of the lobby hospitality-phones that were set in quaint booths with glass doors. She had to be worried since she hadn't heard from us since the day before.

I took the advantage of the glass doors and closed them as I needed the privacy. Considering what we had gone through in the past few days, I didn't want anyone to eavesdrop on my conversation.

Razia picked the phone up before the first ring actually finished. "Tanya! Where are you and Sarah? Shall we come and pick you up?" The words tumbled out of her mouth one after the other. I could feel that she definitely was worried about us.

"I wish you could pick us up." I sighed. I was exasperated with the whole situation.

"Where *are* you?" she shouted. I had to pull the receiver away from my ear because she was so loud.

"I am in Peshawar—" I couldn't say anything further because of Razia's roar of incredulity racing down the telephone lines.

"WHAT?!?!?! What in heaven's name are you doing in blinking Peshawar? You were supposed to be on the morning flight from Kohat to Karachi! I had arranged it for you with the Air Commodore!" She sounded furious. To tell you the truth, I would have been just as livid.

"The Air Commodore, in his infinite wisdom, said that the plane had a volatile cargo; therefore, it wasn't safe to have civilians ride along. He suggested that we go to Peshawar and get a commercial flight out from there."

"Is he *crazy*? A Pakistan International Airlines (PIA) flight crash-landed on the runway last night and damaged the tarmac. The airport is closed for a week, and they are diverting flights to Islamabad. It's been all over the news! I am certain the Air Commodore knew that."

"I think so too. He hardly spoke to us at breakfast before we left. And he hid most of the time behind his newspaper. He must have known about the airport being closed, and yet he sent us here." I stroked my chin thinking about our predicament. "I think he was in cahoots with Farooq's men. We realized there was something not very *halal* with our driver when he stopped in Darra Adamkhel and we saw him talking to one of Farooq's goons. We were able to slip unseen out of the car and catch a bus to Peshawar."

"I hope you both are in a safe place. You never know who is lurking about. No wonder Farooq was so smug when we last saw him. He thought he had you both."

After reassuring Razia that we were safe at the Green's

Hotel and that I would call her back again to tell her what we had planned, I disconnected the call.

Before I went back to the room, I visited the cashier at the reception and exchanged some of my pounds and traveler's checks into rupees. I needed to have enough to pay for our air tickets if we could get them, that is in case the airport opened once more, and any other expense that might pop up in case of emergency. I was still worried that the men would find us. In case they did and we couldn't reach the airport in time, I planned to try to go to the nearby railway station and catch a train to the nearest possible destination —even to go on to Karachi if we were undisturbed. This was turning into quite an adventure! Thrilling, and rather gut clenching, if I may say so.

CHAPTER 11

"To be haunted is to glimpse a truth that might best be hidden." ~ James Herbert, Haunted

Sarah

THE ROOM WE WERE SHOWN TO WAS BEAUTIFULLY decorated. There was an old-world ambience that struck me the moment I walked in. There were some old but polished wood panels at the head of the big double bed and the walls were papered with embossed cream wallpaper. On the far side of the room was a balcony leading from the massive French windows to overlook the inner courtyard, which was resplendent with flowers and vines. The abundance of geraniums created quite a splash of color and the air was fragrant with a bouquet of floral smells. In normal times, this would have been such a nice place to relax.

I turned away from the balcony, walked back into the room, and closed the windows since the air was still a bit crisp. In spite of that, somehow the room started to get even colder. There was a chilly draft that blew through it, and I looked everywhere to see where it was coming from. My skin erupted into goosebumps and the hair at the nape of my neck stood on end. Then I realized this wasn't just an aberration in the weather—it was something else.

I slowly turned around, wondering what I might see or feel. Sometimes I would get irritated when I was made aware of "presences" or other supernatural entities. It was at times quite tiresome.

As I turned in a full circle, I saw a woman sitting on one of the chairs that were set around a small coffee table in a corner of the room. Her face was in the shadows, but her clothes were definitely from the 1950s. Her sleeveless light blue dress had a puffed out skirt, and you could see the scalloped lace of her can-can petticoat peeping out from under the hem. She wore matching pumps and, although she wasn't smoking (I wondered if she actually could), she languidly held a long cigarette holder in her hand.

"What are you doing here? What do you want?" I asked her. She looked quite solid, though the occasional blurring of her outline convinced me that she wasn't completely human.

She looked startled. "Can you see me?"

"Of course, I can!" I was getting annoyed.

"Praise the Lord! I thought that I would have to wander these dusty halls forever. You have to help me. I need to cross over."

"Who are you?" I didn't want to get sucked into another supernatural drama, or any drama as a matter of fact, just as we were trying to unravel our own.

"Oh, excuse me, my name is Mrs. Seymour Fogarty-Hughes. I have been here since 1950."

"Do you have a name of your own? Or are you bound to your husband's name? And would you like to tell me why you are haunting this hotel, and especially our room?"

"Our? Oh, yes, I did see that you were here with tall, dark, and sexy. What is her name? Tanya?" She smirked. I was astounded that she looked so real and not like a regular spirit or ghost. "My name is Margaret," she said finally after a long pause. "Not that you need to know. It's irrelevant. You have to know what I want to tell you and that's all."

"If you want my help you need to tell me your *whole* story. Then, and only then, will I decide whether to help you... or not." I didn't like her smug and superior attitude. It was just like British colonials used to treat the poor "natives." Bloody snobs.

As if reading my mind, she said, "I am not a snob; far from it. Neither am I a racist, so you can wipe that judgmental look off your face." She sighed and took a phantom puff from her cigarette holder. "My husband, Seymour Fogarty-Hughes, was a political liaison officer between the British and the tribes in the Frontier Region. We often stayed at this hotel. It was quite convenient and very up to par with comfortable amenities as we knew them, but he used to leave me alone for days with nothing much to amuse myself. I read most of the books in the library, and I didn't play cards or billiards, so I was completely bored."

There was an undulation in her image as if a gust of wind had blown over a pond of water causing small ripples. Margaret gripped the side of the sofa as if she wanted to steady herself, took a deep breath and continued with her narrative. "Out of boredom, I started to talk to the staff here at the hotel. Everyone was well educated, and I learned a lot more about India and Pakistan from them than at my expat women's clique. It was fascinating. I had studied journalism in Oxford and I was itching to write about this rich multicultural country with different cultures, languages and even clothes in every one of its corners. Seymour wasn't enthusiastic about that. To him, I was the wife and he was the breadwinner, and I shouldn't rock the boat."

I was fascinated by Margaret. She looked so real, and yet there was something ethereal about her, as if the ways and worries of the world hadn't yet touched her.

"The in-house doctor was a handsome man, and I was enthralled with his knowledge. He could talk about so many things and yet make me want to hear more. We would sit for hours just talking over innumerable cups of tea. That too in the lobby, where everyone could see us. I loved him, but I wasn't in love with him—I loved my disreputable Seymour until the end." She looked so sad that, had she had some substance, I would have offered her a hug.

"Dr. Khurram had a fiancé." She continued her story. "Zainab was a beautiful woman and would sometimes sit with us in the evenings on the hotel lawn under the starry sky. She wasn't very educated, but she would chip in many times. I thought that she was also my friend, that she understood the nature of my friendship with Khurram." I saw a ghostly tear make its way down her cheek. "The closer we got, the more jealous she became, and it came to a point that one day she lay in wait for Seymour when he came back from a week-long tour at the Frontier. She told him that she suspected that Khurram and I were having an affair. Which was totally absurd. We were never alone and both of us behaved with absolute decorum."

Margaret got up and started her ghostly version of pacing in the room, which was more like floating, but I didn't interrupt her. I wanted to know where this story was heading. Finally, she sat down again. I could see that she was disturbed, as if talking about what had happened pained her physically as well as emotionally. "I was just getting ready to go down for dinner after my afternoon nap when Seymore barged into the room. His face was distorted in anger, and when he spoke, he was spraying his spittle all over the place.

"Margaret! What is going on? Why are you consorting with a bloody native? Have you no shame? No pride in being English?" He literally spat the words at me and harangued me for a long while because of my "betrayal to country and crown." I was tainted, dirty, not worthy of being Mrs. Fogarty-Hughes... etc., etc." She gave a shudder. I could feel the waves of fear and despair coming from her.

"He didn't even let me get a word edgewise. He just went on and on. When he finally wound down due to fatigue, I told him we were just friends. There was no need to get upset."

"He never gave you a chance to explain," I said quietly, feeling very bad for her.

"No, he didn't, and when I tried to explain, to tell him he was mistaken, he yelled at me for talking back to him. That day, in his rage, he stepped forward and punched me in the face. Just near my cheekbone. Khurram, having heard what his wife had done from the concierge, who saw and heard everything, came to save me. He was too late—Seymore already had his hands around my neck and was squeezing the life out of me. My last words before I lost consciousness were, 'I love you Seymour.' I saw the shock in his eyes when my eyelids finally closed... 'forever.'"

Poor woman...no wonder she haunted this room. She had died here and was looking for justice. She didn't know that there were certain factions that would tell you about power witches or warlocks that would help. However, this wasn't a case for seances and spells. Margaret's ghost was visible and asking for help herself.

"What can I do to help you?" I felt genuinely sorry for her.

"Wait...there is more." She rubbed her ghostly eyes and the bridge of her nose with the fingers of her right hand before she looked at me. I wondered if that was a habit that she had had when she was alive.

"Dr. Khurram was flabbergasted at what Seymour had done. He wanted to call the police, but before he could do anything, Seymour told him that if he didn't help hiding my body, he would tell the authorities that he and his fiancé had killed me. Khurram was pushed into a tight spot. Who would the police believe? The white *sahib*? Or the native doctor who was seen socializing with the white *sahib's* wife? No one would blame him if they thought that Seymour was justified in killing me. He could have spun it into a crime of passion, which in a sense it was."

Both of us were quiet for a few moments. I was wondering what to do to help Margaret. To my knowledge, when a ghost is still tethered to the earth, it was because of unfinished business, or because they had died a violent death and wanted either retribution or have their remains found and laid to rest.

"Do you know where you are buried?" I finally broke the silence and asked her.

"Buried? Hah! No such chance! I am incarcerated into the wall behind the wood paneling. There is a secret switch than can slide the wall open and you can find me there. Not a pretty sight, I am sure."

"In this room? You have been here all these years?" I was shocked. How could that be?

"These old buildings have secret rooms and nooks that were used by the British to hide important documents and other valuables. Their existence was known to very few people. I am sure that the original owners of the hotel aren't around anymore; otherwise, these little rooms would have been common knowledge by now." Margaret had answered my question before I could ask why there were secret rooms in the hotel. She was quite an astute...lady?... ghost? Oh, whatever!

"Yes, and you are the only person who could see me and talk to me. You must have quite strong powers!"

Margaret told me that she had tried to get the hotel guests' attention by moving things, but if anyone noticed, they would leave the room in fright and not come back. The hotel staff themselves had shamans and mullahs come in to "cleanse" the place, but Margaret had stubbornly held on.

Nodding to Margaret as I made my decision, I thought to myself that if I was going to move wall panels, I would need Tanya. I definitely couldn't do it all alone.

Tanya

AFTER MY CALL TO RAZIA, I went to the railway station, which was conveniently behind the hotel. I managed to get two tickets for a private two-person sleeper compartment. At least we would have privacy for as long as we were on the train. The tickets were for that same day, within the next couple of hours and just to Multan. In case anyone asked about us, they would be told that we bought the tickets for there, but once we were on board, I would talk to the conductor and get the tickets extended to Nawabshah, and from there we would extend the ticket once again onwards to Karachi. Although everyone was aware that our final destination was Karachi, I didn't want to make things easy for them, and we didn't know if we were going to be forced off the train somewhere along the line. I knew for sure that my colleagues in Nawabshah would help us if we were in trouble. Nevertheless, I just wanted to go home. No matter how, and fast.

As I neared our room, I heard Sarah talking to someone. I groaned inwardly. I was in no mood to socialize. Sarah always found someone to talk to. She loved learning about peoples' lives and what made them tick.

When I entered the room, I saw that Sarah was facing one of the chairs and talking animatedly with whoever was sitting there. As I neared the chair, I nearly fell over backwards—there was no one there! Sarah was talking to ... no one!

"Who are you talking to?" I looked from her to the empty chair. I didn't think she was losing her marbles; I knew that she always had an explanation for her weird behavior.

Sarah looked up at me and gave me one of her beautiful smiles. The one that melted me, the one where I knew that she wanted something from me.

"Can't you see Margaret?" she asked.

I silently shook my head.

Sarah looked towards the empty room and asked, "Is there any way that Tanya can see you as well?" She cocked her head as if she was listening to someone and nodded. Then she held out her hand to me. I took it and she put her other hand on the arm of one of the chairs, while indicating that I had to put my hand on the other one. Sarah closed her eyes and whispered some inaudible words. Within a few seconds, I saw a form slowly materializing on the chair.

"Hello, Tanya," said the vision. I nearly fell over in surprise.

"Hello," I answered. "What is going on?" I looked from Sarah to the apparition on the chair.

"This is Margaret." Sarah sounded impatient. "She wants us to find her remains so that she can rest in peace."

"Right. And how are we going to do that?" I asked.

"Margaret says that her body is behind the wooden paneling in this room. There is a hidden switch that will slide the wall open. We need to find that switch and get her out of there."

"Oh, no! We don't have time for that. Our train is leaving in a couple of hours." Even though I did protest, I knew that Sarah wouldn't leave until she at least tried to find the hidden switch, and then of course Margaret's remains.

"Come on, Tanya, this could be fun! Didn't you want to do something like this when you read the Famous Five books by Enid Blyton when you were a kid?"

"I never read those books," I grumbled.

"Well, all the more reason that you experience some adventure and fun." Sarah laughed.

"Ok then; let's get over with this," I grumbled and stalked towards the wood panel.

We tapped the panel from top to bottom but couldn't find anything. We pushed and pulled at all of the exposed wood, but nothing moved. Not even a centimeter.

"How about trying lower down behind the bed? Look for a knot in the wood," exclaimed Margaret. It made sense.

After all, the wall was partially covered by the bed. We pulled the bed away and saw that there was a deep knot on the right side of the wall. I pushed on the knot, and we heard a loud click followed by a grating sound. A bit of the wall moved away, but not completely. Decades had passed since it had last been opened, and the mechanism must have been rusty. No matter what we did, we couldn't get it to open further.

Sarah had a brainwave. She took some hand cream from her toiletry bag and smeared it on the exposed runners. When most of the cream had been used up, we felt the panel move and we managed to open it completely. It revealed a space that was large enough for a person to hide... or be hidden. There was a large dusty bundle of rags stuffed into the space. From one corner of the bundle a boney hand peeped out. We had found Margaret!

"Yes!" Yelled Margaret from the chair where she had remained sitting while we did the hard work. "You have found me! Thank you!"

"Now what do we do?" asked Sarah. "How do we tell the authorities about her? We don't even have enough time to deal with this!"

"I would like to bid you goodbye and thank you for freeing my soul," Margaret's voice was getting fainter and she was fading away. We had done what we needed to do.

"Sarah, get your bags. We will check out from the hotel. The staff will see the skeleton in the wall when they notice that the secret door in the wall was open. They can't implicate us in any way because anyone would see that the murder is an old one and we had nothing to do with it. Our train leaves in an hour and I would like to go as soon as possible. We don't have time to be questioned by the authorities."

We gathered our belongings and quickly left the hotel without looking back. I was just as happy as Sarah that we had helped Margaret find peace. Now we needed to work on our own peace. And soon.

The first-class compartment allocated to us was private with an attached miniscule bathroom that had a toilet, a stainless-steel sink, and a shower. There were two bunks, one on top of the other. The top bunk was still folded so that it was easier for us to sit while we travelled during the day. It was surprisingly comfortable and clean.

As soon as we were settled there was a knock at the door and the attendant entered and gave us sheets, pillows, and blankets that had been dry cleaned and vacuum wrapped in plastic. At least we didn't have to worry about bedding.

"I am hungry," said Sarah just a few seconds before her stomach loudly protested.

"We can buy some fruit at the next station, but the attendant has told me that they serve meals to passengers in their compartments if they don't want to go to the dining car."

"Perfect! I was in no mood to brush against other passengers to go to the dining car." Sarah was relieved. I rang the bell for the attendant, and he immediately came with a menu card, as if he was anticipating our requests.

Once we had the passably well-cooked meal, we settled down for the night. The clackety clack of the wheels lulled us to sleep. For now, we were safe. Tomorrow was another day.

CHAPTER 12

"Travel brings power and love back into your life." ~ Rumi Jalalud Din

Sarah

WE SLEPT VERY WELL THAT NIGHT. WHETHER IT was sheer exhaustion or the swaying of the train that lulled us to sleep, there was no doubt that we needed rest. I was sure we couldn't have gone much further without sleep. The best part was that the lower bunk was wide, enough for two people, and we did take advantage of that. Having Tanya close to me that night while we made sweet love to the sway of the train added to the feeling of comfort—a feeling of home. No matter where we were in this world, she was my anchor, my family.

That morning I watched her as she slept. She now looked rested, and I hoped that we would reach Karachi without any hurdles this time. I laughed to myself as I thought what a great adventure novel our travels would make and how, when we retired, we might even co-author our memoirs.

Tanya was adamant that we should keep the blinds on the windows down when the train stopped at the stations, but when we were on our way, it was fun watching the changing landscapes rush by. I remembered a poem that we used to learn in school. The cadence of the stanzas had the same beat as the sound of the train's wheels on the tracks. It was easy to imagine that Robert Louis Stevenson must have written it when he was traveling on a train:

> *Faster than fairies, faster than witches,*
> *Bridges and houses, hedges and ditches;*
> *And charging along like troops in a battle*
> *All through the meadows the horses and cattle;*

There was much more, but these were the stanzas I remembered. It had been ages since I had to learn that poem when I was twelve, and I had mostly crammed my brain with medical stuff since then—we had to learn about Wiscott, Aldridge, Duchenne, Marfan, Edward, Patau, Kleifelter, et al... Pompous names after whom syndromes were named. One would think that the academics would make doctors' lives easier by just calling a spade a spade and name syndromes according to the body parts they pertain to... At least I managed to digest that information with ease, enough to pass the exams. I giggled quietly to myself as I thought of these scholars who took themselves too seriously.

I didn't want to get up to go to the miniscule bathroom because I was so comfortable in Tanya's embrace, but nature called, and quite desperately. I was grateful that we had a bathroom attached to our compartment, even though it was a very tight fit even for one person. I gently extricated myself from Tanya and went to get ready for the morning. I had a feeling that, despite being on the home stretch, our adventure wasn't quite over just yet.

After I changed my clothes I rang the bell for the attendant and ordered breakfast with an extra pot of tea—Tanya loved to have an extra cup after her breakfast.

It was 8:30 am. According to the attendant, we would be pulling into Lahore in half an hour, which meant Tanya needed to get up. The train would be staying at the station for fifteen minutes as it was one of the major railway junctions on the line. We had to be alert and keep in the shadows, but it would have been nice to walk around the station, which was a historical landmark built in the 1800s by the British when the railway first started its operations in British India. I hoped we'd have the chance to come back another time.

Tanya woke with a smile on her face. She held out her hand to me, and as I took it, she pulled me to her and hugged me.

"I am so glad to wake up with you. These past few days were a nightmare. I don't know what I would have done without you." As she bent down to kiss me, I saw the glimmer of tears in her eyes. My strong compassionate warrior. This whole fiasco had without any doubt affected her as much as it did me. We stayed for a while this way, our heads on each other's shoulders, taking comfort in the embrace, until we heard a knock on the door.

"That must be breakfast," I said, jumping up to open the door.

"I hope you ordered extra tea?" Tanya yelled from the

bathroom, where she had hopped into while I took the tray from the attendant.

"Of course. Hurry up while it's still piping hot."

We ate our simple but substantial breakfast while the train was slowing down as it neared the station. Then I called the attendant once more to take away the tray, and he came almost instantly, as if he had been standing right outside our door. I handed over the tray and tipped him, and then I heard a commotion from the next compartment. It sounded as if some women were crying or panicking.

"What is happening next door?" I asked.

"One of the passengers is not feeling well. The women in the compartment are getting upset and no one knows what to do." The attendant looked more exasperated than willing to help.

"Ask them if I can see the passenger. I am a doctor."

His relief was palpable as he hurried away. He came back with a young girl whose tear-streaked face and wild-eyed expression spoke volumes about the situation.

"Please doctor, come and help us. Our mother is not feeling well." Before I could even answer, she took my hand and pulled me towards their compartment. I just had enough time to tell Tanya over my shoulder where I was going.

When I entered the large four passenger compartment, I saw a woman writhing in pain surrounded by eight or nine women. Everyone was trying to help in their own way. Two were massaging her legs and another two her arms. Another was kneading her temples as if she was going to make sourdough bread out of her brains. The ones who didn't have their hands on the hapless woman were offering verbal advice, the decibels of their voices increasing by the minute as they tried to out shout each other over the sound of the wheels of the train.

"Everyone, stop!" I was shocked. It was obvious that everyone was trying to help the poor woman somehow, but she was getting distressed, and her breath was coming out in painful gasps.

"Move away so that she can breathe properly!" My initial observation was that she was having an asthma attack, but she was an elderly woman, so she could also be having atypical symptoms of a heart attack.

After everyone left the compartment, I propped up the old woman, whose name was Nafisa, with three pillows. Her skin was cold and clammy even though she was sweating profusely—definitely a heart attack.

"Do you have any soluble aspirin?" I asked her daughter, Madiha.

"Yes, and I have some other medicines that she usually takes in this pouch." She handed it over to me. Before I inspected the medicines there, I took out two soluble aspirins and put them into Nafisa's mouth. I was relieved that just then we were finally pulling into Lahore station.

"Is there anyone coming to pick you up?"

Madiha nodded. "My father and probably my brother."

I turned to the attendant, who still had a terrified look on his face, and asked if they had a wheelchair on the train.

"We have one with the guard for emergencies." He said and rushed off, presumably to get the chair. In the meantime, Madiha and I tried to get Nafisa as comfortable as possible.

The attendant came back after ten minutes with a decrepit wheelchair, but at least it was something. Nafisa wouldn't have to walk out of the station and her husband could take her to the hospital in his car with no untoward delay whatsoever.

Madiha gathered their belongings and pointed out her father in the crowd. I helped them lift the chair onto the platform and introduced myself to the man who had come forward to help as well.

"She needs to be taken to the hospital immediately. The railway staff will let you take the wheelchair to your car, but you have to bring it back to the stationmaster."

Just as I was saying goodbye to them, the train gave a lurch and started to move with a long plaintive whistle. I was startled, as I hadn't realized how long I had been with my patient. I looked to where our compartment was and I saw Tanya looking at me through the window with a mixed expression of exasperation and fear.

Tanya

THE MORNING STARTED IDYLLIC—JUST me and Sarah in the small compartment after a romantic night and a deep, refreshing sleep. I felt I could take the world on once more. Things were looking up and I hoped that we would be in Karachi soon.

Sarah was off on one of her "savior" stints with the passengers next door. I peeked over the shoulders of the many onlookers trying to get a glimpse of what was happening and was relieved that there were no sinister looking people around. They were mostly women who were either fellow travelers or friends of the woman who seemed to be in distress. Since Sarah was handling the situation in her usual calm way, I went back to our compartment and started to tidy up our belongings and put them back into our backpacks.

I looked out of the window when I felt the train lurch into motion. To my horror, I saw Sarah was still on the platform looking at the slowly moving train in dismay. I picked up our bags, ran to the door just as the train was picking up speed, and jumped off right before the platform ended. I tucked and rolled to prevent any major injury. Thankfully, I only had a few scrapes, but I was getting annoyed with Sarah and her medical side bars. We should be focusing on getting home. I loved that she was so caring, but we were as important as other people, and she couldn't solve everyone's problems on her own.

Growling and muttering under my breath, I stalked towards where Sarah was now waiting for me. She knew that I was angry and had a conciliatory look on her face.

When I reached her, I stood there looking at her for a few moments before I said anything. She tried to take my hand, but I jerked it away. I was sizzling, but at the same time, my mind was working fast to formulate a plan to get us out of this unprecedented situation.

Sarah looked upset and she knew that my being annoyed was justified. There were tears in her eyes, but she refused to look away. She held her head up high because she knew that in her world, she had done the right thing. Though I agreed with her, I was annoyed and wasn't about to tell her that. We needed to be focused on going home and that was all that mattered for me at that time.

"We need to get out of the public eye. Let's go and sit in the ladies waiting room. We can discuss what we can do about our unplanned visit to Lahore."

The waiting room was fortunately empty and had

comfortable chairs to sit in. There was a pay telephone in the corner. I put down my bags and went over to see whether it was working. I was happy to hear the monotonous dial tone when I picked up the receiver.

After putting the required payment into the coin slots, I dialed a number from memory and waited anxiously for the person on the other side to pick up. After five rings, I heard my cousin Javed's familiar voice. Actually, he was my favorite cousin. He was as ostracized from our family as I was, and we always had a strong bond together. Unfortunately, I hadn't kept in touch with him after moving to London, but I knew he would help us if he could.

"Javed," I said tentatively, hoping he would not hold my long absence against me.

"Tanya? Tanya!! Where the hell are you?" he bellowed into the phone.

"I am at the Lahore station, and I need your help. Can you pick us up, please?"

"Of course! I will be there within twenty minutes. Where will you be?"

"We are in the ladies waiting room."

"See you there then," he said in his usual breezy manner, and hung up.

I sat down and started to rearrange my backpack. I knew Sarah wanted to say something, but the expression on my face stopped her. I felt bad for her, but she had to know that she should prioritize... Yet, how could I ask her to ignore a person who needed her? I knew I was being unreasonable, but I wanted to sulk a little bit. We would make up in a little while. I was confident that we would. After all, we did love each other, didn't we?

After exactly twenty minutes, there was a knock on the door and Javed peeked inside.

"Is it safe to come in?" he called out.

"There is no one here but us, so come in," I yelled back.

Javed entered the room, picked me up, and spun me around. That was no mean feat since I was quite tall. "Tanya, Tanya, Tanya, where have you been? How are you? No one tells me anything about you. I just hear snide remarks of how you disgraced the family and ran off to London, yadda, yadda, yadda."

"First of all, let me introduce you to Sarah. My wife. The love of my life." I drew Sarah forward as I introduced her. Sarah looked at me with a mixture of surprise and relief. I winked at her. How could I be upset with her for doing what she was born to do?

"This is my fellow black sheep of my ex-family, my cousin Javed."

Sarah tried to shake hands with him, but Javed engulfed her in a warm hug. Not as exuberant as the one he gave me, but it was rib crushing, or so it seemed from Sarah's expression. She looked at me in surprise when he flipped his hair back from his forehead in a very effeminate gesture and waved a languid hand towards the door saying, "Shall we now leave for our fair city?"

"Yes, Javed is also gay. Our family tolerates him because he is a well-known architect and interior designer. As the saying goes, money talks."

Javed scoffed at that. "You have done very well, little cousin. Not everyone gets the chance to join Interpol and become a well-respected member of that institution. And if people, meaning your family, don't realize what a nice and successful person you are, then it's their loss."

"I don't want anyone to know I am here, Javed, and I mean it." Knowing him, he would be on the phone trying to call all of our mutual friends for an impromptu party. He might also get a misguided idea to reconcile me with my family. Though I would have loved to see my mother, I was in no mood to be insulted by my father or my brothers.

"We need to reach Karachi at the earliest possible chance that we get. We have been held up so many times, and it's only because of a comedy of errors that we have landed in Lahore. Would you be able to help us, please?"

I saw Sarah move towards the door from the corner of my eye. She had that look on her face when she was fascinated by something. She turned back with a smile and said, "Don't worry, Tanya, I won't go out without you. I am just fascinated by this building. It's so similar to the ones in England."

"You are absolutely right," piped up Javed. "Where did you get this delight of a girl? She is too intelligent for you." He took Sarah's hand and kissed the back of it. Sarah pulled her hand away in alarm and looked at me incredulously because I couldn't stop laughing. I knew Javed and his shenanigans very well, but since it was his field of expertise, I let him regale Sarah with his knowledge of the station.

Javed gave an almost girlish giggle, cleared his throat, and started to narrate in a stentorian school master's tone. "The construction of the railway station in Lahore began during the colonial period. It was commissioned by the British, but the contract was awarded to Mian Mohammad Sultan Chughtai, a former official of the Mughal Empire, who constructed the Lahore Railway Junction between 1859 and 1860. It is now one of the oldest railway stations in Pakistan. The building of the railway station boasts a medieval-style structure. It has thick walls, turrets, and giant holes all around it to place guns and cannons during the times of war. This unique structure is like it is because it was built in the post era of the 1857 war of independence and was therefore designed keeping in view any potential future uprisings at that time." Taking a deep breath, Javed picked up our bags and motioned for us to follow him out of the room.

The station was still busy and the crowds on all of the platforms were quite thick, so we all took a collective deep breath and dove into the fray. I made it a point to keep a firm hand on Sarah; I didn't want to lose her again.

Finally, we managed to make our way out of the massive gates of the station and walked towards the parking lot. Javed had parked his Pajero near the building, so we reached his car quickly. It was unlikely that we would see any of Farooq's goons, but I still kept a lookout. It was whenever we relaxed that we got caught, and I didn't want any more hiccups.

We reached Javed's house in Gulberg and I heaved a sigh of relief when we entered his compound. Just as we stepped off the car, an Alsatian dog came running up to greet us. Javed patted him and told us to hold our hands out to him so he could sniff us and know that we were friends. Thereafter, the dog, whose name was Bingo, didn't leave Sarah's side. He kept shoving his nose in her hands, demanding to be petted. Sarah was also flattered that the dog had singled her out.

"Animals always know which person has a good soul, and your Sarah is good. It shows in her eyes. Her truthfulness, and her innocence..."

"Enough with your spiritual mumbo jumbo, Javed. I get enough of that from Sarah." I laughed. The front door opened and a dignified old lady came towards us. "Tanya! Oh my God, Tanya!" she cried out and enveloped me in a warm hug. "Where have you been, my darling? I've missed you! Your parents wouldn't even let us talk about you. It's a miracle that you are here standing before me!"

"Sarah, meet my Aunty Nazira, Javed's mother," I said, pulling her forward gently. "Aunty, this is Sarah. My partner in life."

"Javed didn't mention that you would be here," I added, casting a stern eye towards Javed, who looked as if butter wouldn't melt in his mouth.

"I have been living with Javed since his father died five years ago. This is also my home now. Why are we talking outside? Come in and make yourselves comfortable. Why don't you first go and freshen up, then meet us in the living room?" With that, Aunty Nazira ushered us into the house and called to the maid to get us some fresh lemonade.

Once we had all settled down with the refreshing drinks in our hands, and we finished with the initial formal pleasantries, we started to brainstorm and see what the most feasible solution to our conundrum would be. Javed would throw in some ridiculous ideas like hiring a donkey cart and trotting off to Karachi until his mother told him off.

"I am just joking with Tanya, Ma. It has been so long since I last saw her... I've really missed her. By the way, I have the perfect solution. I have thought about it from the beginning, but I was just enjoying the conversation and that's why I didn't say anything initially." He ducked and laughed when I threw a cushion at him. He lobbed it back to me, and it was fortunate that I caught it before it hit Aunty Nazira on her head.

"I know you want to be on your way, but I want you to

stay the night here. We will leave for Sarghoda tomorrow early in the morning. I have a friend there, Baqir, who is a flight instructor and owns a fleet of Cessnas. While you were freshening up, I called him and he agreed to fly you to Karachi. He will just have to stop once at Nawabshah to refuel. You will hopefully be in Karachi by early afternoon tomorrow."

I got up and hugged Javed. I was touched that he was going out of his way to help me.

"I have only one condition. Actually, it's a condition that both Ma and I agree upon. We want you and Sarah to keep in touch with us. You are part of our family and we love you."

My tears of happiness couldn't be stopped. This was such a nice ray of sunshine and positivity that was emerging from all the turmoil that we had experienced those past few days.

CHAPTER 13

"With the new day comes new strength and new thoughts." ~ Eleanor Roosevelt

Sarah

I WAS WOKEN UP BY THE MYNA BIRD SINGING IN the tree just outside the window. The weather was just right — warm and yet not too warm, typical of a Lahori spring. The flowers had started to bloom, not only in Aunty Nazira's Garden, but all over the city. One thing that I have to say is that the Lahoris took pride in their city. You could see it in the way the gardens were cultivated. What was amazing is that some gardens were as old as the Mughal era, over three hundred years old, like the famous Shalimar Gardens. I wracked my brain to remember what I had learned about this famous garden in school. Oh yes, it was all coming to me. The Shalimar Gardens were planned by the

Emperor Shah Jahan as a Persian garden paradise intended to create a representation of an earthly utopia in which humans co-existed in perfect harmony with all elements of nature. I believe it has been around since 1642! I had read somewhere that in 1981 the Shalimar Gardens were declared to be a UNESCO World Heritage Site I would have loved to go sightseeing, but since we couldn't, I tried to pick Javed's brains for as many historical facts as I could.

Even though it was so tempting to go to 'just one monument,' I had promised Tanya that, no matter what happened, I wouldn't be side-tracked anymore. Our focus was Karachi and nothing else.

Tanya wasn't in bed when I woke up, so I quickly had a shower and then went to look for her. I found Javed, Aunty, and Tanya sitting on the front lawn drinking their inevitable cups of tea. It seemed that it was a family trait to drink gallons of tea, and I smiled to myself as I walked barefoot towards them. The grass with the morning dew was so refreshing on my feet. I felt grounded, as if I was reaffirming my connection with Mother Earth.

"Ah, Sarah! There you are!" Javed called out before I could reach them. "Come and have a cup of tea. Breakfast will be ready in a short while and then we can leave for Sargodha as soon as you both are ready."

Aunty Nazira had already made a cup of tea for me and she handed it over once I sat down on the cane lawn chair beside Tanya. She must have asked my preference from her because it was perfect. Just as I liked it.

"We were just catching up on family news since Tanya has been out of touch for so many years," said Aunty. I looked at Tanya and she had a pained look on her face. I was sure that was something she wasn't very happy to do, but she was humoring her aunt, which I thought was very nice of her.

"Tanya told me that you are a doctor. That is excellent. Now we have a doctor in the family to annoy with our inane questions." She laughed at her own lame joke.

"That is true," I said playing along. "But only if you are a child. You see, I am a pediatrician."

"Well, old people are just like children, so I don't see any problem there," she countered. I groaned inwardly.

We were interrupted by the servants who brought our breakfast to where we were sitting. They wheeled two tea trolleys in front of Aunty. They were laden with more food than four people could possibly eat. It was a mini smorgasbord on wheels! There were eggs cooked in two different ways, and fried potatoes that were prepared with the unique Arabic seven-spice that was growing in popularity in the region. A friend of mine who had a Lebanese mother told me that it was just a unique combination of one tablespoon each of black pepper, paprika, dried cumin, dried coriander, cloves, nutmeg, and cinnamon, but it was a combination that ensured the dish it was prepared with was pleasing to the palate.

Well, the potatoes were quite tasty and I had a second helping. I couldn't resist them. Potatoes in any form have always been my weakness. The chickpeas and *payas* (sheep trotters) were something I usually avoid, but Tanya made me try them, and I admit that they were delicious, but my favorite as always were the piles of homemade *parathas*— piping hot and dripping in butter; just as I liked them.

Once we finished our delicious meal, it was time to get going. We used the facilities one last time and then gathered our meager belongings and said goodbye to Aunty. She kept hugging us as if she didn't want to let us go. After her third hug, Tanya gently disentangled herself and moved away to sit in the front passenger seat of Javed's Pajero. I climbed quickly into the back seat before I was "attacked" again. Finally, after more tearful goodbyes and with Aunty waving with her long white scarf at the corner of the street until we were out of sight, we were on our way.

We drove down the main Mall Road. The massive trees that lined the boulevard were hundreds of years old, especially the banyan trees. The architecture had always been predominantly colonial, since the British were firmly established in Lahore from 1846 to 1947, but if one looked carefully, hints of Mughal architecture could also be found. The real Sikh and Mughal magnificence was seen in the inner walled city. The Lahore Fort, Shahi Masjid and Ranjit Singh's temple were prime examples of the love the Mughals and other rulers of that era had for building monuments with their intricate and unique architecture. In addition to those famous landmarks, there were tombs of Mughal monarchs and queens spread all over the city. These historical buildings were an everyday sight for the people living in Lahore and they are respected and preserved as part of their proud heritage and history.

Javed kept a running commentary on all the historical landmarks we passed them until we left the city. I was impressed by his knowledge, and I told him so.

"I am part of a group that is dedicated to safeguarding our history by preserving the remaining ancient architecture in the country. Therefore, the dates they were built and type of architecture etc. are on my fingertips. It's part of what I do."

"I love history and visiting museums. You and your

group are doing an exemplary job. Thank you." He smiled and nodded his thanks. I could see that Javed was pleased with my appreciation of his work.

The drive to Sargodha was pleasant. We passed a multitude of fields, orchards, and gardens. Everything was either lush green or in bloom. Was this how our ancestors had envisioned heaven?

Once we neared the outskirts of Sargodha, I noticed that the main road was straight and flat with no divider in between, unlike the highway we had just left.

"Isn't that interesting?" I told Tanya. "Look at the road; doesn't it look like a runway?"

"See, Tanya, I told you she was intelligent," laughed Javed. "Sargodha is an air force town and is very near the Indian border. During the times of war when the airport was bombed and the runways were damaged, alternate landing strips were sought. This road was constructed the way it is to be used as such in times of emergencies."

I was about to say something more when Javed slowed down and turned the car into a lane that led to the massive gates of the private airport we were headed to. We were stopped by a burly guard at the security booth.

"Captain Baqir is waiting for us," Javed said imperiously while waving his ID card at the guard.

"Oh, yes, Mr. Javed. He is expecting you. Please drive to the parking place on the left and leave your car there. Someone will come and fetch you. In the meantime, I will keep your ID card with me. It will be returned to you when you leave." With that, he opened the gate and we drove into the parking place, where a man in a civilian flight suit was waiting for us.

Javed hopped out of the car and shook hands

enthusiastically with the man. "Baqir, you old dog! How are you? I haven't seen you in a while."

"Well, whose fault is that?" countered Baqir with a grin on his face.

"This is my cousin Tanya, and her partner Sarah." I was surprised that he was so open about letting a stranger know about our relationship, but he squeezed my shoulder and winked at me. "Baqir is a member of our club. Don't worry; he will take you to Karachi in one piece. I trust him with my life, and in this case, both of your lives."

Heaving a sigh of relief, I looked at Tanya and she gave me a reassuring smile. "No medical emergencies today; just clear skies to Karachi," she mocked gently. I was relieved that there were no professional distractions. I wanted this adventure to be over and start our serene life once again. I would never complain about being bored or wanting change. I loved our life in England and would always be thankful for it.

Since it was lunchtime, Baqir insisted that we eat before we started the last leg of our journey. He had specially asked the cook in his mother's house to make a local spinach-like dish whose main ingredient was the mustard plant (*sarson ka saag*). That was always paired with flatbread made from corn meal and topped with a dollop of hand-churned butter. It is the signature dish of Punjab and is an acquired taste since there is a mild bitter after taste. To counteract that, it is usually washed down with either salty or sweet buttermilk.

After we cleaned up and packed away the debris of our meal, we said goodbye to Javed. Like his mother, he could not hug Tanya long enough. It warmed my heart to see how much she was loved. After so many years without a word from her family, to have her cousin and Aunty in her life once again gave her joy. However, I knew that the years without her mother affected her deeply. Whenever we talked about parents, especially our mothers, we said that if we ever had children, we would love them no matter who or what they were. They would be the children of our hearts and we would be there for them whenever they needed us. I think that not having loving mother figures in our lives affected us more than we knew. It would be so nice to co-parent with Tanya. I was happily overwhelmed with the thought that we could provide a loving home for a child if we were given the opportunity to do so. There was still time, but we were already discussing the possibility, so we might have to practice rearranging our schedules and timings before we got serious about this next step in our relationship.

We walked over to a small aircraft with one rotor engine on its nose. I gulped and put on a brave face. I started a mantra in my mind... do not panic, do not panic.

The first thing that I noticed when we climbed aboard was the prominent first aid kit bracketed onto the bulkhead. That was something I could focus on for a perceived sense of stability, something inherently familiar and comforting to me. I strapped myself in, and as the sound of the engine reached its take off crescendo, I crossed my fingers and hoped for the best.

Tanya

SEEING Aunty Nazira and Javed was a catharsis to my soul. After a very long time, I felt unconditionally loved again. I meant by members of my family. I knew Sarah loved me, there was no question about that, but I always felt a small void in my heart whenever I thought of the people who were genetically related to me and had so cruelly rejected me at a very young age. Knowing that Aunty loved me just as she loved her Javed, with all of our idiosyncrasies and alternate lifestyles, energised me and healed places that I didn't realize were damaged. My greatest wish was to see my mother again one day. She did love me, there was no doubt in my mind about that, but she was a traditional soft-spoken woman, firmly under the thumb of my father and brothers. I was certain that she would love Sarah and just maybe she would accept her as a daughter. Maybe fate will give us the opportunity one day, just like we were unexpectedly able to reconnect with Aunty and Javed.

First, we had to reach Karachi and unravel the convoluted state of affairs there before we could finally go back home to England. It was crazy, but I had a hankering for the greasy fish and chips that we used to buy near Tower Bridge. Since it was close to where Sarah worked, I would sometimes go and pick her up in the evenings and then we would buy our food and eat while strolling along the embankment of the River Thames before we caught the train to go back home. We were happy. I wished to feel that way again and was ready to leave the stress of the past few days behind us.

As we walked onto the tarmac, I saw a small plane starting up its engines. From what I learned by looking at the posters in the waiting area, I knew that it was a Cessna 208 Caravan with a high wing single turboprop utility. It was top of the line and extremely reliable. Our plane could seat six people including the pilot, so it wasn't as small as I thought it would be. I hoped Sarah would manage her fear of heights while we were on board.

Captain Baqir was already in his seat when we strapped ourselves in. Even though I was tempted to sit next to him, I chose to sit with Sarah. Her expression and the way she held my hand tight were affirmations that I had made the right decision.

Once the tower cleared us for take-off, the little plane lifted off quite smoothly. I was expecting bumps and turbulence, but Captain Baqir handled the aircraft expertly. I settled back in my seat, satisfied that now we were on the last leg of our journey. The hum of the engines was lulling me to sleep, which showed how relaxed I was and how much confidence I had in our pilot. It was just a routine flight to a routine destination. Or so I thought.

"There is a bee in the cabin," said Sarah. "I hope it doesn't sting anyone." She looked worried. Even though she wasn't allergic to bee stings, I did know that she had had violent reactions to stings in the past. To distract her from the flying insect, I told her to investigate the first aid kit to see if there was anything that could be used for the effects of a bee sting in case that happened. I then leaned over to tell Captain Baqir about our little "guest." His reaction was astonishing.

"You must keep it away from me, please! Swat it with the newspaper that you will find in the pocket of the back seat. I am extremely allergic to bee stings. I could go into shock!" He was visibly agitated. He was right to be worried. If the pilot of our plane was stung, we would all be in danger because neither Sarah nor I knew how to fly a plane.

Just as I was rooting around in the back to look for the newspaper, the plane gave a hard jerk and I heard a strangled cry from Baqir. "I have been stung! Help me!"

The plane started to nosedive and careen a little sideways. I started to panic.

"Sit in the co-pilot's seat and pull this lever gently. See that the plane levels out. You can monitor that with the dial on the console, the one with the wings emblem on it. Just try to align the wings with the horizontal line." Baqir's voice was gradually fading and his eyes were closing. He was wheezing and sweating, but his hands were ice cold.

"Sarah! Did you find anything in the first aid kit?" I yelled as I climbed over the front to settle into the co-pilot's seat. I shot a quick look over my shoulder and saw that Sarah was rooted in one place, not moving at all. Her fear seemed to increase with every lurch the plane made.

"Sarah!" I shouted. "Help the man, for God's sake!" I had to get her out of her trance of terror. Since I was concentrating on keeping the plane stable, I felt rather that heard Sarah lean over and stab something into Captain Baqir's arm.

"We have to remove the stinger or the symptoms will persist." Sarah, once more in her efficient doctor-mode, started to look for a possible place where the pilot had been stung. "Ah, there it is." She found an area that was red and swollen at the back of his neck. Using the tweezers she had found in the first aid kit, she deftly removed the stinger.

Captain Baqir started to become more coherent and after a short while finally opened his eyes.

"What did you inject into Captain Baqir?" I was curious to know what miracle drug had helped him so quickly.

"There was an Epipen in the first aid kit. It delivers a measured dose of epinephrine for people who have severe allergies. Thank God for that; otherwise, we would have been in trouble." By now Captain Baqir had taken over the controls. He still looked a bit groggy, but when I asked him how he was, he said quite gruffly that he was all right and that he could manage the plane now.

"The Epipen was in the first aid kit because of my allergies. It was clever of Sarah to get it out in time and inject me with it. I could have died if she hadn't done that. We were all in danger in case you couldn't have stabilised the plane. Thank you, Tanya; you did very well."

"Well, I do know it's not the same, but I have flown planes on my computer. It sort of gave me an inkling of what to do. I am glad you are feeling better now." I laughed in relief. Talk about averting a disaster! This was a doozy!

After that hiccup, our journey continued smoothly. We landed in Nawabshah to refuel, but we didn't get out of the plane. Maybe deep down we were scared that something would happen if we did... Maybe by clinging to the plane we were reassuring ourselves that we were finally on the way home.

It was early evening when we flew over familiar ground. Sarah was now more relaxed and pointed out the recognizable landmarks as we flew over them. Captain Baqir had radioed ahead to let Razia know that we would be landing soon. He had permission to land at the air force base, so we wouldn't be delayed by going through the civilian passenger terminal. We asked him to stay with us for a while, but he wanted to fly back to Sargodha right away.

Once we landed in Karachi and we disembarked from the plane, I literally wanted to go down on my knees and kiss the ground. I didn't do it because I didn't want to seem silly, but the sentiment was definitely there. I was glad I didn't give into that impulse because Razia and Adam were walking towards us with huge grins on their faces. It was as if they were reading my mind and were aware of what I wanted to do.

"Finally!" said Razia. "It's about time you arrived. No one said you were allowed to go on an impromptu honeymoon!" She laughed out loud. Adam also sniggered behind his hand.

"Yeah, yeah, do make fun of us; we love it," I said sarcastically.

We bade Captain Baqir goodbye amongst the teasing and hilarity and made our way out of the terminal to Razia's jeep. "I am taking you home with me. The kids can't wait to see you. We will get your passport from Mr. Shah tomorrow, and then we can plan your onward journey."

"Adam, I thought you would have been on your way to London by now?" Sarah sounded annoyed.

"Our flight has been booked for tomorrow. We couldn't get the visas earlier, and Ammi wanted to meet her grandson. We couldn't deny her that since we are leaving the country for a while."

Sarah nodded but she still had a worried expression on her face.

"What news is there of Farooq?"

"From what I hear from my surveillance team, he has gone underground. Or so he thinks. He has not left his house since we returned. Tariq is back from Kohat and we have asked him to be our inside man. Even though he is not in contact with Farooq, he still has friends who are working for him and he has told us what he knows, but there is nothing of significance going on so far. Farooq seems to be biding his time. Maybe he was just waiting for you to come back from up north, but don't worry—we are prepared this time. Nothing is going to happen to you. I only just hope your Ammi won't interfere."

I wanted to leave for home as soon as possible, but I knew that we had to address the "Farooq problem." If we let it go, he would think we were weak and would try again and again to not only make our lives miserable but also that of Gulnaz and Adam's. We needed to brainstorm together and see what we could do to stop him from ruining any more lives.

CHAPTER 14

"A journey is like a marriage. The certain way to be wrong is to think you control it." ~ John Steinbeck

Sarah

THE WINDOW OF OUR BEDROOM WAS FACING EAST, and the first rays of sunshine were trying to edge their way under my eyelids to wake me up. However, I drifted in and out of sleep because I was still physically and mentally exhausted from our travels, or should I say ordeals?. Tanya must have felt the same because whenever I looked out from under half open eyelids towards her, she seemed to be fast asleep. We were finally woken up by two identical wiggling bodies trying to come under the covers with us. "Wake up, Aunty Sarah! Aunty Tanya! Wake up!" The little boys were giggling and there was no way we could feign being asleep at their innocent exuberance. They were such dear little boys. I loved them as if they were my own family. We were there that fateful night when we had to rush Razia for her c-section to the hospital. Tanya and I were the first persons to hold them in our arms when they were born, and now they were active and robust six-year-olds. How time had flown.

Saad and Saeed were identical twins. One could barely tell one from the other, but Saad had a mole on his chin which helped us single him out from the pair. They were so mischievous that I was sure they would still be playing tricks on people when they grew older. They were on the threshold of being boys, but still holding on long enough to babyhood to let us snuggle with them under the covers in the morning.

"Aren't you supposed to go to school?" Tanya looked at the pair in mock annoyance. They just giggled and burrowed even deeper under the covers. I was grateful that we had our pajamas on. I giggled at my own naughty thoughts.

Razia knocked on the door and entered before we could invite her in. She knew that her sons had already woken us up, so one more person in the room didn't make a difference.

"Go and get ready for school. Now!" she said sternly to her boys.

Both boys slid obediently off the bed and went to kiss their mother, but Saad winked at me before he turned away. Such a little imp!

"It's going to be a difficult day for you today, Sarah, but let's play everything by ear. We don't know where Farooq is as he has eluded our surveillance team today, and we definitely don't know what your mother has planned at the moment, but we need to see your parents to finish this lingering drama once and for all." While she spoke, Razia bustled around the room tidying up and folding our clothes.

I knew that she was as nervous as we were, but we drew solace in the fact that we were all together, and in that way, we were strong. Tanya was aware of my growing anxiety and came to sit next to me on the bed.

"We will always stand by you." Tanya looked at me with such love in her eyes as she gently held my hand and kissed my knuckles. I was so blessed with Tanya's love and Razia's friendship. I just knew that things would only get better.

"While I was waiting for you to arrive from up north, I told my superiors about your situation, and they were able to inform the High Commissioner in London about the role their staff members played in abducting you. You will be happy to know that they have been terminated from their posts there. You won't have to worry about anyone bothering you in England anymore. As a matter of fact, I have a written apology from the Minister of Foreign Affairs himself for you. The office regrets the inconvenience that any of their staff members has caused both of you in any possible way." Razia handed over a large envelope with the embossed seal of the Government of Pakistan on it. I took it from her with a skeptical look on my face, but in my heart of hearts, I did appreciate that the officials were trying in their own way to mend the strange and volatile situation created by that reprobate Farooq.

Since we hardly had any luggage with us, Razia lent us some clothes while her maid took our crumpled, soiled laundry for washing. My ensemble was a soft pink cotton *shalwar kameez* suit with delicate embroidery in white on the neckline and the edges of the sleeves. It was very comfortable and I felt fresh and cool wearing it. Tanya wore a similar suit in white. It did suit her very well. I have always loved her in white and pastels—the light colors make her skin glow, and...well, no time at the moment for my salacious thoughts. We needed to tackle our dilemma head on. If we wanted to live in harmony in the future, we had to make peace with our family. Otherwise, we would be looking over our shoulders all the time, and that was definitely not the way we wanted to live, neither in England nor in Pakistan.

The maid, Hamida, had laid out our breakfast on the big dining table. It was a lively meal with Razia trying to get the boys to hurry up before their school bus stopped outside their gates and started a cacophony with its obnoxious pressure horns. Her husband, Irfan, was sitting at the head of the table and just smiled benignly while he ducked behind the inevitable newspaper till it was time for him to go to work as well. His hand snaked out occasionally from behind the paper to pick up some toast from his plate or take a sip from his cup of tea.

We heard the school bus stop at the gate, and the boys first hugged their mother and then ran to me for a hug as well. I didn't want to let them go. I couldn't. The hair on the nape of my neck was standing on end and I had a serious sensory awareness regarding the boys' safety. Razia looked at me with a quizzical look in her eyes. She knew that I was getting one of my "feelings" once again.

"Don't send the boys to school today," I whispered to her. "Please, it's not safe!"

Razia hesitated for a fraction, looked at Tanya and at me, and then quietly nodded and went out to talk to the bus driver. Just as she stepped out of the gate, she heard a whistling sound as something whizzed by her left ear. She ducked automatically when she felt the air move, and we saw a bullet smash into one of the ornately carved wooden posts of the balcony.

"Take the children and go into the shed in the back garden! It is surrounded by a high stone wall; you will be safe there!" Razia shouted at us. Tanya and I grabbed a child each and ran. Irfan on the other hand ran into the study, where they kept their guns in a strong box, and unlocked it with his fingerprints. He stooped low and literally crawled to where Razia was crouching behind the hedge to avoid being shot and handed her one of the guns. He kept the other one and crawled a bit further on, all the while taking care to stay behind the cover of the thick yew hedge.

"I have called the precinct and the headquarters; help is on the way," he whispered to Razia. "These people must have a very low IQ if they are attacking a police officer and her family at her own place of residence!" He was justifiably appalled.

Within a few minutes, the sound of the plaintive whine of the police sirens came closer and closer. Razia looked over the hedge and saw that the men who had been shooting at her were now running towards their car. They flung themselves inside and sped off. The oncoming police car didn't miss a beat and followed the perpetrators immediately. When we heard the sirens, we left the twins in the care of the maid and came out of our hiding place to see whether we could help Razia. We watched as the police caught up with the gunmen and cheered when one police car blocked their way. Another police car rammed them from the rear, but the little blue Suzuki FX was as light as a tin can and crumbled under the impact of both cars. The men stumbled groggily out of the wreckage, both of them bleeding from their heads, while one of them painfully supported his arm, which he held in a very unnatural position. I hoped that the failed efforts of these two men would be the last we heard of Farooq trying to terrorize us and our friends who were helping us. Razia in this case. I shuddered to think what would have happened if my intuition hadn't kicked in. The poor twins would have really been traumatized, and maybe even injured. Farooq had delusions of perceived power and was a dangerous psychopath. He was a menace to his own self as well as others. It was now even more essential that we settled things with my parents, especially with my mother. I needed to make her realize that I would never marry Farooq. Ever! I knew that my father was already softening his stance towards me. I think that in the past he was probably influenced by Ammi, and just wanted to keep the peace in the house.

Razia sent Irfan and her sons with a police escort to her parents' house in Nawabshah. They were able to get tickets on the next flight out, which was safer and much better than travelling by car. We told Razia to go with her family, but she insisted on helping us bring this weird situation to its final conclusion. She had shown us time and again what a wonderful and loyal friend she was to both of us. Now it was time to deal with my mother and Farooq head on. Enough was enough! We couldn't let pettiness and fear of what people would say or do rule our lives and our peace of mind anymore.

Tanya

THE DAY HAD STARTED SO well. It was an almost idyllic morning, and Razia's family always made us feel welcome when we stayed with them. I had looked forward to a quiet chat over breakfast and my usual extra cup of tea with Sarah and Razia.

Then Farooq's men had to rear their malevolent heads and spoil what would have been such a nice, relaxing start of a day that in all fairness could have ended by repairing or severing the relationship we had with Sarah's family.

We were however very grateful for Sarah's "feelings" because they had saved our lives many times. This time, it was Saad and Saeed's lives. If anything had happened to them... I couldn't even think of anything negative regarding the little boys; they were precious to all of us.

Once Farooq's men were in police custody and Razia's family were on their way to Nawabshah, we quickly drove in her official jeep to Sarah's parents' house. Razia insisted that she would wear her full-dress uniform even though she was off duty. These official trappings were to intimidate people and to make a point that whatever was happening should be taken very seriously. Farooq might have ingratiated himself with Sarah's mother, but he was dangerous and should be treated as such.

Razia had a spare Glock that I borrowed. She knew that I had trained and was licensed to use these small handguns. Having a hidden weapon on my person made me feel safer and more confident that I could protect Sarah if it was necessary.

We reached the cul-de-sac where Sarah's parents lived without anyone stopping us, and there wasn't any other untoward delay like the inevitable traffic jams that usually occurred in Karachi. The lane was quiet, with none of the hustle and bustle of the faux preparations for the wedding that was to take place earlier. Was that actually just a few days before? It felt like we were in a continuous nightmare, trapped within a toxic never-ending loop. Without hesitation, as if she was eager to get things rolling, Sarah jumped out of the jeep as soon as it came to a halt, and pressed the bell that was partly hidden by a bough of bougainvillea, lush with the red blooms the plant is famous for.

The maid, Hira, opened the smaller side gate. She saw Sarah and put her hand over her mouth whispering in surprise. "Sarah *Bibi*!" She looked pleased to see Sarah, but there was a frisson of fear that rippled over her eyes.

"What is it, Hira?" Sarah was, as usual, very aware of changing emotions in people. "Why are you afraid?"

Hira stepped out onto the road, looked around furtively and whispered, "Dr. Farooq is here. He has been threatening your parents and brothers. He has a gun! I am so afraid. The other servants are hiding in their rooms. No one has been able to get to the telephone yet, so we couldn't call the police."

She glanced at Razia and the official jeep and continued to whisper. "His car is hidden around the corner so that you wouldn't know that he was here, and he has threatened to take you away. Please go and save yourself. He is mad. He will hurt you!" Hira was visibly distressed. Sarah hugged her and told her to go to the kitchen and act as if there was just a vendor at the gate. Sarah instructed her to leave the gate open for us to quietly come inside.

Before we made a move, Razia went to her jeep and radioed her team to come and help us as soon as they could. She also told them to come quietly, without using their sirens.

Razia and I drew our guns and held them steady in our

hands, but we left the safeties on. We didn't want to shoot anyone by mistake. We instructed Sarah to go and look for her family, and we would cover her with our weapons and only make ourselves known if we thought that she was in danger.

Sarah entered the main living room, where she knew that her parents, brothers, and grandmother would be at that time of the day. As we neared the large room, we heard Farooq's loud voice raised in anger.

"You will bring your whore of a sister to me, Adam, or I will shoot your wife and child. No one will implicate me if I kill them in the tribal areas. They are not important there. They are just a woman and her child. The people will believe me, or at least cover for me, because they know of my wrath and they fear me in Parachinar!" He laughed manically. It was even more clear now that he was mentally imbalanced. Bullying Sarah's family, or Sarah's family allowing him to bully them, gave him a delusion of self-importance and faux power. And yet... I heard Sarah's mother appealing to Adam.

"Adam, tell this man where Sarah is. Let him take her and we can then all live in peace! She turned away from our family five years ago. It won't matter if she is taken away by this man. After all, what harm is there in that since he wants to honorably marry her? She would be much better off than cavorting around England with that weirdo Tanya. At least we will all have some peace and quiet. I am sick and tired of this situation. Isn't the sacrifice of one child worth peace for the rest of the family? You know that Sarah doesn't care about us. She isn't even here!"

"Hey!" Adam and Mr. Shah shouted together. They sounded appalled. Didn't Gulnaz's and Sarah's lives matter? Were they expendable?

"Sarah is my daughter! YOUR daughter! Is this how you treat her? This man is a cruel maniac! How do you want her to live in the future? Your little girl? You used to love her so much!" Mr. Shah was distressed. You could hear the hopeless frustration in his voice.

Razia and I signaled Sarah to walk into the room.

"Ah! There you are! Are you tired of being with that despicable woman? Have you come so that I can show you what a real man is?" Without any modicum of shame, he cupped his crotch and laughed at the horror in Sarah's face.

"Salaam, Dadi, Baba, and Ammi," Sarah said calmly. She turned and went over to the other side of the room and hugged both of her brothers and Gulnaz. "I am surprised that you are all still entertaining this psychopath even though he has put all of our lives in danger time and again," she added.

"Of course, they are!" smirked Farooq. "I am the only one who would take their freak daughter and sister off their hands. I am the only one who can whip you into shape and tame your headstrong personality. So yeah, they still let me come and try to get you when I find the time to do so." He made that sound as if he was doing her parents a great favor by being there. "Where is your bodyguard today? No one to shield you from big bad Farooq?"

"Sarah! Just give up. This drama has lasted long enough. Let us live in peace. Go with Farooq and leave us alone!" Mrs. Shah sounded just as maniacal as Farooq.

Sarah walked up to Farooq and held her hand out. "Give me your gun. Do you think I will listen to you if you threaten my family?" She kept holding her hand out, but he just looked at it as if it was a snake or something similarly obnoxious. "You want to marry me and take me with you, yet you are standing there threatening us all with a dangerous weapon in your hand?" She continued to mock him, but he stood there stubbornly and refused to budge. "You do know that you have committed federal as well as international crimes against us, right? You could be locked away for a long time. Just give me the gun and we will forget what you have done. Let us sit down and discuss everything like civilized people."

She turned towards Adam and Gulnaz as she looked pointedly at the clock over the large mirror which seemed to dominate the center of the room. "Don't you have a flight in a couple of hours? Go quickly before you miss it. We will meet you in London."

"No one is leaving!" screamed Farooq while waving the gun haphazardly around. From my vantage point, I could see that he had a wild look in his eyes. Was he on drugs? Or was he just getting more and more psychotic? I was worried about Sarah, who just continued to calmly talk to him. As a doctor, she understood his mental condition and tried to quieten him down. She kept his focus on her and discreetly signaled to Adam and Gulnaz to leave the room. They sidled towards the door and were nearly out into the hallway when Ammi saw them and called them back.

"Where do you think you are going? No one leaves this house till we have settled things here. The driver has gone to the mosque and will bring the *imam*. Farooq has promised to leave us alone if we have an impromptu wedding ceremony this morning." That woman just didn't give up... What was her problem?!

"Let Adam and Gulnaz go, Ammi," Sarah said bravely, though I could now detect a mild tremor in her voice. "They have a small baby and need to take care of him. Just let them go. This has nothing to do with them." Ammi scoffed and tossed her well-coiffed head, but with an arrogant wave of her hand dismissed the relieved coupled. Adam saw us in the hallway and came straight away towards me.

"Go! You have to think of your family," I whispered as soon as he came within hearing distance. "We will meet you in London. Hopefully, in the next day or two. Please go. At least we won't have to worry about you if you are on your flight." I had to continue to persuade Adam for a while, but he finally agreed and left the house with his small family and the luggage that was already stacked in the driveway. The driver was still there. He hadn't obeyed Ammi to go to the mosque because he had known that Adam had to go to the airport, and I was sure he didn't want to leave the house while Farooq was there threatening the family. I was grateful that Adam and his family would be on their way to England while we were still trying to work out how we should deal with the potentially volatile situation in the Shahs' living room.

Sarah continued to try to persuade Farooq to give up the gun, but to no avail so far. Ammi was adamant that Sarah "surrender" to Farooq for the good of the family. He sat back on the recliner with a smug look on his face enjoying the perceived adulation from the older woman.

Razia and I still kept watch from the corridor through the glass doors of the sitting room. We saw Sarah's reflection very clearly in the large mirror over the ornate faux fireplace. We didn't want to suddenly appear in the room because we noticed that the safety of Farooq's gun was off, and he consistently, almost lovingly caressed the trigger with his finger as he spoke. We were worried that if we startled him with any sudden movement, he would press the trigger and shoot someone. There were lives at stake and we wanted to be as cautious as possible. Razia left my side for a few minutes but came back almost immediately. She told me that her team had arrived and the house was surrounded. Just as I was about to signal that we go and make our presence known to the family, I heard Mrs. Shah shout and then there was the sound of a loud slap.

"You ungrateful girl! We gave you the best medical education available in Pakistan and *allowed* you to finish your post graduate studies in England. Now it is about time that we were paid back. It is your duty to marry well so that our final responsibility is over and we can spend the rest of our days in peace without worrying about you or that your weird shenanigans may cause scandals."

Sarah gasped in surprise. No one had ever slapped her before. Even when she was a young child. To my horror, I watched as Mrs. Shah lunged towards Sarah with her hand outstretched as if she wanted to slap her again, but her sudden movement startled Farooq, who yelled indignantly. The retort of the gun was very loud in the room as his finger jerked involuntarily on the trigger.

Razia radioed her team to come in while we both rushed into the room. Sarah was lying crumpled on the floor. She had been shot! The cream-colored carpet was already soaking up her blood as it flowed out of a wound on the upper right side of her chest. Farooq stood there open mouthed, and Mrs. Shah just looked down at her daughter with a contemptuous look on her face, but it was very strange that no one was helping Sarah.

"Farooq! You are a doctor! Help Sarah!" I barked. I shook him out of his stupor, grabbed some cotton napkins and put them in his hand. He started to apply pressure to

Sarah's wound, but she was fading fast. She desperately looked around and when she caught my eye she said very faintly, "I love you, Tanya. I will always love you." Then she lost consciousness.

Mrs. Shah screeched in frustration and would have kicked Sarah on her side if Razia hadn't stopped her in time. The police had called for an ambulance and Razia waited to formally arrest Farooq until the EMTs arrived and took over trying to stop the bleeding from Sarah's wound. I was beside myself. I knew that we had Farooq on a tangible charge, but my prime concern was Sarah. I just held her hand and kept repeating long forgotten prayers and Quranic verses over and over again. "Please, Allah, don't take my Sarah away from me! Don't just show me beautiful glimpses of love and what my life could be, could have been, and then snatch them away so cruelly. I will do anything! Just give me my Sarah!" I didn't care what was going on around me. I was just focused on Sarah, my prayers, and my God.

The EMTs took Sarah to the main government hospital. I rode with her in the ambulance, still holding her hand. I couldn't let go even if I wanted to. Razia had left the formalities of arresting Farooq to her second in command and accompanied me. As soon as we reached the hospital and Sarah was wheeled into surgery, we went to look for our friend Professor Jahan Ara. We were lucky that her husband, Professor Yunus, was the surgeon on call and was operating on Sarah. She came to the operation theater waiting room and spoke to us in her usual gentle manner. Sarah always thought very highly of Professor Yunus's surgical skills, and I knew she was in good hands, but until we knew that she was safe, I couldn't sit down and relax.

Baba and Dadi joined us in the waiting room an hour

later. Azaan, Sarah's other brother, was with them as well. He had a rueful expression on his face. And so he should, because he was the one who would always side with his Ammi and actively encourage her vendetta against Sarah and me. I was surprised when he walked up to me and indicated that he wanted to talk to me in private. We left the waiting room and stood facing each other in the deserted corridor.

"I am so sorry. I didn't realize the degree of madness that Ammi had whipped herself into. I never liked Farooq, but I always thought that because everyone was so against Ammi, someone had to be on her side. When I saw how she wanted to kick Sarah when she was lying there injured and bleeding profusely, I realized that she had gone completely insane. Please forgive me. I would also like to apologize to Sarah when she is out of surgery." He seemed sincere. There was a shimmer of tears in his eyes when he opened his arms to hug me. I looked startled towards Abba, who was watching us from the doorway and smiled benignly while nodding his approval. When Azaan hugged me, he started to sob like a little boy. I just patted his back awkwardly hoping that he would calm down soon.

One of Razia's colleagues walked in and whispered in her ear. She nodded and then came over to talk to us.

"Farooq has been arrested on charges of attempted murder, kidnapping, fraud, and endangerment. Judge Murtaza Ahmed has also informed Interpol and Scotland Yard about his arrest, and he will be charged by them as well. Mrs. Shah has been admitted in the psychiatric ward here in the hospital. She has been sedated but is under police guard. For now, the charges against her are assault, along with aiding and abetting a criminal, but we will see how it plays out once she has her court ordered psychiatric assessment."

Now we just had to wait for Sarah to come out of surgery. Razia asked Baba if he wanted to see Mrs. Shah in the ward, but he said he would as soon as we had news about Sarah. He was as worried as we all were and refused to leave the room.

After countless cups of tea and coffee and five long hours of surgery, we saw Professor Yunus walk out of the automatic double doors of the operation theater. He looked exhausted and his scrubs were stained with blood. My Sarah's blood...I felt faint at just the thought. He tiredly pulled his surgical cap off and ran his hands over his short, cropped salt and pepper hair.

"Sarah is in the recovery room. The surgery was very difficult because some major arteries in the chest were nicked. If she hadn't received first aid immediately, she could have died. At one time it was touch and go and we had to resuscitate her, but she is a fighter and came back after a few minutes. We had to give her a few pints of blood, and she is by the Grace of God now stable. She will have to be in the hospital for a few days, but I am sure that she will make a full recovery.

What do you know? Farooq had saved Sarah's life, albeit reluctantly.

"May we see her?" I asked.

"Yes, one at a time. And just two persons today. The rest of you can visit her tomorrow."

"May I stay with her tonight?" I asked tentatively. Professor Yunus knew of my relationship with Sarah. Jahan Ara had told him about us when Sarah was still an intern. He smiled and ushered me towards her room.

"I will ask the charge nurse to set up a small cot for you

in here." With that, he nodded and waved to the chorus of thank yous that followed him without looking back.

I silently thanked Allah for saving my love. Sarah was alive and would get better! I resolved that I would feed some poor people as a thank you to the Almighty.

Farooq was in custody and in deep trouble not only locally but also with the international law agencies. What a waste of a well-educated doctor. He could have done so much good for his people. Such a shame and such a waste. Hopefully, that was the last of his shenanigans that we had to bear. And yet there was still Mrs. Shah...

CHAPTER 15

"A great many men are mad, and no one knows it.
They do not know it themselves." ~Agatha Christie,
The Secret Adversary

Sarah

I HAD NEVER FELT SO FRAGILE AND IN PAIN IN MY whole life. From what Tanya told me, I had surgery to remove a bullet that hit me on my upper chest. Darn that idiot Farooq. Our lives would have been so much more peaceful if he had just let us be.

The weird drugs that they gave me were disturbing. They made me phase in and out of consciousness. It was curious, because whenever I closed my eyes, I was in a beautiful garden and I saw my grandmother sitting on an ornate bench in an alcove. She kept signaling to me that she wanted me to come over and listen to her. For some odd reason, I would feel very afraid and I would try to forcibly open my eyes. I wanted to look at Tanya—my anchor to life. I needed to see her desperately. I understood that my life was in turmoil, but Tanya was the only familiar person, the only one my inner subconscious knew I could trust without fail.

The next time I opened my eyes and saw Tanya looking at me with love and concern in her eyes, I forced myself to stay awake. I gestured with my hands that I wanted to have a drink of water, and almost immediately a drinking straw was at my lips and I took a few greedy sips to lubricate my throat.

"I am scared..."

"Professor Yunus said you were on the mend. Why are you scared, sweetheart?"

"It's not my physical recovery that I am worried about. I know that I will get better soon. I am worried about my mental well-being. Will I become as disturbed as Ammi one day? Am I on the way to mental instability? Will you still love me if that is the case?"

Tanya looked at me pointedly. She knew me well enough to know that something was bothering me more than what I was saying. I took a deep breath and started to tell her about the visions I had of my grandmother in the beautiful garden.

"Why don't you listen to what she has to say? Maybe she knows what's bothering you and can help you from the other side." I was at that point extremely grateful that Tanya knew me so well and she knew that even after all those years I was still struggling with my powers. Without any doubt, I couldn't have had a more understanding or loving partner.

"You are right, my love. This time, when I sleep, I will not struggle to wake up. I will try to talk to my Oma. She might be trying to get a message to me, or maybe she will help me get back my equilibrium and peace of mind. Thank you for your support, as always. I love you, now and forever." I lifted her hand and cupped my cheek with it. I turned my head and gently kissed her palm. The look of love in her eyes just washed over me like a panacea to my bruised and uncertain feelings.

My feelings for Tanya grew stronger every day; it was the Farooq/Ammi situation that had definitely put me off balance. I had always thought that deep down Ammi loved me no matter what. After all, I was her only daughter, but seeing the hate in her eyes when she looked at me those past few times when we met was deeply disturbing.

We continued to talk about many things, including our journey back home, which would be inevitable whenever my doctor gave me the green light to travel. I was dreaming of sitting and recuperating in our beautiful garden. The flowers would already be in bloom and the weather quite mild. When I closed my eyes, I could hear the bees buzzing and the birds singing. That was definitely my idea of heaven.

My chest started to ache once again. I shifted uncomfortably but didn't say a word. I didn't want to act like a weak cry-baby, but Tanya realized that I needed my pain medications. She looked at me with a silent question in her eyes, and when I nodded tersely, she pressed the button to call the nurse. "This time, when you fall asleep, just let things happen. Listen to your grandmother. Maybe she can let you know something about your Ammi's behavior? Maybe what she can ultimately tell you will help you mend your bridges with Ammi as well?" Tanya was right. I needed to know. I was desperate to know. This was a journey that I had to have enough courage to take on my own.

The nurse came and injected the prescribed pain medicine into the IV line, and I floated off once more into oblivion, but this time I felt different because I had resolved that I wouldn't fight it. I drifted along, subconsciously anticipating a meeting with one of the few people I had loved dearly in this world. My Oma, my maternal grandmother, who left this earthly plane when I was just thirteen years old.

Since I was more receptive this time, I felt as if I was drifting on something light. Like a dandelion. I floated along for a short while and then I was deposited on one of the softest and greenest grassy knolls that I had ever seen or felt. It was dotted with daisies and there was a distinct fragrance of fresh chamomile—a scent that I had always corelated with my grandmother. I looked around at the sunny vista, basically enjoying the warmth and the inherent feeling of being loved. The place looked familiar to me, and I tried to wrack my drug addled brain to recognize the area.

Then I remembered. This was a forest glade where my Oma used to take me for walks. To the right there was a picnic area where we used to stop and have a snack that she would pack before we left the house. I loved this place and came here many times even after she passed away to pay silent homage to the happy times we had together. The picnic area was just a few meters away from where I sat, so I stood up slowly and turned to look at it. I was aware that I didn't feel any pain at that moment. I only had a hollow feeling in my heart. As if I was missing something profound.

"Ah, there you are! You are a tough person to get through to, even though you have inherited my gifts!" Oma merrily called over to me. There she was, sitting in her usual place with a picnic spread out in front of her. "Come on, we don't have much time and I need to tell you some important things. Maybe if you know what I am about to tell you, it will bring you a modicum of peace, and maybe, just maybe, you will forgive your Ammi's behavior."

I walked over and hugged Oma. I felt such warmth, such peace with her arms around me. I didn't want to leave her. I wanted to stay with her forever.

"Oh, no, no, no! You will not think like that!" she admonished me gently.

"Can you hear my thoughts?" I was astonished.

She winked as she pulled away and patted the seat next to her. "Come sit down. Your time will come one day. But not now. You still have a lot to do in the world, but remember this—I will always be there for you. I love you, my sweet little girl."

As I sat next to her, I noticed a dark cloud to the left of us. It was swirling and undulating as if some evil entity was trying to come forward and neutralize the good vibes I could feel around me. Within the murky gloom I saw the dark figure of a woman with her back to us. She had her hands folded over her chest and her back was stiff, stubborn, and yet she didn't turn around. God help me, but I thought she looked just like my Ammi. Why would Ammi be enveloped in such an evil cloud? She was my mother and I did love her no matter how she had behaved towards me.

Oma watched me as I looked in horror at the figure that was supposedly representing my mother.

"Forgive her, my darling. Her behavior is my fault. She is the child of her times. They really were difficult times, and I didn't realize how much they affected her until I saw how she behaved towards you and Tanya."

I couldn't stop my tears of sorrow as I continued to look at that dark, unrelenting figure that was supposed to have loved me unconditionally. Oma put her arm around me and wiped my tears away with an embroidered muslin handkerchief that was scented with lavender.

"It's all my fault," she repeated sorrowfully.

"How can you say that? You are kind and loving, and Ammi has been vindictive and cruel to me. So much so that she didn't even care if I lived or died. She wanted me to marry that horrible man so that her standing in society was reinstated." I was sobbing uncontrollably now. The hollow in my heart was throbbing with emotional pain.

"Don't blame her completely. Listen to what I have to say. We don't have much time." I nodded and laid my head in her lap as she lovingly stroked my hair.

"The Second World War was horrible. Many lives were lost, and unnecessary restrictions and violations caused even more sorrow in our day to day lives." Oma sighed and pushed a lock of hair back into the neat bun that she had on the nape of her neck.

"Your Ammi must have told you that I lost seven sons in the war. All of them died defending a Reich they didn't believe in, a Fuehrer who had started with a good ideology for the Germans, but ended being a homicidal megalomaniac and a self-serving menace. I tell you, nearly everyone was pleased with the dishonorable way he died. He deserved it many times over."

"But what does that have to do with Ammi? She must have been quite young at the time." I turned my head to look at her.

"Yes, she was very young. But you are a doctor, and you know that the young mind is the most impressionable. There are things that an adult might think won't affect a child, but unless one is aware of it, the hurt can burrow quite deep and fester in many ways. In your Ammi's case, her behavior to you. Her only daughter."

Taking a sip of her apple cider, Oma continued. "My youngest son, Peter, was always a delicate child. I used to overprotect him because he was born preterm and would get very sick nearly every winter. I tried my best to prevent his annual bronchitis with herbs and medicines, but without fail, as soon as the weather became colder, he would get sick and I would helplessly see how he became weaker and weaker every year. I wouldn't let him out of the house to play like the others because I was always afraid that he would get ill, so he was often indoors with your mother and your Tante Waltraud. One day, when he was just fifteen years old, he was sitting at the dining table with his sisters cutting some cloth to make a dress for one of their dolls when I was visited by my neighbor, Frau Meier. She was a rabid Nazi and was always looking out to find fault and report her neighbors. Her standard of living was much better than ours because she was rewarded whenever she snitched on anyone. It could have been something really small like not having Hitler's photo hanging on the wall, and she would be rewarded with extra rations or a bolt of cloth."

Oma had tears in her eyes as she recalled that day, but she went on with her narrative. "We were so used to Peter's ways that I didn't think of telling him to stop or go outside and play. He just sat there and continued to cut and sew the doll's dress. Frau Meier didn't take her eyes off him and I could see her mind working. What could she possibly think about a young boy playing with his sisters? The whole neighborhood knew that he was a sickly child and was indoors most of the time because of that.

"Just before she left, she said cryptically to me, 'Now I

know why you keep your boy indoors.' Then she smartly turned around and walked away before I could reply. I didn't think much of it. If I had known what that evil woman was up to, I would have sent Peter away to my brother in Switzerland."

Looking at the dark cloud, my Oma's voice softened. "Your Ammi loved Peter. He was her favorite brother. They were very close and shared everything. They were always together, ate together, and basically did everything together. Therefore, what happened next was very difficult for her." Shaking her head with regret, Oma continued to stroke my hair.

"The next day, quite early in the morning, before your Opa went to work, there was a loud banging on the door. 'SS! Open up!' What was that all about? I quickly took Hitler's photo out from the drawer where we usually hid it and hung it up while your Opa hastened to open the door before it was kicked in.

'Heil Hitler!' said the leader of the group in the dreaded black uniform. He briskly gave the Nazi salute and looked expectantly at us to see if we reciprocated the greeting. There was nothing we could do. We had to, and quickly, or that would have also been a violation and a cause for harassment by the soldiers.

'We have been informed that there is an infraction of the military law of 1935 version of Paragraph 175! We have a warrant for the arrest of Herr Peter Huber!' the soldier shouted.

'Paragraph 175? What is that?' your Opa was confused. He was wracking his brain, thinking that what could a child like Peter have done to be noticed by the SS since he was at home most of the time. And what in heaven's name was paragraph 175?

"Paragraph 175 states that the practice of overt homosexuality or anyone who shows signs of this perversion is pronounced socially undesirable and subject to the will of the Nazis. In this law, it was decreed that the deaf, the blind, the physically disabled, homosexuals, the mentally ill, and alcoholics were either to be sterilized or killed because they were viewed as genetically defective to propagate a strong German Nation. The soldiers forced their way into the room and pulled Peter from his bed.

"'Peter is just a child! He has been very ill since birth. He is not a homosexual!' I shouted. I tried to pull Peter back from them, but one of them hit Opa on the head with the butt of his rifle and another one pointed his gun at the little girls. Peter, however, was brave and stood tall and proud.

"'Mama, it's ok; God is with me.' Then he looked at the soldier and asked whether he could at least change his clothes. Giving him a terse look, the soldier consented and Peter hurriedly put on his clothes. We didn't hear from him for days, but then after nearly a month went by, one of the soldiers came again to our house and flung an envelope with something heavy inside on our table.

"'We could have killed your son, but since you were so loyal to the Reich we allowed him to enlist and fight for his country. He was killed on the Belgium front. Here is a letter of thank you from the Fuehrer himself and his medal. You should be proud of him. We all thought he was useless, but he is now a hero. *Deutschland Über Alles*! Heil Hitler!'

"That was too much! Poor Peter! My beautiful little boy! He was just fifteen years old when they took him away! Your Ammi couldn't speak for months. His death affected her very deeply. On top of that, the disreputable Frau Meier was gossiping about Peter's homosexuality and was proudly telling everyone how she had told the SS about him. People started to talk about him behind our backs. They even went so far as to say he was molested by us, and that's why he was like he was. Your Ammi just couldn't take it. I am sure if she had been an adult at the time, she would have harmed Frau Meier. Believe me, if it weren't a crime, I would have killed her myself. And what did she get out of it? A new Mercedes? For the life of an innocent boy? Shame on her!"

I looked once more towards the dark cloud. The effigy of Ammi was looking over her shoulder. "Oh, Ammi! I feel your pain and I forgive you. I love you!" As soon as I said that, the cloud disappeared and Ammi along with it.

"Where has she gone?" I asked. What had I done? Why did she leave?

"You will find her; just give her time. She loves you." Her voice started to fade away...

"Oma! Don't go!"

"We will meet again one day, my darling. Go now; the rest of your life awaits you."

I watched as she slowly faded away while giving me one of her loving smiles. I felt a tug on my body and opened my eyes. I saw my Tanya looking at me with love and understanding. She knew that I was ready to at least think about forgiving my Ammi. Hopefully, we would be able to live in peace and harmony once more.

Tanya

SARAH LOOKED both tortured and at peace, if that makes any sense. When she resurfaced from her drug induced sleep she just lay there. Her eyes were very expressive, but I didn't say anything because I wanted her to speak only when she was ready to. It was painful to see her in her silent torment. I could only share her pain if she told me what was going on in that beautiful mind of hers. I was sure that she must have experienced the psychic visit from her grandmother just as we had thought she would.

I got up to leave the room. I thought that maybe Sarah wanted some space, but just as I was moving away from the bed, I felt her hand pull at my clothes.

"Don't go. Just give me a moment. I am processing what I've just experienced. I want to tell you everything. Please wait; I will need your help, as always." She looked at me beseechingly. How could I resist that?

I sat down again and took her hand in mine. We were silent for a few minutes, and then Sarah began to speak. She told me how wonderful it had been to see and talk to her beloved Oma. She also told me of her Ammi's harrowing experience with the Nazis and about her uncle Peter. I began to slowly understand her Ammi as well. Her childhood trauma had spilled over onto our lives, and it would be only through compassion and forgiveness that the rent in all of our souls could be mended.

"What do you want to do now?" I asked Sarah as I gently wiped her tears from her cheeks.

"I want you to take me to see Ammi in the psychiatric ward. Knowing what we do now, I feel that is not where she should be. I would like to recommend a second opinion from a psychiatrist that I know. Many times just counseling is more beneficial than being monitored and drugged for no proper reason. Ammi has been carrying this trauma with her since she was a young child. She needs love and understanding. The medicines they might be pumping into her could be harmful rather than beneficial for her. She also needs to know that we are not in danger like her brother was, and that we will always try to forgive her because we love her."

Sarah lay back down on the pillows, apparently exhausted by her outburst. I understood what she was feeling and I was proud that she wanted to help her Ammi and exonerate her. I don't know if I would have been as forgiving, but then Sarah always had a soft heart. That's why she was the healer while I was the law enforcer in our partnership.

Sarah wanted to get up and go to see her mother immediately, but with a little bit of persuasion I was able to make her rest a little more. Just talking to me had worn her out. I wanted to stall her as long as possible because I needed her to be strong when she faced her disturbed parent. However, first of all, there was her stubborn streak that had to be overcome, and gently. Maybe in such a way that she would think it was her own idea. While she slept, I called Baba and her brother. I would let her tell them what she saw in her dreamscape and what she planned. It was possible that she might be a bit annoyed with me, but in her weakened state she needed support. And what better way to support her than to get her family to rally around her?

Baba, Adam, Gulnaz, and Azaan came to the hospital within the hour. We were all surprised to see them because we thought that Adam and his family would be 35,000 feet above Turkey en route to England by then.

"We met one of Razia's deputies at the airport who told us that Sarah had been shot. We turned back and came to the hospital, but the nurse didn't let us in because visiting time was over. We were relieved to hear from her that Sarah was out of danger. We then went home to support Baba because we were sure that he would have been almost ill with worry. We can go to England any other day. Being here for our family is more important."

With that Adam sat resolutely back in his seat with a sigh and looked speculatively at Sarah, as if he was expecting her to contradict him.

Sarah had by that time woken up and eaten her tasteless soft hospital diet. She wanted to eat something substantial and almost cried when she saw the gruel on the tray, but we couldn't take the risk of giving her some fast food with the extent of her injuries. She needed to follow the doctor's orders, difficult as it was for her.

As soon as she was finished with her meager lunch, Baba sat down next to her and held her hand just like I had before. It seemed that to get Sarah's complete attention one had to do just that, and I smiled to myself at that thought.

"Little one, how are you feeling today?" His concern was very sincere, and you could see the love he had for his daughter in his eyes. If I had any doubts before about Baba's love for Sarah, they all flew out of the window in that instance.

"Getting better, Baba. But this wound hurts like a b.... ummm... like hell."

"That is understandable. You have been through a lot."

Baba smiled as he continued to lovingly stroke his daughter's hand.

"Why are you all here at the same time? I thought you were visiting in shifts. Not that I don't like your being here. I enjoy your visits." Sarah glanced at me and caught my guilty look. Uh oh, busted.

"Oh, now I understand. Tanya, did you ask all of them to come?" She looked at me in mock annoyance. I gave a small nod and looked at her anxiously, hoping that she wasn't upset with me.

"It's all right. I should have thought to speak to the family as well. That is before I go on my mission of mercy. After all, it does concern all of us. Baba, you do know that sometimes I 'feel' and 'see' things?"

Baba nodded and so did her brothers. Gulnaz looked puzzled and turned to Adam, who whispered in her ear that he would tell her later.

"Well, I know it sounds weird, but I met Oma in one of my dreamscapes and she told me why Ammi is the way she is. I need to go to her and make peace with her, tell her I that understand her fears, and maybe get the family together. I don't like that the family has been pulled apart because of me." She held up her hand when there was a murmur of protests from everyone present. "I know it is indirectly because of me, because Farooq wouldn't have had the guts to even come near our family if he hadn't set his beady eyes on me. So first of all, I would like to apologize to all of you for what you had to go through. Especially you, Gulnaz and Adam, because you were also dragged apart because of Farooq, and I am so sorry that you had to suffer. Especially you, Adam, since you couldn't be there for Daniyal's birth." Sarah took a deep breath and indicated to me that she wanted a drink of water. Once she had moistened her lips she spoke again.

"I want Tanya to take me to the psychiatric ward to visit Ammi. I want to take a chance and see whether she would talk to me. I want...no, I need this tension in our family to stop so that we all can live a relatively normal and happy life together. She doesn't need to be in the psychiatric ward, Baba. I firmly believe that keeping in mind her childhood traumas, just compassionate counseling would do a lot for her. Of course, as I told Tanya earlier, we would need a second opinion from another psychiatrist."

Baba tried to say something, but Sarah held her hand up indicating that she wanted to continue. "I need to talk to Ammi alone. Maybe I can get through to her. I need to tell her that we don't take her fear and her loss lightly, but that we have to move on. She should also know that we will all always be there to help and support her if she needed us in any way."

Baba had tears in his eyes and he tried to discreetly wipe them away, but he failed miserably. As unobtrusively as possible, I handed him a handful of tissues which he took gratefully without looking up.

"I am so proud of you," he finally said once he had composed himself. "I love your Ammi dearly and I knew she had suffered physical and mental traumas during the war, but I didn't realize that they were festering in her so much that the vitriol spilled over to you. I blame myself; I should have found help for her when we arrived back in Pakistan, but in those days the concept of counseling was alien to most of us." He sat there with his head in his hand. I signaled to the others, and we all rallied around him and gave him a group hug.

"You aren't a doctor; how could you know? Psychiatric medicine is so specialized that even a regular doctor needs to look twice before they find anything out of the ordinary. So please don't blame yourself. We will all get over this hiccup in our lives. We love each other and that is what counts."

We spent most of the afternoon planning various scenarios of how we could approach Ammi without causing another psychotic breakdown. Plans were made and discarded and then made again. I noticed Sarah's strength was flagging and her eyes had started to droop.

"Let us call it a day and continue tomorrow," I told everyone. Just in time. Sarah's bland evening meal was served by a cheerful cafeteria lady who eclipsed the tasteless meal on the tray with her happy banter.

"We will give you some fish tomorrow," she said as if she was bestowing a rare portion of ambrosia to Sarah.

"I know, I know, steamed with no salt or pepper!" Sarah had a disgusted look on her face. The cafeteria lady just laughed and left with a cheerful wave of her hand. She was obviously used to grumpy patients. Everyone else hugged or kissed Sarah goodbye and promised to be there in the morning bright and early.

"Are you sure you are up to talking to Ammi so soon? You aren't fully recovered and I worry about you." I sat next to her on the bed and held her gently as I talked to her. I didn't want to jolt her injury and cause her pain.

"I am fine. I want to get this out of the way; otherwise, it will keep on festering. Most of all, I feel that we need to help Ammi. Her childhood traumas have affected her more than she even realizes. If we leave for home before anything is done, I would simply mull over the situation all the time and make myself ill with worry."

That was definitely true. Sarah always wanted to heal the world. She was often successful, but I hoped this wouldn't be one of the times when she would have to concede defeat. I hoped against hope that she would bring happiness once more into the family. It was important for both of us to live in peace without fear and looking over our shoulders all the time.

CHAPTER 16

"Yet, it is in this whole process of meeting and solving problems that life has its meaning. Problems are the cutting edge that distinguishes between success and failure. Problems call forth our courage and our wisdom; indeed, they create our courage and our wisdom." ~ M. Scott Peck, The Road Less Travelled

Sarah

TANYA, BABA, AND THE REST OF THE GANG WERE making plans on how to "tackle" Ammi. My opinion was to talk directly to her. No matter what we tried to do, the outcome would be the same—either she would soften her stand against me, or she would continue to look at me with the mixture of hate and pain that I had seen the last few times I had been near her. I needed to talk to her. I wanted to know if there was still love hidden inside her, the love that she had showered on me from the time I was born, while I still was a "good, obedient daughter." I wanted her to know that no matter what, I would always love her.

I persuaded, or rather argued with Tanya to let me visit Ammi in the psychiatric ward that morning. I didn't want to wait for the rest of the family. I felt that if our conversation was spontaneous rather than rehearsed, we might have some progress. Tanya reluctantly asked the ward sister to arrange for a wheelchair to take me to Ammi's ward. I was dressed in one of those weird hospital gowns that don't close from behind. I had never realized how uncomfortable the poor patients must have felt by having their derrieres exposed to all and sundry. Understanding my predicament, Tanya placed a soft shawl around my shoulders. It was large enough to cover my whole body. She knew that I hated to be exposed and that was really kind of her.

Tanya insisted to push the wheelchair herself, but I told her that I wanted to go alone so that Ammi wasn't intimidated. I asked the nurse who had brought the wheelchair to take me to the other ward. I knew that Tanya wasn't very happy with my decision.

"I need to do this alone. I have a feeling that this way there will be a lesser possibility of triggering Ammi. I know you are concerned, my love, but don't worry; all will be well. I have a good feeling about this."

"Fine, but I am coming with you and I will wait in the waiting room until you come out from the ward."

That was a fair compromise and we arranged to meet after twenty minutes no matter the outcome—even if my discussion with Ammi was prolonged, I would come out for a short interval and let Tanya know how things were going.

Once we reached the outer door of the psychiatric ward, I hesitated. A medley of emotions flowed over me, from hope to fear and everything else in between. Tanya gently squeezed my shoulder. I looked up and smiled as she bent down and kissed my forehead.

"Best of luck, sweetheart," she said quietly. I nodded and signaled to the orderly to push me into the ward and towards the nursing counter.

"May I please visit Mrs. Anna Shah?" I asked the martinet behind the counter. She looked quite intimidating, and my voice trembled a little bit as I spoke to her. I hoped that she hadn't noticed it.

"Mrs. Anna Shah? Let me see..." She consulted the chart in front of her.

"Oh, yes, she is in the recreation room. She does the crossword in the newspaper every morning. She says it calms her down." As she spoke, she gestured to the ward orderly to take me into the recreation room. I was glad and relieved that he was pushing the wheelchair for me, because I was sure that just the small distance from the door to the counter would have exhausted me if I had wheeled myself in.

As I entered the area, I saw Ammi sitting at a table at the far end of the recreation room. There was a large window overlooking the hospital garden, and the room would have been quite pleasant to spend time in if there weren't sturdy black iron bars on the window. Those were the only subtle reminder that we were in the psychiatric ward. The orderly rolled me towards her table and set the brakes so that I didn't roll away. Ammi didn't look up as I approached; she continued to focus on her crossword puzzle, just like she used to do at home. The only difference was that she had a crayon in her hand instead of her pen. They probably thought she would hurt herself or someone else with a pen or pencil. Her brow was creased in a frown as she concentrated on the clues given in the paper. I actually thought that she was deliberately ignoring me.

I put my hand on her arm and softly called out to her. "Ammi."

She abruptly shrugged my arm off but still didn't look at me and continued with what she was doing. I waited a few minutes and then tried again. I didn't want to startle her or trigger a breakdown if she still had negative thoughts or feelings about me. It was a delicate balance, and until I knew what her present mental status was, I didn't want to be too intrusive.

"How are you feeling today? Are you better?" I finally asked after staring at her for more than five minutes with no response whatsoever from her. She started, turned, and looked at me with a strange expression on her face. It looked like she was sneering as well as mocking me. I had never seen her look at me that way before. It was chilling!

"Oh, you are still here! I thought if I ignored you, you would go away. You are a persistent little thing, aren't you, Sarah? Actually, that shouldn't surprise me; you always were, even when you were a little girl."

"I wanted to talk to you before I left for England. You know that I have been admitted in the same hospital. I am sure you remember that I was shot and nearly died." I sounded truculent, like a little child now. I shook myself out of this strange melancholy. I had to act like an adult if I wanted her to take me seriously.

"I know you were shot. I was there." She scoffed. "It would have been better if you had died; then all these problems of ours would be gone. No Sarah, no problems.

You know that you are the cause of all that has happened to our family these past few days, don't you?"

That was very unfair, and even though I knew that she was mentally unwell, it still hurt to hear her cruel words. Each one was an excruciating stab to my heart, but I tried to rein in my temper and be patient. This woman was my mother, and she didn't seem to have any compassion or any sliver of love for me. She didn't even ask how I was or why I had come to visit her. It was now time to take a direct approach.

" Ammi...Mama..." I reverted to the way I used to call her as a little child. "Mama, I talked to Oma..."

Ammi twisted her head towards me so suddenly that I thought she would injure herself with whiplash. "Oma? Don't be ridiculous! She died years ago!"

"You know what I mean. You were there too!"

Ammi looked at me with dawning understanding in her eyes. "My dream... you were having a picnic with your Oma, and I was standing some distance away... but how is that possible?"

"It is possible, and you know that. You have also inherited the gifts of sight and intuition from Oma, but you have always denied them. Why, Ammi?"

"Because you can see what you sometimes don't want to, and it hurts too much. I don't want to have anything to do with Oma's mumbo jumbo." Ammi sounded angry and yet almost desperate.

At least she was talking to me, even if it wasn't what I wanted our conversation to be about.

"Oma told me about Uncle Peter and how upset you were when he died."

That sparked a sudden fire in Ammi, and she abruptly

stood up and clasped her hands to her head as if she was trying to block out the sounds of hidden voices.

"Of course, I was upset!" She was shouting now, and the orderly who was sitting in the corner started to move towards the door, probably to get the nurse. I signaled to him to wait. I didn't want the nurse to come and sedate Ammi before we could finish. Thankfully, he seemed to understand and sat down again.

"It was my fault that that horrible Frau Meier saw Peter sewing with us girls that day! He didn't want to, but we teased him and forced him to play with us. He loved me so much that he hardly ever said no to me. Can't you see, Sarah? I killed my own brother!" Ammi started to sob quietly. I went over and put my arms around her. She shrugged me off angrily, but I persisted. I wanted my Ammi back and it seemed that the longer I sat there, the more distant she became. As a matter of fact, I was concerned that she was on the brink of a psychotic break. I lowered my voice and continued to talk quietly to her.

"Oma said to tell you that no one blames you. It was a troubled time; Germany was at war with a madman at its helm. There was nothing you could do; you were a child and history tells us that all weak people at the time were 'culled' so that a strong German nation could be created. Uncle Peter would have anyway been taken away by the Gestapo because the Reich needed soldiers, especially towards the end when they tried to recruit as many as possible. Even though they were struggling and defeat was inevitable. You do remember that six other brothers of yours also died in the war?"

"Oma said I wasn't to blame? Hah! What does she know!

She is dead and gone. She is at peace while I am still struggling with my demons of guilt. I have carried this guilt within me since I was a child." Ammi paused to hiccup and wipe her tears. "And then to find out that you are just like Peter! That was the straw that broke the camel's back!" She clasped her arms around her abdomen and rocked to and fro as if she was trying to soothe herself.

"When you told us that you had fallen in love with Tanya, it was like being back in Nazi Germany. I was reliving that awful day when they took Peter away. I was so scared for you. I was also scared for myself. More so for our family. In this society, people are very quick to point fingers. They will smile and talk nicely to your face, but the backbiting would be atrocious, and at times even debilitating. Something like your overt filthy aberrations could be social murder of our family's good standing. Your coming out would just ostracize you, or worse, kill you. How could you do that to our family? How could you selfishly go traipsing off to England and leave us behind on the brink of being social pariahs?" Ammi took a deep breath and for a short while continued to focus on her crossword. I thought she had forgotten about me, but then she turned back to face me. There was a thunderous expression on her face.

"I had to harden my heart and I tried to give you a way out of this convoluted situation by making you marry Farooq. I thought if he wanted you with such passion then he would surely love you and give you a good life. The way he behaved in front of me gave me all indications that he was a good man from a good family. Moreover, he was a doctor who trained in the same institution as you had. You just needed to be persuaded. Now I realize what a mistake that would have been. He is a cruel and ruthless man, and I am glad he is behind bars." She spoke almost absently, as if she was letting the words justify her actions.

I was puzzled at her blow hot blow cold attitude. She went from ranting at me to being almost affectionate.

"I realize you acted out of love although it didn't feel like it at the time. However, you need to understand that Tanya is my soul mate. We have created a good life for ourselves in England. I have a well-respected job in one of the largest hospitals in London, while Tanya is a decorated agent of Interpol. We have a lovely home, a home where we would welcome you whenever you wanted to visit. Maybe even be the loving grandmother of our future children? Please, Ammi, accept us as we are. I would love for us all once again to be together, as a close-knit family just like we were before."

Ammi shook her head violently in anger. I could see that the wild expression in her eyes was slowly receding and my old Ammi was trying to emerge, but it seemed she couldn't get rid of her anger. If she would only give us all a chance, life would be easier. I hated that there was a rift between us.

"Baba has reconciled with my being with Tanya. He has given us his blessings, especially after what has happened these past few days." Ammi still had a stubborn expression, but I could see a mixture of emotions ranging from anger to frustration to resignation. I think she held on to her anger like an emotional blanket. It was something that had been an inherent part of her ever since she was a little girl. Maybe she needed more time to come to terms with me and Tanya.

Then she surprised me. She looked at me for a long time. I thought she would tell me to leave her alone. Her eyes filled with tears and spilled over onto her cheeks. Did she really love me? Was that all an act to hold onto her childhood fears and anger?

"Where is Tanya? I think I owe her an apology." Ammi was now trying to smile through her tears. "I am sure she is not very far. I would have been surprised if she had let you come to see me all alone."

I laughed at her astute remark and signaled to the orderly to come over.

"Could you please be so kind and ask the lady who came with me to come in here?"

Tanya arrived within a few minutes. She looked worried but gave me a smile of reassurance as she approached us. To our surprise, Ammi held her hand out to her. What was happening? What was she playing at?

"Tanya, I would like to apologize for all the trouble you and Sarah have had. I want to say that I wish I was more open minded five years ago, but you have to understand that I am a product of a very difficult time. I hope you will accept my apologies for rejecting your bond with my daughter and for encouraging that idiot Farooq." Ammi spoke in a semi defiant tone and didn't sound very convincing . I felt that she would still need counseling for a while to completely come to terms with our situation.

Tanya took her hand and respectfully kissed it like one did to an older member of the family. Ammi was at first taken aback but then she slowly placed her trembling hand on Tanya's head in a gesture of blessing. Now I fervently hoped that all would be well. I prayed that Ammi, who had always been unpredictable in the past, would stand by her apology to Tanya. I just wished she had said some kind words to me as well. I felt hurt, but for now, I had to go back to my ward. My pain killers were wearing off, and the excruciating pain of my injuries was starting to cloud my perception of time and space.

"I will talk to you again later. I have to go." I could hardly speak because of my mental and physical pain. Tanya understood that I needed to leave to mull over this strange situation. And I needed my medicines, and fast.

"We will be back, Mrs. Shah," she said with a smile as she swiftly wheeled me out of the ward.

Just as the doors were closing behind us, we heard Ammi call out to Tanya, "You may call me Ammi!"

Tanya

I HAVE NEVER LIKED WAITING. I get impatient and irritable. As it is, I was worried for Sarah. I hoped that her Ammi was in her proper senses and wouldn't attack her daughter. Even a verbal attack would devastate Sarah, and I knew how much that would hurt her. I was worried that there wouldn't be anything I could do to help her. That thought increased my anxiety and frustration, so I started to pace in the small, shabby waiting room. Occasionally, I would hear Mrs. Shah's voice raised in anger and that worried me even more.

I was surprised when I was summoned to where Sarah and Mrs. Shah were sitting. I hoped everything was all right. When I laid my eyes on her, Sarah seemed to be all right, though she didn't look too happy. I went in ready to defend her in every possible way, but I was happy to see her give me a watery smile.

Mrs. Shah's apology, even though fairly reluctant, was a panacea to both of our souls. We hoped that we could live in peace once more. I was surprised that she had asked me to call her Ammi! Sarah said to take her apology with a pinch of salt. She didn't completely trust her yet. She was hurt that Ammi hadn't said a word of reconciliation to Sarah herself. She thought that Ammi had apologized to me to keep her "face" and then she would be able to go back to her society friends with a clear conscience. Sarah said she still needed to talk a bit more to Ammi and work things out. Her empathic feelings were all over the place. She was upset that she wasn't completely sure of her own mother, and I didn't know how to help her. I promised that I would be there for her in any way that I could, but first of all, Sarah had to concentrate on getting better. Her adventure that morning had taken a lot out of her. She was exhausted and fell instantly asleep once she was given her medicine and her head connected with the pillow.

After reassuring themselves that Sarah was out of danger, Adam and Gulnaz had finally left with Razia for London. Farooq was in prison awaiting sentencing, but he still had a lot of cronies who could cause mischief for them if they stayed in Karachi, so I was relieved that they were out of immediate danger. As we had discussed before they left, they would stay with us for a short while until they found their own place. Sarah had told Gulnaz where she could find the books to study for a UK practicing license in our home.

She was enthusiastic and wanted to start studying while Daniyal was still small and didn't need as much attention as an older child. I was happy that Razia stuck to her plan to accompany them since this was the first time they were traveling to the UK and having someone know their way around was always an advantage. She was going to settle them in our home and then come back as soon as she could. After all, she couldn't leave her boys for long periods of time. I would have liked her to stay a bit longer because I enjoyed visiting the museums with her whenever she came to London.

Both of us literally craved to go back to the sanctuary of our home, but Sarah now needed to get physically and mentally better first. We wanted to go home the moment we got the green light from her doctors.

Baba and Aazan came to visit us in the hospital by midday. Sarah had finally woken up from her drug induced nap and I thought she looked a bit better. Talking to Ammi might have helped, but she was not very optimistic. She insisted that Ammi may have apologized to me, but she was still holding back. She knew her mother better than anyone else, and she knew that, unless her mother came completely to terms with our relationship, there would always be the chance that she would revert to her old self.

"I am glad you talked to your Ammi." Baba was pleased.

"I am glad too, but I am still waiting for the other shoe to drop. I feel she needs more treatment. Like I mentioned to you before, I was telling Tanya that psychological counseling will do a world of good for her."

"I understand, but don't worry, dear. I will keep talking to her. Just accept her as she is. The trauma that she suffered as a child is deep. Take what she has offered now, and I am sure she will come to talk to you when she is better. Much better."

I understood why Ammi had apologized to me. In her mind, I was still an outsider and not a member of the family.

It was just a façade to stop people from talking, or maybe to make me stop talking about her? As if I would. I had no interest in doing so. My interest was and always would be Sarah's wellbeing.

EPILOGUE

"All roads lead home as home is where the heart is. So Love. Simply Love. For love is home to all of us." —— *Wald Wassermann*

Sarah

WE WERE HOME AT LAST. THE WEATHER HAD BEEN remarkably good for days, so much so that Tanya strung a hammock for me between the two medium sized apple trees in our garden. Even though I was on the mend, I still felt a bit weak, and the pain of the wound plagued me off and on, especially when it got cold. My boss at the hospital told me to take a month off and come back with enough energy to work as much as two people. His words, not mine. Anyway, I was grateful for the respite. Tanya and Gulnaz pampered me to no end and I felt loved. I never had a sister, but I had always wanted one, and Gulnaz fitted into our family perfectly. When she wasn't looking after her little family, we would get together and I would help her study for her upcoming PLAB exams so that she could start working here in the UK. I suggested that she should apply for short term locum jobs. They paid quite well, and one wasn't tied down to one place. When an assignment finished, one could go onto the next one at their own pace. It was an ideal solution for a young working medico mom. I was actually thinking of doing the same once Tanya and I decided to have children. I had already researched in advance, and that was why I could give Gulnaz all the relevant information she needed.

Adam found work almost immediately. He had been an IT manager in Pakistan and apparently, his skills were quite in demand in London. Just within a few weeks, they moved to a comfortable two-bedroom apartment a few streets away from where we lived. It was walking distance away and, to tell you the truth, it was nice to have our family nearby. Gulnaz was also happy to have two aunts babysit Daniyal whenever we could. He was growing well and was such a sweetheart. He looked exactly like Adam when he was that age. All was well for their family, and I was glad. Being far away from under Farooq's dark cloud brought out a funny side in Gulnaz. We loved hearing her jokes and she was a good conversationalist. I told her that she would fit in and definitely do well in England.

Tanya had also applied for a few more days off. She wanted to be sure that I was well and physically fit before she started her international travels again. I reassured her that I was all right, but she still stayed. Obviously, I relished this extra time with her. Our "adventure" had shaken her to the core, more than she wanted to admit, and I still saw a glimmer of fear in her eyes when she looked at the ugly scar on my chest. I knew that she was thinking how close she had been to losing me. I understood. I would have been devastated if anything had happened to my intrepid policewoman.

As we spent lazy days gently swinging on our two-person hammock, we talked more than we had in the past few months. Our busy schedule used to keep us flitting in and out of our home, but we relished this reconnection we had at least for a few weeks. The most important topic we discussed was having children. We debated whether we wanted to adopt or have a donor. Since our family, mostly Ammi, was still flabbergasted with our relationship, we thought the best option was to adopt a child. I would have loved to carry my own child, but there were so many orphans in this world who would benefit from being part of our family. We decided that we would research the feasibility of adopting in the UK or whether it was better to get a baby from Pakistan. That would be the next adventure for us, and just the thought was heartwarming.

Tanya

I FELT as if I had aged ten years. The emotional toll those past days had us feeling like we had been spinning on a high-speed roller coaster. I tried not to show my anxiety and concern to Sarah, but she knew me too well. We sat down and really talked to each other. To my mind, for us that was the best form of therapy. Talking definitely avoided the suggestion or even a hint of having post-traumatic stress disorder. I would have gone mad if I had lost Sarah. She was who I lived for. I was so glad that she hadn't given up and fought to stay back in this world for me. She was on the brink of death, and yet she came back to me. It was absolutely mind blowing and yet humbling.

I was delighted that we both wanted children. It was time for us to think about expanding our family. We talked about donors, and Adam said that he was willing to be a donor if I carried the baby, but we had already shaken the family foundations away from their cultural norms. We couldn't rock the boat more than we already had, so we decided that adoption was the best option for us. Actually, if I had still been in touch with my brother, I would have asked him to be a donor and I would have loved to see Sarah blossom into motherhood, but by adopting we would be initiated into parenthood at the same time. And I was sure... well, I hoped that we would be good parents one day.

A few weeks after getting back home, I had a call from Andy, my colleague at Interpol. They had received information about a child smuggling ring, that spanned Europe and Asia, and they wanted us to look into it. The demand to adopt children was growing day by day and the fees were exorbitant, making it a lucrative business. The sad part was that not all of the children were orphans. Many were kidnapped and never saw their families again. It was strange that just when we were contemplating to adopt a baby, this case fell into my lap. Kismet?

AUTHOR NOTES AND GLOSSARY

"BADLANDS"

The journey of Agent Tanya and Doctor Sarah in **Bloodlines** takes them deep into Pakistan's "Badlands." This area, known as the FATA (Federally Administered Tribal Areas) and later renamed as Pukhtunkhwa, is located along Pakistan's north-western border with Afghanistan, and consists of seven autonomous agencies. The Badlands notoriously have their own laws and traditions, which is why they have been left more or less alone by the different governments, which just had their representative political agents in each district, since the British separated this area from India in 1893 by the 2,500-kilometers-long (1,553 miles) Durand Line. To enter legally, one had to go through a whole rigamarole of permits and paperwork, and that explains why our team had to go in under the cover of night. The only place that offered some sense of safety was the Kohat air force base.

This beautiful part of Pakistan is bordered by the Hindu

Kush mountains and is famous for the Khyber Pass, where a multitude of conquerors have entered ancient India, including Alexander the Great. Many areas have been likened to Switzerland and Austria and considered maybe even more beautiful because of their raw ruggedness. There were places where Sarah wanted to stay longer and explore, but the adventure and the chase of the story didn't give her much time to do so. Maybe next time?

I am lucky that I was able to travel to nearly every corner of Pakistan because of my parents' wanderlust and my father's job, so when I write about any of these places, I just close my eyes and travel there while my fingers start to move on my keyboard on their own volition. Therefore, I do hope you enjoy reading **Bloodlines** as much as I have writing it.

∽

CHAPTER ONE

Congenital hydrocephalus:
Congenital hydrocephalus is a build-up of excess cerebrospinal fluid (CSF) in the brain at birth. The extra fluid can increase pressure in the baby's brain, causing brain damage with mental and physical problems.

Gojra: a small agricultural town in Punjab, Pakistan

Consanguinity: Two individuals that are "blood relatives" or "biological relatives."

NICU: Neonatal Intensive Care Unit

ESP: Extra Sensory Perception

CHAPTER TWO

MRCPCH: Member of the Royal College of Paediatrics and Child Health

Forced Marriage Unit: The Forced Marriage Unit was set up in the UK in 2005 and provides support to victims as well as expert training and guidance to professionals. It is jointly run by the Home Office and Foreign and Commonwealth Office. In 2011, they dealt with over 1400 calls in relation to forced marriages.

CHAPTER THREE

Ammi: Mother.

Baba: Father.

Shalwar kameez: A pair of light, loose, pleated trousers, usually tapering to a tight fit around the ankles, worn by women from Pakistan typically with a kameez or tunic (hence the two together being a *shalwar kameez*).

CHAPTER FOUR

Mazar of the Quaid: Mausoleum of Mohammad Ali Jinnah, the founding father of Pakistan.

Pushto, Sindhi and Punjabi: Local regional languages spoken in Pakistan.

Pathan: Person from the North of Pakistan who speaks Pushto.

CPR: This is an emergency procedure consisting of chest compressions often combined with artificial ventilation to manually preserve intact brain function until further measures are taken to restore spontaneous blood circulation and breathing in a person who is in cardiac arrest

Reiki: This is a form of energy healing, a type of alternative medicine. Reiki practitioners use a technique called palm healing or hands-on healing through which a "universal energy" is said to be transferred through the palms of the practitioner to the patient to encourage emotional or physical healing.

Defence Society: or Defence Housing Authority (DHA) is an upscale residential neighbourhood located within the Clifton Cantonment of Karachi. It was originally established as a residential town for retired military personnel by the Army in the mid 1950s, however, currently the majority are civilian families that reside in this town.

CHAPTER FIVE

Dadi: Usually, a term used for paternal grandmother.

AK47 rifle: This is officially known as the Avtomat Kalashnikova and is a gas-operated assault rifle that is chambered for the 7.62×39mm cartridge. Developed in the Soviet Union by Russian small-arms designer Mikhail Kalashnikov, it is the originating firearm of the Kalashnikov family of rifles.

C-130 Hercules: The Lockheed C-130 Hercules is an American four-engine turboprop military transport aircraft designed and built originally by Lockheed. Capable of using unprepared runways for take-off's and landings, the C-130 was originally designed as a troop, medevac, and cargo transport aircraft.

Kohat: is a city that serves as the capital of the Kohat District in the North of Pakistan. It has a well-established air force base there.

Parachinar: is a small Pashtun town which is the capital of Kurram District in the province of Khyber Pakhtunkhwa. It is situated on a neck of Pakistani territory west of Peshawar, that juts into the Logar and Nangarhar provinces of Afghanistan

CHAPTER SIX

Salam: Shortened form of the Islamic greeting Asalam alaikum which means peace be upon you. The shortened form loosely translated means peace.

Bell AH-1 Cobra: is a single-engine attack helicopter developed and manufactured by the American rotorcraft manufacturer Bell Helicopter. A member of the prolific Huey family, the AH-1 is also referred to as the HueyCobra or Snake.

CHAPTER SEVEN

Mingora: is a city in the Swat District of Khyber Pakhtunkhwa, Pakistan. Located on the Swat River, it is the 3rd largest city in Khyber Pakhtunkhwa and the 26th largest in Pakistan

Cutaneous Horn: is a type of lesion or growth that appears on the skin. It's made of keratin, which is a protein that makes up the top layer of the skin. The growth may look like a cone or horn, and it can vary in size. The name comes from the growth sometimes resembling an animal's horn. It is a skin condition that is more common in older adults.

Mullah: is an honorific title for a Muslim mosque leader. The term is also sometimes used for a person who has higher education in Islamic theology and sharia law.

Kishan Gul Mountain Trail: A steep and treacherous trail leading to remote little villages and scattered dwellings in the mountains of Parachinar.

CHAPTER EIGHT

Peritonitis: is an inflammation of the peritoneum — a silk-like membrane that lines your inner abdominal wall and covers the organs within your abdomen — that is usually due to a bacterial or fungal infection.

CHAPTER NINE

Meconium: is a new-born baby's first poop. This sticky, thick, dark green poop is made up of cells, protein, fats, and intestinal secretions, like bile.

Political Liaison Officer: Intermediary official between the Government of Pakistan and the Tribes in the area.

CHAPTER TEN

Chaddar: a large sheet-like cloth used as a head covering (and veil and shawl) by Muslim women and covers them from head to toe.

Peshawar: is the capital of the Pakistani province of Khyber Pakhtunkha. It is the sixth largest city in Pakistan. Situated in the broad valley of Peshawar east of the historic Khyber Pass close to the border with Afghanistan, its recorded history dates back to at least 539 BCE, making it the oldest city in Pakistan and one of the oldest cities in South Asia.

Darra Adamkhel: is the main town of the Kohat District of Khyber Pakhtunkhwa. It has gained fame and notoriety for its bazaars packed with gunsmiths and weapons merchants. The town consists of one main street lined with multiple shops, while side-alleys and streets contain workshops.

Halal: Halal is an Arabic word that translates to "permissible" in English. Or kosher.

CHAPTER ELEVEN

Sahib: A term used especially among the native inhabitants of colonial India when addressing or speaking of a European of some social or official status. Nowadays its used as a form of respect e.g. Doctor Sahib.

Multan: is a city located in Punjab, Pakistan. Situated on the bank of the Chenab River, it is Pakistan's 7th largest city and is the major cultural and economic centre of Southern Punjab. Multan's history stretches deep into antiquity.

CHAPTER THIRTEEN

Lahore: is the capital of the Pakistani province of Punjab and is Pakistan's second largest city after

Karachi. It is the 26th largest city in the world. Lahore reached the height of its splendour under the Mughal Empire between the late 16th and early 18th century and served as its capital city for many years.

Mughal: A member of the Muslim dynasty of Indian emperors who originated from Afghanistan and established by Babar in 1526.

Parathas: Golden-brown in colour, flaky and layered, a paratha is a type of Indian/Pakistani bread that is typically consumed for breakfast.

Sargodha: is also known as the City of Eagles. It is one of the few planned cities of Pakistan. It is an agricultural district, wheat, rice, and sugarcane being its main crops.

CHAPTER FOURTEEN

Bibi: A name of Farsi and Persian origin, means "young lady of the house".

Imam: The person who leads prayers in a mosque and conducts religious ceremonies like weddings and funerals.

CHAPTER FIFTEEN

Oma: A term of endearment for grandmother in German.

Reich: The term is derived from the Germanic word which generally means "realm," but in German, it is typically used to designate a kingdom or an empire, especially the Roman Empire.

Führer: a tyrannical leader. In this book pertaining to Hitler.

Heil Hitler!: used by the Germans or their supporters during the Nazi regime as a greeting or an acclamation of the supremacy of Hitler.

Deutschland über Alles!: Germany above all: German unity above factionalism. A common Nazi slogan in WWII.

CHAPTER SIXTEEN

Gestapo: abbreviation of Geheime Staatspolizei (German: "Secret State Police"), the political police of Nazi Germany. The Gestapo ruthlessly eliminated opposition to the Nazis within Germany and its occupied territories and, in partnership with the Sicherheitsdienst (SD; "Security Service"), was responsible for the roundup of Jews throughout Europe for deportation to extermination camps.

EPILOGUE

PLAB: The Professional and Linguistic Assessments Board (PLAB) test provides the main route for International Medical Graduates (IMGs) to demonstrate that they have the necessary skills and knowledge to practise medicine in the United Kingdom (UK).

Kismet: 'this comes from the Arabic word 'qisma', which means "portion" or "lot." The word Kismet was borrowed into English in the early 1800s from Turkish, where it is now used as a synonym of fate.

ALSO BY SHIREEN MAGEDIN

The Journeys Series:

Book 1: Lifelines

Book 2: Bloodlines

ABOUT SHIREEN MAGEDIN

Dr. Shireen Magedin is a practicing pediatrician who has studied in Pakistan, England, and Ireland. She has always had psychic abilities, and in the beginning they scared her, until she received guidance from trainers and connected with people who had similar abilities, thus knowing she wasn't alone. Connecting psychically and intuitively with her patients has helped her hone her medical skills.

She lives with her cat Pompi (aka Madam Pompadour) and enjoys visits from her daughter Sharmeen, son Nadir, and daughter-in-law Mariam.

Connect with Shireen

Official Author Site
https://shireenmagedin.com

Email
https://shireenmagedin.com/contact-us/

Facebook
https://www.facebook.com/groups/shireenmagedin

www.ausxippublishing.com

AUSXIP Publishing publishes quality fiction and non-fiction with strong female characters that inspire, strengthen and enrich the soul. Stories that build up, create a sense of achievement and most importantly to entertain.

AUSXIP Publishing Newsletter
https://newsletter.ausxippublishing.com

AUSXIP Publishing Store:
https://store.ausxippublishing.com

Facebook:
https://facebook.com/ausxippublishing

Twitter:
https://twitter.com/ausxippublish

www.ingramcontent.com/pod-product-compliance
Lightning Source LLC
Chambersburg PA
CBHW020347120726
47904CB00002B/485